Sweetest Mistake

A Nolan Brothers Novel ~ Book Two

AMY OLLE

Ebook ISBN: 978-1-944180-02-7
Print ISBN: 978-1-944180-03-4

DEDICATION

To my Luke.

ACKNOWLEDGMENTS

This book would not have been possible without the love and support of so many. To my husband, my rock. To Lori Nelson Spielman for suffering through the first draft of this book, and to the wonderful women at Hot Tree Editing, particularly Olivia Ventura, for your awesomeness in editing achievements. Thank you all!

Chapter One

Emily Cole's entire life, when tightly folded and stuffed, fit into two suitcases and one overburdened carry-on bag.

A buzz of activity swirled around Cherry Capital Airport's Baggage Claim B, where Emily waited to retrieve her luggage. The four-hour flight from Tucson to Traverse City, Michigan, had been blessedly uneventful, but Emily was eager to collect her belongings and make the hour-long drive in time to catch the last ferry out to Thief Island.

She pulled her cell phone from her purse and scrolled through her e-mail, searching for her car rental reservation.

Lost in her task, Emily was only dimly aware of the ripple of unease that ran through the small cluster of travelers until, over the whine of the baggage carousel, a smattering of nervous laughter pierced her concentration.

Her head came up, and a sympathetic groan eased from her. Heaps of clothing littered the baggage conveyor belt and the shredded remains of a black suitcase lay among the carnage, as if a grizzly bear had mauled it. An array of dark cotton yoga pants and crumpled T-shirts inched by. A pair of dingy socks. A lone sneaker–

The air sucked from Emily's lungs.

That was *her* canvas sneaker amidst the black and gray loungewear. A caretaker's wardrobe.

Her wardrobe. She spotted *her* plastic-handled hairbrush, teeming with the bright strands of her strawberry-blonde hair, and the red plastic case that held *her* bite splint.

Emily's legs turned to pillars of cement and affixed to the hard concrete floor. A pair of shabby panties she should've replaced months ago paraded along before the watchful gazes of her fellow travelers.

It was all there. Her entire life. For anyone–for *everyone*–to see.

With a horrified moan, she squeezed her eyes shut.

Including *her* seven-and-a-half inch, twenty-speed, hot pink vibrator.

A woman detached from the crowd and crept forward. She plucked a brown leather bag off the carousel and melted away again into the crush of bodies. Bolstered by her act of courage, a white-haired man in neatly pressed slacks and a crisp dress shirt stepped up to the turnstile. He lifted a black suitcase and, giving the luggage a little jiggle, shook loose one of Emily's serviceable white bras, which had snagged on the bag's zipper.

Emily bit back a whimper. She stayed rooted to the spot while her life rolled along the winding carousel, watching helplessly as, one by one, suitcases disappeared along with their people.

When only a few pieces of luggage remained on the conveyor belt, Emily snuck a glance left and right. The baggage claim area absent of prying eyes, she scrambled toward the massacre on wobbly legs.

Her heart thrashed against her ribs as she scooped up an armful of clothing. She dumped the load on the ground at her feet and turned back for another armload. Her course set, she snatched up clothing and objects with frantic urgency.

A hum of noise pierced the fog of panic surrounding her. She shot a glance over her shoulder, only to witness a fresh horde of people spilling through the gate and into the baggage claim area. She wrenched back around and, swallowing a sob of frustration, grabbed blindly at the scattered remains of her pathetic little life.

Her fingers brushed over the silky silicone vibrator, but it slipped through her grasp. She pitched forward, stretching to snag BOB before he slipped behind the black rubber flaps and back into the bowels of the airport.

A large, tanned hand clamped around the hot pink shaft.

For a split second, she stared at that hand, and then she lifted her gaze.

Heavily lashed bright green eyes ensnared her.

She reared back. *Oh, shit.*

His full, pouty mouth pushed up at one corner.

Ohshitohshitohshitohshit.

She recognized Luke Nolan immediately. Hard to forget the most beautiful man she'd ever seen in real life. Words log-jammed somewhere in the circuits between her brain and mouth while she gaped in horror at his perfect face.

The sharp, sculpted lines of his nose and jaw stood in

defiance to the plump softness of his lips and the smooth, rounded planes of his high cheekbones. His richly dark hair and bronzed skin acted like a canvas that only intensified the brightness of his deep-set emerald eyes.

He pointed at something over her shoulder. "You might want to grab those."

Emily whirled. A gasp tore from her as she lunged to snatch a bra and trio of panties off the belt before they disappeared behind the rubber curtain flaps.

With a broad sweep of his arms, he scooped her shredded suitcase with the last of her belongings from the carousel. Stooping low, he rescued the heap off the cement floor and hauled it, along with her mangled luggage, to an isolated corner of the terminal.

She wrestled her still-intact suitcase off the belt and scurried after him just as the throng of travelers descended on the baggage claim.

He straightened. "Is that everything?"

"I th-th-th-think so." She winced at the stammer.

She'd worked hard to overcome the embarrassing speech impediment, but sometimes when she was flustered or frustrated it reappeared, leaving her to turn over words and clauses like an engine that wouldn't start.

If Luke noticed, he pretended not to. "Is someone picking you up?"

She sagged against the wall and pushed a puff of air through her lips, lifting a strand of hair off her forehead that'd escaped her ponytail. "I r-rented a car."

She felt his eyes on her like a caress. "Do you take cream?"

Emily blinked at him. "Wh-what?"

"With your coffee?" His smile turned mischievous. "We're doing this all out of order, I admit, but now that I've fondled your panties, I think it's expected that I at least buy you a cup of coffee."

She frowned.

"I'll take that as a no." He appeared unfazed by her rejection. "How about your name then?"

Her frown twisted into a scowl. Either he didn't recognize her, or he didn't remember her. For someone who'd spent her life trying to stay invisible, that should make her happy.

It should, but it didn't.

She dropped to her knees and began tidying the upheaval of her life.

He cleared his throat. "Let me help you get all this to your car."

Emily shook her head. "I c-can m-m-m-manage–" She stopped when the spasm hit, and swallowed painfully. Her hand shot to the necklace around her neck.

She'd worn the silver chain with the small amethyst pendant for as long as she could remember, using it as a sort of talisman to calm herself when the stutter took over.

"Go on." He crouched beside her. "I'll watch your things."

His gentle tone stabbed a pang of longing into her heart, but she pushed to her feet and set off in search of the car rental counter. She wanted to leave the airport well behind her more than she didn't want to accept his help.

In the tiny five-gate airport, she quickly located the desk and secured her reservation. When she steered the royal-blue sedan up to the terminal, she spotted Luke waiting at the curb, her suitcases perched at his feet, and rolled to a stop in front of him.

She pulled the trunk release latch the car rental clerk had pointed out to her and climbed from the car. Luke met her at the back, and when she propped open the trunk, he plunked her undamaged suitcase inside. He returned to the curb to attack the wreckage.

She grew a little lost in watching him struggle to cram

the bulk of her suitcase and clothing into the compact trunk space. His soft green T-shirt hugged the muscles of his back and biceps and the sunlight picked out threads of rich auburn hiding amidst the strands of his dark hair.

With a grunt and one last hard shove, the bundle dropped into the vehicle. He slammed the trunk shut and patted the roof. "All set."

"Th-th-thank you." The tips of her fingers brushed across the solid pendant.

His gaze tracked her hand. "You're welcome," he said softly.

Her heart jumped into her throat as she scurried round to the driver-side door.

On the curb, he leaned a shoulder against a large structural column and pulled a cell phone from his hip pocket. He bent his head over the device.

She wavered. "Do you, uh, need a ride?"

Over the roof of the car, his green gaze landed on her face and the force of it knocked her back a step.

"I'm sure I'm out of your way, but thanks for the offer."

"Aren't y-you h-h-headed to the island?"

Confusion clouded his well-formed features. The lines between his brows deepened and she imagined he struggled to place her among the multitude of women whose panties he'd no doubt fondled.

Struggling to recall her, or worried he might?

Suddenly, his features cleared as recognition struck.

A practiced smile teased up the corners of his mouth. "I didn't recognize you without the pub lighting."

At his naked relief, she frowned. "Do you w-want a ride or not?"

"Are you here visiting your cousin?" He pushed the cell phone into the front pocket of his worn jeans and straightened away from the column. "'Cause I'm pretty sure she's still out of the country with my brother."

"I'm not visiting. I'm m-moving to the island." Saying

the words out loud, a jumble of emotions whipped through Emily. Excitement and fear.

Mostly fear.

No, not fear. Anticipation?

Whatever. It didn't matter. It was a change, and more than anything, Emily needed something in her life to change. Any change would do, as long as it amounted to a life different from the one she'd been living the past nine years.

The playfulness vanished from his face like mist burning off with the morning sun. All the softness disappeared, replaced by a hard glare. "I didn't know you enjoyed our little oasis so much. Not many people find island life to their tastes."

She'd only visited Thief Island twice before deciding to make the permanent move. Sweeping views of sand and sea, rolling hills, and a quaint downtown were all she recalled.

It was vastly different from the desert of Tucson. Nearly the exact opposite, in fact, which was fine by her. Preferred even. Maybe the foreign environment would distract her from the painful memories she'd hoped to leave behind in the desert.

She lifted her shoulders. "What's not to like?"

His eyes narrowed to dangerous slits. "Have you spent any time here in winter?"

"I have." It'd been unseasonably warm when she'd visited last December, but she didn't share that tidbit with him.

"When the lake ices over, the ferry can't run. No one can come to or leave the island for days, even weeks, at a time."

"It's too late to talk me out of it." She yanked open the car door. "I bought Mina's house."

His expression turned incredulous. "Why did you do that?"

Her scowl deepened, and not only because she didn't have a ready answer.

She had a lot of almost answers, though none she wished to voice for Luke Nolan's examination. Answers such as because her cousin, Mina, one of the few family members Emily had left in the world, had lived in that house and lived on the island still. Or because last year, the most excruciatingly difficult year of Emily's life, she'd buried her mom on that island.

No, she didn't wish to share those answers with him, especially considering her most compelling answer amounted to "why not?" She didn't have anywhere else to go.

She settled on the facts instead. "I'm opening a bed-and-breakfast."

He studied her for one heartbeat, two. "We don't get a lot of tourists."

Her throat constricted around a rush of unspoken words. She focused on her breathing. "I'm h-hoping to ch-change that."

His inscrutable expression suffered a crack and she glimpsed some fleeting emotion. Though gone too quickly for her to identify, it appeared suspiciously like panic.

Just then, a sleek black Chrysler rolled to a stop behind Emily's sedan.

The woman at the steering wheel had honey-blonde hair and oversized sunglasses. She lifted her hand and wiggled her fingers at Luke, jostling the gold bangles stacked on her wrist, before she stepped from the luxury car with the ease of a long-legged gazelle. Her red dress barely gained mid-thigh, and its stretchy fabric clung to her shapely figure in all the places men seemed to find most interesting.

Luke bent to retrieve his backpack and slung the bag over his shoulder as she bounded onto the curb. His hand slipped to her waist when she kissed his cheek with her red-painted lips.

They were perfection made manifest.

Emily shoved her hands into the pocket of her drab gray sweatshirt while Luke guided the woman to the passenger side and pulled open the car door. The woman slid into the vehicle and he closed the door behind her before rounding the car.

His hand on the driver-side door handle, he lifted his head. "You okay? Do you want to follow us?"

Emily shook her head. "I'm okay." She pointed at the sedan's interior. "GPS."

With a fluid motion, he slid behind the wheel of the gorgeous woman's car.

Emily ducked into the shelter of the rental car and hauled the door shut. She slunk down in her seat. Not until the Chrysler eased past her side window and disappeared among the congested traffic did she release the breath she'd been holding.

For the first time since she decided to move across the country, unease prickled. She'd made the move, in part, because she envisioned living out her life in relative peace and quiet in the isolated small town. Now she wondered if that'd be possible with Luke Nolan prowling the streets.

A thought struck. Dread swept through her and she bounded from the vehicle, leaving the car door wide open in her haste.

In the trunk, she plunged through the mound of her clothing and toiletries. Frantic, her horror rose to the back of her throat as a whine of dismay.

BOB was missing.

CB

Waves crashed over his head. He thrashed and kicked his

9

legs, but the torrent pulled him under. Water burned through his nose and lungs. His body grew weak and the dread of what was to come filled him.

Luke jolted awake.

Disoriented in the darkness, he reached out for... something, but there was nothing to grab on to and he collapsed. He sucked in large gulps of air. Fresh air. He turned his head.

Through the patio door, stars dotted the blackened sky and the rhythmic churn of Lake Michigan endured. He'd left open the slider door to allow the warm summer air inside his loft apartment. The sheets, drenched in sweat, tangled around his legs. He kicked free of them and stumbled from the bed.

He trudged to the kitchen on legs made weak from a grueling workout earlier in the day. The clock on the stove screamed the hour in neon-green digits as he retrieved a tumbler from the cupboard.

It was 3:13 a.m. He'd slept almost an hour that time. He couldn't recall the last time he'd slept longer than a couple hours, and he no longer felt the exhaustion that plagued him.

As he snatched up the bottle of whiskey on the counter, his hand brushed against something unexpected.

In the dim room, he could make out the unmistakable shape of the shocking pink vibrator lying on the counter where he'd tossed it. He hadn't meant to steal it from the woman at the airport, but with the crowd rushing in to swarm them and her eyes filling with panic, he'd shoved the phallic object into his hip pocket so he could scoop up her far-flung belongings and haul them away to safety. He hadn't recalled the vibrator until he'd climbed behind the wheel of Kate's car and the fleshy device had poked him in the thigh.

Filling the glass past halfway, Luke drank the contents

in a long, deep swallow. The liquid burned a path down his throat to his gut. He refilled and drank until he gasped for breath. Then he gripped the bottle by the neck and crossed the darkened room to the patio doors.

With his elbow, he slid the screen open and stepped out onto the balcony. It'd be some time before he settled down enough for sleep, and he wouldn't be able to do it at all without the whiskey.

The apartment complex, an old factory converted into studio lofts, sat overlooking the harbor on the island's sunrise coast. Sparse, tiny lights winked at him from the mainland across the lake. He dropped into the wrecked recliner, its leather cracked and duct taped in several places.

He sat in the dark, taking nips of whiskey, the way one might chat with an old friend. When the first fingers of dawn peeked over the horizon, he stared into the light, daring the sun finally show itself. His eyes burned but he didn't look away. The pain felt good. It was all he had to remind himself he still lived.

He threw back the Jack in his tumbler and poured the last remaining trickle of liquid from the bottle, both frightened and relieved to see the bottle run dry.

Only then would he sleep.

Chapter Two

The sun threw light across the room and Emily rolled to her side to escape its harsh glare. It was well past noon, and the nagging voice inside her head badgered.

Get up.

I don't want to.

You have to.

Why?

You haven't bathed in two days.

So?

Get up.

No. Go away.

What would your mom think if she could see you like this?

Emily got up.

The hardwood floors were cool beneath her feet as she trudged across the bedroom. In the bathroom, she turned on the shower and brushed her teeth while steam filled the room.

In the week since she'd arrived at her new home, she'd fallen into one of her now-familiar funks. They'd happened every so often since her mom died. Periods of gloom that often lasted several days, or sometimes, weeks. Unable to muster the will to eat or get out of bed, she'd sleep more hours than she'd spend awake, yet exhaustion never left her body.

After her shower, she rummaged through her suitcase for a clean pair of yoga pants and a T-shirt. She tugged a comb through the long mass of her tangled hair, but the humidity coaxed waves into her normally straight, fine locks and she soon gave up the fight and ventured out of her suite of private rooms.

Located off the home's gourmet kitchen at the back of the house, the cozy suite boasted a living area, a bedroom with an en suite bath, and a wall of French doors through which she enjoyed the same expansive views of Lake Michigan as the rest of the house.

Not that the seven-bedroom, seven-thousand-square-foot Winslow mansion wasn't cozy. It was lovely. Lovely and massive. Cavernous, really. Which only exacerbated Emily's utter distaste for living alone.

Nothing a houseguest or two couldn't help fix.

She started a pot of coffee brewing and distracted herself from her melancholy with thoughts about the inn.

Despite Luke Nolan's lack of enthusiasm, the hour-long drive from the airport had given her some reason for optimism about her business venture, spurred by sweeping views of the lake, charming coastal communities, and an abundance of road signs directing traffic to nearby wineries and antique shops.

No doubt, the tourists weren't far away. All she had to do was lure them onto the island. Located a short ferry ride from the mainland between Traverse City and

Ludington, two of Michigan's most popular tourist destinations, how hard could it be?

When the coffee's aroma filled the spacious kitchen, she filled a to-go mug and scooped her purse and keys off the kitchen counter on her way out the back door. She shoved a pair of dark sunglasses over her eyes to shield against the intense sunlight. In the rented sedan, she traveled south along the island's western coastline.

The lake appeared a brilliant blue-green color she couldn't ever before recall seeing. At the southern point, she rounded the bend and soon turned up the drive to the old stone church. She parked atop the gentle hill overlooking the graveyard and snagged the watering can off the backseat.

Since she'd buried her mom here a year ago, the church sign had changed from St. Patrick's Catholic Church to Little Stone Church, a name that perfectly described the building.

Her mom's tombstone rested at the edge of an ancient oak tree's shadow. As she filled the watering can at the spigot, a bird chirped in the tree overhead and a warm, freshwater-scented breeze gusted off the lake to kiss her skin and lift her hair off her shoulders.

At Audrey's resting place, Emily tipped the can and water trickled over the pink geraniums. When she'd first learned of her mom's wish to be buried in Michigan, she'd been shocked. Audrey had brought Emily to visit Thief Island a few times when Emily was young, but never thereafter and Emily had assumed her mother felt no love lost for the town where she grew up.

Just one more thing she wished she'd thought to ask Audrey before her death. Who was her first love? Was her heart ever broken? What subject did she enjoy most in school? What was Audrey's favorite thing about the island? The breathtaking views? The smell?

In the end, they'd run out of time.

As Emily descended the hillside, a seagull screeched above her head.

So very many questions, and she'd never know the answers to any of them.

og

Luke dragged a hand through his wet hair and pushed open the door to the station.

The rookie officer, Dominic Newberry, hunched over a file on his desk. "Chief's looking for you."

Luke grunted. He was late to work, and while he hated disappointing Chief Brown, he couldn't muster the will to give a shit about the recent string of write-ups filling his personnel file.

Dominic looked up from his paperwork. "They've posted the position."

Weariness clawed at Luke.

The kid snuck a glance over his shoulder before his gaze slid back to Luke. "Sloane's applying for it."

The hairs on Luke's neck lifted and he rolled his shoulders. "Is that right?"

A figure took shape out of the corner of his eye. "Welcome back, Detective."

Luke turned toward the sound of the chief's voice. "Good to be back."

Cynthia's chocolate-chip-brown eyes studied him over the rim of her glasses for one long, uncomfortable moment. "Come talk with me."

A heavy sigh rattled through him and he followed her into her office. He remained standing beside the chair positioned before her desk while she rounded the oversized faux-mahogany bureau.

"How was your weekend?" She dropped into the vinyl-covered chair.

His weekend consisted of a three-day confinement at

a farmhouse somewhere in the backwoods of Georgia, where he'd been forced to talk about his feelings with a crotchety bunch of maimed, disturbed, and, for all he could tell, utterly broken men.

Needless to say, his weekend sucked balls. Definitely not his idea of a good time. Not his idea at all, but Cynthia's. Somehow, she'd gotten it into her head Luke was suffering from post-traumatic stress or some such shit.

"Glad I went," Luke lied. "I hear the position's been posted."

Best part of his weekend was that little mishap at the airport. He bit back a smile when he recalled her small face with huge, horror-struck brown eyes. He'd never forgotten a girl before. What was her name? Amy? Emma?

"Are you interested?"

Luke corralled his meandering thoughts. "Is Sloane up for it?"

Cynthia appeared to measure her words. "He expressed an interest, yes. Does that impact your decision?"

"Not at all." He fabricated a wicked smile. "Just scouting the competition."

Cynthia made a noise that Luke recognized as the closest she came to laughter. "So, tell me about the retreat."

"I'd love to." He took a small step back and his heel caught on a chair leg. His hand shot out to grip the chair back. "But I'm buried in paperwork. How about we chat later?"

Her gaze strayed from his face to his hand on the chair. "Come find me when you've caught up."

At his desk, he attacked the stack of files he'd been shifting around for months. Words swam before his eyes, as they'd done since that day six months ago.

He shoved the paperwork into a corner of the steel desk and, rather than seeking out Cynthia, careened toward the front door. In the parking lot, the sun-warmed asphalt radiated heat. He climbed into his SUV with the Thief Island Police logo and cranked the air-conditioning.

Pulling out onto Main Street, he thrust a hand through his hair, as if he might soothe his agitated mind.

He didn't need therapy. Therapy wouldn't bring Anthony back.

He pumped the brake when the island's lone stoplight caught him with a red signal.

Therapy couldn't fix what was broken. Therapy would only reopen the wounds, but he didn't want to revisit them. He wanted to forget, and to forget, he had everything he needed—women, workouts, and whiskey.

Unfortunately, he couldn't indulge in any of those things while on duty.

Before him, a royal-blue Jetta passed through the intersection. Through the windshield, the driver's strawberry-blonde hair shone in the sunlight.

A smile tipped up one corner of his mouth.

Whatshername would have to do.

ℭ

Emily peered through the windshield to read the name on the street sign. Brandywine? She collapsed back in the seat. She was officially lost.

Thinking to learn the layout of the island, she'd taken a different route home from the cemetery. She'd even managed to confuse the GPS, which kept guiding her around the same loop. At a stop sign, she pulled a paper map from the car's glove compartment and laid it across the steering wheel while she studied it. A bead of sweat broke out on her brow and she lowered the car window.

With a plan in mind, she eased through the stop sign. Just then, a sudden strong breeze kicked up, snatching the map from her fingers and sucking it through the car window. In her rearview mirror, she watched the map dance in the wind.

A curse shot from her. Leaning forward in her seat, she squinted to read the road signs as she passed by, hoping one of them might ring familiar. Absorbed in her crisis, she failed to heed the lights flashing in her rearview mirror until the police siren's sharp chirp punched the air.

Emily groaned as she eased off the accelerator and maneuvered the car to the side of the road. The white police vehicle drew up snug behind her.

In her side mirror, she watched the officer unfold from the SUV and amble up alongside her car. The navy-blue uniform hugged his lean, well-muscled frame.

A niggle of unease chased up her spine. She reached through the window opening and adjusted the driver-side mirror so that she could see his face.

Her heart plummeted to her stomach.

Mirrored sunglasses obscured his eyes and the white stick of a sucker dangled from his pouty mouth, but he was instantly recognizable.

Luke withdrew the sucker from his mouth, leaving a kiss of moisture on his lips. "License and registration."

She started out of her dumbstruck state. Stretching, she popped open the glove compartment and rummaged around until she located the vehicle's registration. She handed it over.

He pushed the sunglasses on top of his head and green eyes pierced her. Her mouth went dry.

"Your license?"

She snatched her purse off the passenger seat, dug out her wallet, and slid the State of Arizona driver's license from the laminated holder.

He studied the documents. "Do you have any idea how fast you were going?"

She licked her dry lips. "Twenty-seven, I think."

"I clocked you at twenty-six."

She breathed a sigh of relief.

Sea-green eyes landed on her face with the force of a tidal wave. "Speed limit is twenty-five, Ms. Cole."

Ms. Cole?

He flipped open a notepad. "I'm afraid I'm going to have to issue you a ticket."

Her jaw dropped. "You're going to w-w-write m-me a ticket? For going o-one mile over the speed limit?"

He pointed at something in the distance. "This is a school zone, Ms. Cole."

"A single mile per hour?"

"You could've hit a child."

"It's Sunday."

He sliced her with a look. "Safety doesn't take a day off."

Laughter burst from her.

Which he quelled with a look.

"You're kidding." She searched for signs of humor on his face. "Aren't you?"

"It says here you're five feet four inches tall." He looked at her beneath lowered lashes; their length so long they tangled at the corners. "That seems awfully generous."

She floundered for words while he scribbled something in his notepad. Then he tore the sheet from the tablet with a flourish. He held out the ticket, along with her license and registration.

She reached for the papers, but at the last moment, he pulled back and she missed.

He leaned close and the scent of soap and sun-warmed skin teased her senses. A soft light shimmered in his eyes.

She swallowed.

"Unless..." His tone, deep and penetrating, sloped through her. "You'd like me to get you off?"

The seductive smile on his flawless face set off a series of alarm bells inside her skull. An image of his long fingers cradled around a pink vibrator came screaming to life in her mind.

Her face flushed with furious heat. "Is this about BOB?"

His brows snapped together. "Who's Bob?"

"Y-you haven't confiscated him, h-have y-y-you? I didn't think they were illegal."

"Are we talking about your vibrator? No, no, vibrators definitely aren't illegal." He frowned. "Though it probably depends what you're doing with it."

"I'm sure it was an oversight. If you'll kindly return him to me–"

"It wasn't an oversight." A knowing light danced in Luke's bright eyes. "I thought I could make you come for it later."

She gasped.

His lips parted and the red sucker disappeared inside his mouth.

She stuck out her hand. "I'll take the ticket."

∛

Two days later, as Luke made his way along Lakeshore Drive, the familiar tension built in his shoulders. He tilted his head from side to side, trying to loosen the corded tightness in his neck muscles, and exhaled a few sharp breaths–part of a relaxation technique they'd taught at last weekend's retreat.

Then he spotted the royal-blue Jetta. His racing heart skidded to a stop at the cliff's edge when he recalled her bowtie mouth moving in wordless frustration. If he weren't a seasoned professional, he might feel a twinge of pity for her.

It wasn't his fault—or at least, that's what he told himself—it was his job, and he took his job very seriously.

A cop and all-around good guy, he pledged to keep the quiet, sleepy island community quiet and sleepy. No drama. No shocks or surprises. No tragedies.

Never again.

To that end, it was his job to know, with intimate detail, what was going on in the private lives of the citizens living on the island. Each and every one of them. What mattered to them most? Who were they sleeping with, and who or what did they ache to possess? He needed to know their weaknesses. Their vices. The thing they could not live without.

It was his duty to keep his eye on Emily Cole.

The thought delivered a smile to his lips.

He cranked the steering wheel and swung the SUV around to follow her. What the hell, he was already late to work. He flipped on his police lights.

She spotted him immediately and eased the sedan over to the curb. He approached her window, surprised by the effort it took to keep his stride slow and measured.

Once again, she wore a shapeless gray sweatshirt and her red hair drawn back from her face in a tangled mass. She looked as though she were coming from a particularly grueling session at the gym. Or, after a long day, was on her way to bed. To sleep.

Her deep scowl as she glared up at him was so severe it came off as insincere.

He bit the inside of his cheek. "City ordinance forbids frowning at an officer of the law."

"That's a lie." A thread of uncertainty tinged her assertion.

"License and registration."

"Is there a reason y-you p-p-pulled m-m-me over?"

"I was concerned by your erratic driving. You were clearly distracted with something."

She flushed an attractive shade of pink. "I wasn't."

God, this was fun. She was fun.

He tapped a finger against the corner of his mouth. "You got a little something right here."

Her pink tongue darted out to lick the smudge of ketchup.

A punch of lust hit him like a kick to the nuts.

She handed him her documents. He took a moment pretending to study her vehicle registration while he grappled with his confused lust. What the fuck was that, anyway?

"Are you aware you have ninety days to apply for a state-issued driver's license before you are in violation of the law?"

Her throat worked and she gave a curt nod.

With an exaggerated motion, he pulled the notepad from his breast pocket, licked his index finger, and flipped it open. He paused with pen poised above the pad. "Have you applied for a new license?"

The sound originating in the back of her throat sounded suspiciously like a growl.

He started to write.

Her mouth opened, as though she might argue, but then snapped shut again.

He ripped the top sheet from the pad with a large sweep of his arm. "This will just serve as a little reminder. When you have your license, take it to the clerk's office and the violation will be dismissed."

She lobbed toffee-brown daggers at him. No woman ever looked at him like that. All he ever saw was adoration and longing.

A whiff of disappointment wafted through him. "You don't talk much, do you?"

Her brown eyes cooled like an autumn frost. "Wo-

would you, if y-you talked like m-me?"

A pang struck his chest, but he ignored it. "I wasn't complaining. A quiet woman is like a mild winter. Both a rare and welcome relief."

"Have I d-d-done something to offend you?"

"Not at all." He leaned against her car. "It's my job to protect the good citizens of this town from harm. I take my job very seriously."

"And you think I'm going to hurt someone?"

"The problem is, I don't know. I have to assume the worst until I'm shown otherwise."

"You don't *have* to," she muttered.

"I mean, what do I really know about you? You're five foot *three* if you're an inch, thirty-two years old, and you recently bought an insanely large house." He lowered his sunglasses to peer at her. "Oh, and you're a Wildcat."

Her sharp gaze swung to his face. "You've been spying on me?"

No, he hadn't, though the thought had occurred to him. Rather, he'd obtained a wealth of information in a brief conversation with his brother, but she didn't need to know that.

He shrugged. "I'm a cop."

"You're a terrorist."

It occurred to him then that the more he tormented her, the less she stuttered. "You were one semester shy of graduation when you quit. Why is that?"

She stared up at him with soulful, brown eyes. A sliver of softness sloped through him.

"My mom got sick and I moved home to take care of her."

He straightened away from the car. "I'm sorry," he said softly.

Her hand shot out and she plucked the ticket from his grasp. She put the Jetta in gear and whipped out onto the road.

That night, while he sat up with his bottle of whiskey, he contemplated the fact that his encounter with Emily Cole was the best part of his whole day.

24

Chapter Three

Emily dreamed of a green-eyed man.

A naked green-eyed man, with a well-defined bare chest and a flat plane over his stomach. The fuzzy hair of a happy trail disappeared into his low-slung blue jeans while pink fuzzy handcuffs swung from his fingertips.

She leapt out of bed at first light.

In the kitchen, she started coffee brewing and settled in front of her laptop at the center island. She pulled up the bare-bones website she was in the midst of designing and connected her digital camera to the computer.

She spent the next hour uploading photos she'd taken of the home and its breathtaking views—she still couldn't believe they called the body of water outside her door a lake. To Emily, a lake was an inland body of water she might swim or paddleboat across. No one would dare attempt to paddleboat across Lake Michigan, as the waves crested and crashed to shore as ocean waves might.

She fussed with the web layout, searching for a design that pleased her. In college, she'd studied photography and graphic art, and it felt good—really, really good—to use this particular skill set again.

Once done with the website, she kept working, relishing the distraction from the disturbing dream and the even more disturbing real man. She searched the web to find other bed-and-breakfasts in the northwestern part of the state and studied their websites, taking notes on everything from their web layout to their prices and general marketing strategy.

By mid-afternoon, an angry growl in her stomach roused her from her spot hunched over the laptop. A quick search for food turned up a bag of potato chips leftover from the sub sandwich she'd picked up at a deli in town a few days ago. She snagged the bag off the counter and returned to the computer.

She crunched on a chip and logged in to check her e-mail. She had a new message from her cousin, Mina. In two weeks, she'd return to Michigan, along with her boyfriend, Noah, for an extended stay and wanted to rent the apartment over the carriage house.

Having grown up two thousand miles apart, Emily and Mina didn't know each other all that well. Not yet, anyway.

Emily sent an immediate reply stating the apartment was hers, free of charge, for as long as she wanted it, and that she couldn't wait to see them when they arrived.

She fiddled with the website some more and sketched out a few ideas for a sign to place in front of the inn. A web search turned up the website of a sign shop she'd noticed in town, and she sent an e-mail requesting a quote for a sign with customized design work.

An hour later, she'd discovered Michigan had a robust

tourism campaign and had registered the Winslow Inn and Bed-and-Breakfast with their databases. She e-mailed the city to request the house and the archaeologically significant eighteenth-century dwelling on its premises be added to their list of local area attractions.

Whenever possible, she sent texts or e-mailed. She despised the phone, as her stutter intensified severely when she tried to use it.

Soon, her stiff muscles demanded she step away from the laptop. The chips had done little to slacken her hunger. The fridge remained mostly empty, as did the cupboards. She needed to make a large shopping trip to stock up on essentials.

She hesitated. What if he lurked around town? She'd rather go hungry than face Luke Nolan. She shook herself. Who was she kidding? Chances were, he'd had his fun at her expense and would now move on. Certainly by now he'd have forgotten all about her.

On the drive into town, she rolled down her windows and enjoyed the warm breeze. Her lightheartedness sagged a little when she turned onto Main Street.

No signs of the Thief Island police when she eased through the traffic light. The sign for Mike's Country Store sprang into view. She was going to make it.

She peeked at the speedometer and the red gauge sat on top of the twenty-five. She flipped on her turn signal.

Red and blue lights winked in her rearview mirror.

Anger rose up to choke her.

She sidled up to the curb with expert ease. Before he arrived at her window, her arm flopped out, her license and registration poised between her fingers.

His stern scowl only intensified his dark beauty. He took the license and registration from her hand. "A rolling stop is not a stop, Ms. Cole."

"You're right. Must be the dead body in my trunk. I

didn't account for the extra weight."

"I'm glad you find this funny."

Her jaw clenched tight. "I don't find a single thing about this funny."

"I'm relieved to hear that."

She wiggled her fingers at him. "Ticket, please. I need to get back to the lab to check on the meth."

"Oh, come now." He tore a sheet from his notepad. "You wouldn't want to give me probable cause to follow you home and conduct a search of your... premises."

Feverish heat burned her cheeks. "You can't keep pulling m-me over. It's harassment, and it's not legal."

"This is a small town, Ms. Cole. A tiny, isolated island, to be more precise." He lifted his broad shoulders and let them drop. "I can pretty much do whatever I want."

She snatched the documents from his hand. "Good day, Officer."

Her tires spun on a patch of gravel when she tore away from the curb.

In the rearview mirror, he shook his head, a wide, sparkling smile on his face.

He was laughing at her.

ß

She refused to live like a prisoner. For the second day in a row, she remained trapped, a captive in her seaside resort mansion without wine or potato chips.

Enough was enough.

She waited until dusk to make her move, hoping the cover of night and the potential for a shift change would confuse his overzealous radar and allow her to carry out her shopping trip undetected. She stepped into her flip-flops and tugged a baseball hat over her distinctive hair.

Outside, the hot, muggy air licked her skin while the last rays of sunlight danced atop the cresting waves.

She'd been on the island two weeks already and hadn't so much as stuck her big toe into the lake. Tomorrow, she resolved, she'd go for a swim.

A few minutes later, she stole into town like a thief. She saw no sign of Officer Bright Eyes when she rolled down Main Street. Maybe it was her lucky day. Her lungs stopped expelling air until she slid safely into the parking lot of the small market store and the breath she'd been holding burst from her.

She scurried inside the store. Learning how to cook a proper meal remained on her list of things yet to do, so she loaded up on frozen dinners and prepackaged foods. Mike's produce section was a thing of beauty, and she filled her cart with an array of colorful, oversized fruits and vegetables before winding her way to the checkout lanes.

At the car, she flung the grocery bags onto the passenger seat, darted around the front end, and fell into the driver seat. She crouched low and yanked the cap down over her forehead, unable to repress the urge to hide even knowing Luke would recognize her car whether he glimpsed her behind the wheel or not.

She steered out into traffic, and as she neared the stoplight leading out of town, her adrenaline soared. This time, she would make it. Victory never tasted so sweet.

The light changed. She bit back a curse and eased to a stop. And that's when she spotted him. The white SUV, with its dark green lettering, sat tucked beneath an elm tree on one of the neighborhood side streets, no doubt stalking innocent civilians going about their legal affairs.

While the car idled, she kept her eye on the SUV. Would he harass her today? Was there any chance he had actual police work to do? Had he been spying on her some more? Her knuckles turned white on the steering wheel.

Let him snoop. Some things he didn't know. Couldn't

know.

Like the fact that she'd been a painfully shy child with a torturous stammer. Or that, in all her thirty-two years, she'd slept with exactly one man, and him only a handful of times.

Or the real reason she'd dropped out of college.

While it was true her mom had started to show symptoms of the disease that would kill her, Audrey hadn't yet required full-time care when Emily left school, nor did they yet know how serious her illness would turn out to be.

Emily left school because, in order to graduate, she had to complete a public speaking course, which required her to give a ten-minute speech in front of 250 of her classmates. Rather than subject herself to that cruelty, Emily dropped out, nine credits shy of a earning her Bachelor's degree.

The old wounds stung anew. She scowled at Luke's police cruiser. He'd been having a good laugh at her expense. Well, no more. She wasn't that painfully shy, stuttering girl anymore. Well, she still stuttered, but she'd worked hard to overcome her deficiencies, and she'd be damned if she was going to let him drag them back out into the light.

It was time she put an end to his bullying ways.

A car horn honked and Emily startled. The traffic light glowed green overhead.

She punched the accelerator and the car lurched forward. Painful memories hounded her and she pressed down on the gas pedal.

The needle on the speedometer bobbed past twenty-six, through twenty-seven and twenty-eight, to top out at thirty miles per hour as she bore down on him. She continued to push down on the accelerator.

Out of the corner of her eye, the bottle of wine she'd bought at the store peeked out from one of the grocery bags. In a moment of sheer reckless rebellion, she snatched it up and, tipping it high so he could make out its unmistakable shape, pressed the unopened bottle to her lips.

"Cheers," she muttered.

Predictably, red and blue lights flashed in the darkening sky. With a self-satisfied smile, she pulled off to the side of the road and killed the car's engine.

The police cruiser pulled up snug behind her and a moment later a man stepped from the vehicle. In the glare of his headlights, she lost sight of him. She readjusted her rearview mirror until he came into view.

His tall frame seemed less lean than she recalled, and he had a hitch to his walk she didn't remember noticing before now. Her smile faltered.

Then fell away completely.

The air wheezed from her lungs. With a groan, she slunk low in her seat.

The officer's hand came up and he knuckled a sharp rap on her window.

Her hand trembled when she pressed the electronic control button. With a soft whir, the glass between them disappeared and she looked up into a face that was very distinctly *not* Luke Nolan's disgustingly handsome mug.

Chapter Four

Luke stuffed the last bite of the fast-food hamburger into his mouth and checked his blind spot before easing out over the centerline to pass a tow truck angled on the shoulder of the road.

The truck's safety lights flashed in the night sky as the driver hitched to the front end of a Jetta.

Luke twisted in his seat. The sedan appeared unscathed, with no mangled fenders or busted glass. Maybe a mechanical failure? A flat tire? He'd missed the license plate, and there was no sign of Emily.

At the station, he parked near the front door and bore a straight path to the main desk. "You know anything about a Jetta getting towed on Main Street?"

Dominic swiveled on his chair, a wide grin on his baby face. "I got a fish in the tank."

Luke stretched, trying to get a look through the glass

partition into the jail's cellblock. "What's the charge?"

"OWVI."

"Drunk driving?" An alarm bell sounded inside Luke's skull. "Who's the suspect?"

Newberry launched into his brief. "A female, thirty-two years old, no prior arrests. She said something about outstanding citations, but I can't find any record of that."

Probably because Luke never turned in those ridiculous tickets.

"Did you perform a field sobriety test?" Luke's voice sounded thin and strained to his own ears.

Newberry cleared his throat. "Yes, sir, I did."

"And?"

Newberry shifted his weight in the chair. "She passed."

Relief rushed over Luke. "So she isn't drunk?"

"Upon questioning, the suspect exhibited incoherent, slurred speech and her face appeared flushed."

Luke stalked toward the cellblock door, his long strides eating the ground beneath his feet. "Buzz me in."

The grating buzzer sounded, followed by the hard clank of the lock's release, and he burst through the steel door. At the second holding cell, he lurched to a stop.

She sat huddled on the gray-blanketed cot, her back pressed to the concrete wall. Her brown eyes appeared huge in her pale face.

Another jarring buzz split the air and the door latch to her cell released.

A heavy silence hung in the air inside the cell, and with it, an odd sensation surged in him. Something gross and squirmy. It felt kind of like uncertainty, but that didn't make any sense.

He shuffled forward. When he dropped onto the cot beside her, she jostled. She risked a sideways glance at him.

"Are you okay?" he asked softly.

A shaky sigh eased through her lips, and she nodded.

"What happened?"

"I w-w-was teaching y-y-you a lesson."

At the stutter, he felt a pinch in the center of his chest. "What lesson would that be?"

"I saw a cop car and thought it w-was y-y-you. I figured if y-you w-were going to pull me over again, I should give y-you a reason to do it."

He swallowed the dryness in his throat.

"I w-was speeding and–" one hand flitted through the air as if to grab the words, "I p-p-pretended to drink from a w-wine bottle I'd just bought. It w-w-wasn't open," she struggled to add.

Despite himself, a low chuckle slipped from him.

She searched his face. He allowed her assessment of him, and indeed, he performed one of his own, noting for the first time the smoothness of her fair skin and the smattering of freckles across the bridge of her small, straight nose. She was tragically cute.

"I really w-wish it'd been y-you in that cop car."

"So do I." He nudged her with his shoulder. "Sounds like you violated three, maybe four laws. A strip search might've been warranted."

Her shy smile caught him off guard. Then she lifted a hand to push a hank of bright hair behind one ear, and the sleeve of her oversized sweatshirt dropped back to expose her forearm.

He stilled.

Slowly, he reached for her hand and gently turned her palm up. He pushed her sleeve up to her elbow. His fingers traced over angry red marks marring the fair skin around her wrist.

"What's this?" There was no softening the hard edge to his tone.

She pulled free from his grip. With her other hand, she rubbed at the marks. "I guess the handcuffs did that."

He noted similar bands of irritation on her other wrist

as well and a cold violence stirred in him.

He climbed to his feet. "Can you sit tight a little longer while I go fix this?"

Her head snapped up. "You can fix this?"

"Do I hear doubt in your voice?"

She cut him with a look. "Yes."

He laughed. "Give me twenty minutes. Half hour at the most. You okay that long?"

She nodded.

"Is there someone you want to call to come pick you up?"

"M-Mina's out of the country. I don't know anyone else."

He frowned. He hoped she meant she didn't know anyone else *on the island*. But that wasn't what she'd said.

The knife of regret twisted. He stood. "I'll be back as soon as I can."

He left the door to her cell wide open and returned to the reception area.

Dominic cradled the phone against his ear and hunched over a computer. Luke sat at the other workspace, where Dominic had left open Emily's arrest file.

The final report not yet written, Luke combed through the rookie's notes. He'd clocked her at thirty-three and gaining speed in a twenty-five before she came under suspicion of drinking while driving. The alcohol container visible, as she'd described.

Upon contact, Dominic observed her speech was jumbled, and at times incoherent, and then described her behavior as uncooperative.

Uncooperative?

Luke continued to read, trying to untangle the disjointed account of events. By the time he'd come to the end of the file, he had a clearer picture of Emily's conduct, not as defiant or insolent, but increasingly withdrawn and panicked under duress.

His chest squeezed.

Behind him, Newberry shuffled papers.

"Didn't you administer a Breathalyzer?" Luke asked without turning.

"Sloane did."

Luke's fingers froze over the keyboard. With a push, he swiveled in the office chair. "Sloane?"

"He booked her before his shift ended." A defensive edge crept into Dominic's tone. "And gave her the Breathalyzer."

Luke's scrambled brain attacked the information like a pit bull. "Where are the results?"

"They should be..." He shoved some papers around on the desk. "Here."

Luke waited while the kid squinted down at the report.

A moment later, two bright pink spots stained his cheeks. "Oh."

Luke pushed to his feet. "I'm releasing her. She isn't drunk. Can you get her things ready?"

Halfway to the jail entrance, Luke turned. "And try to keep an eye on the handcuffs next time. If they're digging in, they're too tight."

Dominic blinked. "I didn't cuff her."

Luke blinked back. "You didn't cuff her?"

"No, sir." He cleared the squeak from his throat. "I meant to, but I forgot and put her in the backseat. I didn't want to get her out of the car just to put the cuffs on."

"Sloane cuffed her?" Luke repeated.

Dominic's expression turned sheepish and he scratched the crown of his head. "Yeah, and he already gave me a pointed lesson so that next time I don't forget to do it."

Uneasy tension situated on Luke's shoulders. "How about you and I go over it one more time later, just to be sure?"

"Yes, sir."

"I'm gonna drive Ms. Cole home. See if you can get her car out of the impound tonight, would ya?"

Luke returned to the holding cell to find Emily pacing the small enclosure.

"Ready to go?"

She nearly leapt into his arms. At the front desk, she signed the receipt for her personal effects and shot toward the exit like a pinball from its launcher.

She didn't speak on the ride, and for once, Luke couldn't think of a single quip or barb to lighten the heavy silence hanging over them.

He walked her to her front door and waited while she fumbled with her house key in the dark.

"You should consider installing motion-activated lighting out here."

In the faint moonlight, he could make out the severe scowl screwing up her features.

He held up both hands. "Sorry. It's a safety issue. Bad habit, I know."

Finally, the dead bolt gave and she pushed inside. She turned back.

He waited, but she said nothing.

"I'll be in touch as soon as I hear something about your car," he said.

Another awkward silence descended. She unsettled him. He had no idea what she was thinking or feeling. He could guess, but he didn't want to guess.

He waited, desperate to hear what she'd say.

She shut the door in his face.

ოჳ

Emily pressed her forehead against the solid wood door and listened to the sound of Luke's footsteps fading away.

She waited for the bang of a car door, the growl of an engine, and finally, silence.

This was supposed to be her fresh start. Her new life free of sorrow and stigma and self-doubt, where she could be more than the girl who stuttered.

But Luke Nolan ruined that.

Okay fine, it might not be entirely his fault.

With a frustrated sigh, she whipped around and pressed her back to the door.

But it was mostly his fault.

She rubbed her sore wrist, only to recall his gentle touch. Her stomach gave a gleeful flip.

Dammit. She didn't want to soften to him. Even if she didn't really know him, she knew she didn't like him. With his mischievous smile and lighthearted ways, he was trouble for her. Like the cool kids in school, he flustered and unnerved her to the point she lost her composure. If she were lucky, they'd looked right through her, but on those occasions when luck had abandoned her and they'd drawn her out to stand beneath their perpetual spotlight, she'd suffered mightily, whether through taunts and humiliations or their piteous regard.

Never trust the cool kid.

Her stomach released an angry grumble, but in the kitchen, the cupboards remained bare, her groceries languishing in the passenger seat of her car, wherever it was.

She stared unseeing into the empty refrigerator.

She was an idiot, which was a belief she'd held most of her life, beginning with her earliest memories.

Like the time she was five years old and three weeks into speech therapy. Her progress was slow, if not altogether absent, and Emily's father, Harrison, grew frustrated. He accused her of not trying hard enough to overcome her stutter, an accusation she adamantly denied.

Thinking to teach her a lesson in determination, Harrison had locked her out of the house. She remembered begging to be let inside while tears rushed down her cheeks. It was getting dark, and she was afraid of the dark. Hours passed. She was hungry and tired, and she had to pee.

By the time she'd slunk to the neighbor's house to ask if she could use their bathroom, she'd waited too long and had wet her pants on their porch.

Heat swept over her skin with the memories. She slammed the refrigerator door shut, as if to block her mind's journey down torturous paths.

But her thoughts forged new routes around her barriers. She rubbed her temples and paced. When she'd arrived at the house, the size of the kitchen alone had overwhelmed her. Now, the room felt cramped. Oppressive.

Escape. She needed to escape. She flung open the back door and plunged out into the night. A large moon hovered low in the night sky and she raced toward it. Only the steady sound of waves crashing against the shore assured her the lake was out there in the dark.

Hard ground gave way to sand and she kicked off her sandals. She didn't stop running for fear she'd think. Her lungs burned, but another memory chased her. Cold water splashed her feet. She wriggled out of her yoga pants, discarded the remainder of her clothing, and plunged into the blackness.

A scream tore from her throat when she smacked into the frigid water. Gooseflesh broke out over her skin, but she was naked, so she leapt into the waves and dove for cover.

She swam down, down through the dark silence, where humiliation and regret didn't exist. Shame drowned away.

Out of breath, she burst through the water's surface

and gasped for air. She turned onto her back and floated while her breathing slowed. Stars punched holes in the black sky. Looking up at them, her small worries washed away.

Laughter piled in her throat. Not all that long ago, she thought she'd forever lost the ability to laugh.

Then a shout rent the air. "What in the hell are you doing?"

Emily sank like a stone.

She splashed and spluttered her way back to the surface. "Luke! Wh-what are you doing here?"

On shore, he stood with his feet shoulder-width apart, his body rigid. Ready to pounce.

"I heard a scream."

"That was me." She swam closer to shore so that her feet touched the spongy seafloor. "I'm sw-swimming."

His stance visibly relaxed. "Swimming? Sounded more like cats fighting. Or dying."

Emily frowned. Her teeth started to chatter.

He crouched in the sand and she squinted, trying to glimpse his movements through the dark.

His head cocked to one side and he pushed to his feet.

Her yoga pants were clutched in his fist.

Emily gasped. "Uh, you can just leave those there."

White teeth flashed in the shadows of his face.

"Oh, no," she whispered.

03

Luke rescued a pair of white cotton panties from the sand swirls at his feet.

He raised his voice over the rush of wind and sea. "I'll just wait here for you. Until you're ready to come out."

After a beat, her reply carried across the water to him. "That isn't n-necessary."

"Oh, but I insist." He fought to banish the laughter

from his voice. "Did you growl?"

"Wh-what are you doing h-h-here?"

"Good news. Your car's been released from the impound." He'd received the call from Dominic while on the return drive to the station and, wishing to make it right for her, had turned around and headed straight back to her place. "I can take you to pick it up now, if you want."

"Great!" The word erupted as a yelp. "I owe you o-one."

"Now isn't that an interesting thought," he murmured.

"Wh-what?"

"Nothing. Any idea when you'll be done? I need to get back to work."

All kinds of amusing squeaks and grunts drifted across the water's surface. "Uh... I'll meet you up at the house in a few m-minutes."

"I'll wait."

"No, really—"

He rescued her bra from the beach and lifted it in front of his face. He waited for her eruption of indignation, but it didn't come. Instead, something happened. Something changed.

She changed.

Right before his eyes, her frantic movements eased. Her breathing quieted. She swam closer to shore, pushing forward through the water until her shoulders emerged, pale and pure in the moonlight. She kept coming.

Until the mounds of her breasts rose above the surface.

Luke's mouth swent dry.

The two beaded nipples poked through the water and he sucked a hiss of air between his teeth. Water scuttled down her body, over the erotic flare of her hips.

Gripped by the slow reveal, his gaze became riveted

on the juncture of her thighs. He licked his suddenly parched lips.

Holy fuck.

Was that—? Was she—? He squinted to see in the dark. Was she a natural redhead?

His senses misfired. He could taste the color of her gold-brown eyes. Hear the soft whisper of her thighs brushing together as she walked toward him. Smell the aroma of her uncertainty and obstinacy.

Her breasts and hips swayed in time to the beat of his pounding heart. The hypnotic rhythm held him captive. Never once had he suspected a body like that existed beneath the pajamas she wore. Bountiful and toned, with lush breasts and hips offset by a narrow waist and shapely thighs.

He unabashedly drank in every naked, glorious inch of her body. He couldn't have hidden his reaction to her if he'd wanted to. He was spellbound.

She came to stand before him.

He searched his mind for something—anything—to say, but nothing would come. He swallowed to dislodge the lump of lust and shock jammed in his throat.

A bemused smile twitched at the corners of her plump mouth and one arched eyebrow inched upward.

He shoved her clothes at her.

She drew the T-shirt over her head, foregoing her bra, and tugged her yoga pants over the exaggerated swell of her hips. His cock took notice of every swing and jiggle.

She straightened and her puckered nipples screamed at him through the wet cotton.

With a knowing smile, she plucked the bra from his hand and carried the delicate undergarment along with her sandals as she turned toward the house.

The swing of her hips as she walked away caused the circuits of his brain to fry. Regret that he'd been deprived a glimpse of her lush ass filled him.

She shot him a look over her shoulder. "Aren't you coming?" Her husky purr wrapped around his cock and squeezed.

Then she left him standing alone on the beach in the dark.

With her panties dangling from his fingertips.

Chapter Five

On Friday, Mina came home.

Emily bounded across the foyer and flung open the front door.

Mina wrestled a suitcase over the threshold. She dropped the bag and threw her arms around Emily. "It's good to see you. How are you?"

"I'm good. H-How about y-y-you? How was Ireland?"

Noah appeared in the doorway. He let two black suitcases hit the floor with a thud. "Did you tell her?"

"Tell me wh-what?"

Mina's smile could've lit up the entire island. "We're getting married."

Hugs bounced around the trio.

"Have y-you picked a date?"

"Halloween." Noah smiled down at Mina. He flicked a strand of hair out of her eyes. "It's kind of an anniversary for us."

At the tender lilt to his voice, Emily's heart gave a little wrench of longing. She cleared her throat. "Halloween is less than two months away."

Mina dragged her gaze from Noah. "It's going to be a small wedding."

"If you need anything—"

Mina brightened. "Would you mind helping with the menu? And the flowers? You have an eye for color and I have no idea what I'm doing."

"All you need to do is show up," Noah interjected. "No one cares about the rest."

Mina's features twisted into a frown. "I care."

Noah ignored her. "We were hoping to have dinner here after the ceremony. In the ballroom, if possible."

A bloom of pleasure unfolded in Emily's chest. "It's all yours, and if there's anything I can do to help, just name it."

Mina bit down on her bottom lip. "Actually, there is one more thing, but I totally understand if you don't want to do it."

Emily's gaze trailed to Noah. "Now I'm worried."

He grinned. "You should be."

Mina elbowed him in the ribs. "Will you be my maid of honor?"

Shock and an upswell of emotion clogged Emily's throat.

A frisson of worry chased across Mina's face. "I promise not to put you in an ugly dress." She rolled her eyes. "Oh, who am I kidding? They're all ugly. And uncomfortable, and overpriced, and no matter what we say when we pick it out, you will not be able to wear it again. Anywhere. Ever."

Around her watery laugh, Emily nodded.

"You'll do it?" Mina asked.

Emily nodded again.

Noah clapped his hands. "Great. I say we celebrate. I'm starved. Dinner and drinks at the pub?"

While Mina and Noah disappeared to the carriage house to change, Emily dug out the breezy black blouse she'd worn to her mom's funeral and yanked her lone pair of blue jeans over her hips. They were more than a tad snug, but they were the only pants she owned that couldn't reasonably be mistaken for pajamas, so she ignored the way they cut into her flesh and slid her feet into her shabby sneakers.

At Lucky's Irish Pub, Emily and Mina settled in a booth at the back of the restaurant while Noah headed to the bar.

"How do you like life on the island?" Mina asked.

Emily only just stopped herself from launching into a full-blown tirade detailing the hell that'd been her life on the island thus far. As Noah's brother was in large part the root cause of that hell, she swallowed her outburst.

"It's been an adjustment," she said carefully.

Mina shot her a knowing smile. "How's the bed-and-breakfast? Have you had many guests?"

Emily sagged against the booth. "Not even one."

"Really? I thought for sure you'd be booked this time of year?"

Emily shook her head. "There aren't as m-many tourists taking the ferry out here as I expected."

A frown pulled down the corners of Mina's mouth. "Yeah, they mostly stay on the mainland."

"Maybe if it weren't called Thief Island, but something more... enticing," Emily said. "Like Paradise Cove or Safe Harbor."

Mina laughed. "How about Temptation Island?"

"I'd be booked nonstop if we lived on Temptation Island."

Noah appeared at the table, balancing a large tray loaded down with a pitcher of beer, a heaping platter of nachos, and plates and mugs.

He slid into the booth next to Mina. "Hope you two are hungry."

The aroma wafted over the table.

Mina reached for the pitcher and began filling mugs. "To be fair, by the time we completed the sale of the house, it was a little late for you to take full advantage of the tourist season. Next year will be better, I'm sure."

Emily hoped that was true. In the meantime, it'd just be her and ghosts of the Winslows who'd passed. Although she disliked being alone, she derived comfort from the home's long history.

Mina reached for a nacho chip, but then snatched her hand back. She sighed and deflated in her seat.

Noah quirked an eyebrow at her. "What's wrong?"

"Oh, nothing." She sighed.

"Why aren't you eating?" Noah asked.

Twin pink spots stained her cheeks. "I'm getting married next month. The diet needs to start now."

His brows snapped into a frown. "Shut the fuck up." He slopped a healthy serving of nachos onto a plate and shoved it at her. "Eat. Or I'll force-feed you."

Mina bit her lower lip to hide her smile. Eyes shining, she ate.

Emily ducked her chin to conceal her own smile and filled a plate. As she bit into a chip loaded with beans and cheese, Noah lifted a hand and waved at someone over her shoulder.

"There's Luke," he said.

Emily jerked around in the booth. Her knee knocked into the table leg and their drinks rocked precariously. She dove to steady them and then twisted back around to confirm Noah's pronouncement.

She spotted him near the front entrance. Her worst nightmare.

He moved across the pub, a long-limbed, large-breasted woman decorating his right arm. Even without the oversized sunglasses, Emily recognized the woman from the airport. Her face was even more lovely than her outrageous body.

Emily swallowed back bile, recalling the last time she'd seen Luke.

Or rather, the last time *he* saw *her*.

Naked.

A groan slipped from her. He must've had a great laugh at her average-breasted, short-legged, butt-naked expense. Her satisfaction at having managed to wipe that smug smile off his face, if only momentarily, disintegrated like cotton candy on her tongue.

On the drive to rescue her car from the pound, he hadn't said more than three words to her, spiced with a few grunts and overlaid with one long, deep, menacing scowl. While he was tense and snarly, for once, all Emily felt around him was relaxed. Peaceful.

The peace was long gone now as Luke and the woman curled their way through the tables. The palm of his hand rested at the small of her back. An intimate touch in a public place.

Emily sighed and turned away from the sight.

To find Mina and Noah watching her.

She tossed up a weak smile, which quickly sputtered out. She stuffed a chip into her mouth.

Mina cradled her chin in one hand and gazed in the direction of the bar. "He is awfully pretty, isn't he?"

Noah frowned thoughtfully. "You think?" he asked, showing no signs of jealousy.

"Oh, yeah." Mina snagged a chip off her plate. "It's not really debatable."

Emily lifted one shoulder in a peevish shrug. "Too bad the effect is ruined the moment he opens his mouth."

Two intelligent gazes sharpened on her face.

Mina lifted her glass and took a small sip. "You don't

like him?"

Emily studied her plate, pretending the interest she'd had in the nachos just a moment ago.

"They say he's a hero," Mina said.

Emily's head snapped up. "Who says?"

"Yeah, who says?" Noah wanted to know.

Mina waved a nacho through the air. "Everyone."

Emily risked another glance over her shoulder. Luke, having dropped the blonde at the bar, was in close-quarters contact with a petite, dark-haired woman in the middle of the room. He peered down into her face as she spoke, a soft smile curving his puffy lips while he listened intently to her.

Emily's stomach gave a little wrench.

"He's been nominated for an award."

"What kind of an award?" Noah asked.

Mina lifted her shoulders. "Some award given to police officers."

Noah rolled his eyes. "It's bad enough he's a cop. They have to give him an award for it now, too? And why am I always the last one to know about these things?"

Mina consoled Noah with a soft pat on the back. While he soaked up her touches, Emily toyed with her ponytail. When she was satisfied they were thoroughly absorbed in one another, she whipped around for another glimpse at Luke and the woman.

Only to find her view blocked by the planes of a flat stomach.

She looked up, past the span of a gray T-shirt hugging lean muscles, and into the chiseled perfection of his face. Her heart dropped into a frenzied rhythm.

"I just heard the news," he said, his charmer's smile firmly in place. "Congratulations, you two."

Noah stood and pulled Luke into a man hug. "About time you made it over here. Your admirers are a voracious bunch."

Side by side, the resemblance between the two men was striking. There was no denying their beauty, but as gorgeous as Noah was, next to Luke, he appeared as merely a blurry copy of the original.

"Nothing could keep me away. I hear wedding bells and I'm as giddy as a schoolgirl."

"Glad to hear that, since you'll be there, too." Noah's smile flashed bright. "As a groomsman."

Luke winced. "Not content to be the only miserable bastard in a tux, huh?"

"I believe in sharing my good fortune."

Luke's mouth bent with a wry twist. "I'll be sure to return the favor someday."

Noah slid into the booth next to Mina. "You remember Mina's cousin, Emily?"

Luke's unnerving green eyes swiveled to Emily. Caught by surprise, she made the mistake of looking directly into their emerald depths. His gaze caressed her face, and then dropped lower, down the column of her neck to settle on her breasts. Her pulse skittered.

"How could I forget?" he murmured, almost as if the thought truly puzzled him.

"And yet that's exactly what you did." The words traveled straight from her brain to her mouth, unfiltered.

"A mistake I intend never to make again."

A shiver passed through her. Seeing it, a green spark lit in his eyes, and as if by some dark magic, transported them to the beach, where she stood before him with every inch of her naked body exposed to his hungry stare.

"So, we're to be cousins, are we?"

His words crashed into her and she blanched.

His gaze swung back to Noah, severing their connection. "I always doubted the rumors about you, but if you aren't a genius, you're obviously not a complete buffoon. You'll forever be my hero for bringing two such lovely women into our family."

Emily snorted.

At the same moment, Mina's soft smile warmed and she looked so happy, Emily couldn't begrudge her.

"Let me buy the next round."

"It'd be impolite to refuse." With Noah's remark, Luke slipped away.

Emily sagged in the booth. She snatched up her glass, downed a large gulp, and returned the mug to the tabletop with a graceless clunk. She tossed a pointed look at her cousin.

Mina's hands shot up. "No, you're right. He's perfectly wretched."

℞

Her light scent stayed with him as he crossed to the bar. He hadn't been able to stop thinking about her.

Naked.

Her nipples hardened against the cold. The soft fuzz between her thighs beckoning to him in the dark.

The images, unwanted and unnerving, kept coming like that, one after another. They stalked him, until his head ached with the effort he exerted to banish her from his mind.

She'd even tormented him while he slept. He'd dreamed of her in his bed, her pale skin translucent atop his dark sheets. She'd called to him, but he'd refused her.

So she'd teased him. Her knees had parted and she'd drawn a shocking pink vibrator to her body. Her head dropped back when pleasure overtook her. A chorus of her greedy moans rained down on him, threatening to wrench the orgasm from his body.

He'd jolted awake and, throwing back the sheets, shot from his bed. In the shower, he'd cranked the nozzle and shoved his face under the spray, trying to cleanse her from his mind. The water had rushed over the sensitive skin of his back and torso, but only served to call forth the memory of her emerging from the lake.

His cock had given an agonizing jerk and he regarded his erection with baffled surprise, both at its appearance after so long and at the fact that Emily Cole was the cause of it.

A lot of women had tried to stoke his desire. Beautiful, available women. Not one had succeeded. At least, not fully. Not since That Day.

Not until now.

The shower had done nothing to wash away his want of her, and instead, one hand had slipped down his body, over the clenched muscles of his abdomen, to stroke his rock-hard length. Exquisite sensation had torn through him. He'd pressed the flat of his palm against the shower wall and with his other hand, pumped his rigid shaft.

His body roared with the knowledge. Her. He wanted her. He had to have her.

With one final tug of the long hardness between his legs, his thoughts had scattered with the orgasm screaming through him.

Now, as he approached their table with the round of drinks, he pondered how it'd happened. How, in a single night, she had turned everything upside down. How, in a single, erotic power grab, she'd gone from the woman he wanted to fuck with to the woman he wanted to fuck.

His gaze bored into the back of her head. His face felt weird, stiff and twisted in an odd, scrunched up kind of way. Like he was scowling, except he never scowled. He was far too good-natured for such petulant displays.

He slid into the booth beside her and her light, flowery scent reached out to him. His body grew taut and molten at once.

He glared down at her.

She shot him a pitying look. "What's the matter? Bad

hair day?"

He laid a hand over his heart. "*Daaaamn*, prison changed you."

"Prison?" Mina and Noah said together.

Emily offered them a weak smile, and then lanced him with toffee-brown daggers.

He could pick out at least three distinct shades of brown in her eyes. His favorite, near the center, was a deep, burnished whiskey. His balls tightened.

He bared his teeth. "You don't like me."

She shrugged her dainty shoulders and took a diminutive sip of her drink. A kiss of moisture remained on her small mouth when she returned the glass to the table.

"Everyone likes me," he felt compelled to point out.

Her snort of disbelief rankled. "Because y-you're so modest, no doubt."

That was it. Time to hit the reset button on this debacle and return things to the way they were before she showed him every delicious inch of her naked body.

He eased back in the booth and folded his arms over his abdomen. "Ah, I get it. There's something wrong with you, isn't there? A personality disorder, maybe?"

A lick of fire flared in her eyes.

An answering spark shot to his groin.

"It is odd, I'll admit," she said. "I mean, w-why w-would I dislike the cop who, w-with zero evidence and even less reason to be suspicious, has accused me of an array of grievous crimes ranging from distracted driving to frowning?"

"Are you still mad about that? I apologized, didn't I?"

"I'm sure you were just doing your job to the best of y-your abilities."

"That's right," he said. "It's hard, thankless work keeping the streets of Thief Island free from thugs and hoodlums."

"Is it hard work keeping track of all the w-women you accuse of felony frowning?"

He wanted to kiss her.

"Don't be silly. Lack of respect shown to a public servant isn't a felony. Tactless and repugnant, maybe, but not a felony."

She sighed. "Experienced as you are with moral corruption, I trust you're right."

From across the table, his brother and soon-to-be sister-in-law watched the exchange with wide eyes, their heads volleying like spectators at a sporting event.

Over Noah's shoulder, Kate emerged from the women's restroom.

Luke tilted his pint and downed the last drop of Guinness. He pushed to his feet. "Speaking of moral corruption, I need to talk to our brother about his children."

Noah straightened. "What about them?"

"Their obsession with My Little Pony has gotten out of hand. It's time for an intervention."

Noah laughed and Luke clapped him on the shoulder. "Congratulations again, you two. Let me know the details when you have them."

He turned to go, but pulled up at the last second. With an exaggerated snap of his fingers, he swiveled toward Emily. "Oh, I almost forgot."

She regarded him with dark mistrust. Smart girl.

"I have your panties with me. Would you like them back?"

She choked on the chip she'd just popped into her kissable mouth.

"You were in such a hurry to get dressed, you must've forgotten all about them."

Her damnable mouth moved with little pinches and odd twitches while she struggled to find and form words. Insults she wished to hurl at him, most likely.

Except she didn't.

In a flash of movement, she bounded from the booth and made to move around him. He shifted his weight and blocked her. Startled Tootsie Pop-brown eyes flew to his face.

He braced for her retribution. Would it be a cool dressing-down or a fiery tongue-lashing? He hoped the latter.

Instead, her expression crumpled and she shoved her way past him.

Disappointment sliced through him. He turned in the direction she fled.

"Hey."

Luke looked down at Noah's hand clamped on his arm.

"Are you two going to be able to play nice?" Worry shimmered in Noah's dark eyes.

"No worries, brother." A cruel smile twisted Luke's lips. "I always play nice."

Chapter Six

Emily banged through the back door and burst into the parking lot. A wall of humidity smacked into her. Clouds had rolled in with the night and a light, warm mist kissed her skin.

Footsteps sounded behind her.

She knew he'd followed her even before she whirled on him. "Wh-why did y-y-you do that?"

"Tell me why you don't like me."

"I didn't start this, y-y-y-you did. Y-you've hated m-me from the b-beginning."

His hard expression splintered. "That's not true."

"It is." She loathed the ring of anguish in her voice. "Why are y-you so against m-m-m-me?"

His hand came up and she shrunk back.

He went still. His green eyes locked on to hers, and with a slow, deliberate motion, he showed her his palms.

She sucked large gulps of air into her lungs while her fingers grappled for the pendant around her neck. He made a soft, soothing sound and slipped closer. His hand slid beneath the curtain of her hair and kneaded her nape.

Rain began to fall in a steady patter. Soon, her muscles eased under his warm touch.

"I am not against you." He spoke softly next to her ear.

"Y-you pulled me over three times in four days."

A lock of his dark hair, now wet with rain, fell across his forehead. "I was curious about you. So I made up reasons to pull you over and talk to you."

Shock siphoned the stinging frustration from her. The intensity in his eyes pulled her in, sweeping her out to sea.

Many long moments passed before she was able to unscramble any words. "W-will you stop?"

"Yes. I promise." He untangled his hand from under her hair. "Is that it? Is that why you don't like me?"

At the hitch of vulnerability in his voice, her heart constricted. She shook her head. "Never mind. It doesn't matter."

"It matters to me."

She startled at the snap in his tone.

"Please." He took a measured step back. "I want to know."

Her gaze fell to his throat. "Sometimes... you m-m-make me feel..."

"What? What do I make you feel?"

Her hand flitted over her collarbone. "Sometimes y-you make me feel s-s-stupid."

She barely registered the slash of devastation that ripped across his face before he was on top of her, pressing her back to the brick wall.

"My God, Emily. How could you think that?"

"Y-you're always laughing at m-m-me."

A curse slipped from his lips and his shoes scraped across the gravel parking lot when he pushed away from her.

He shoved both hands through his wet hair so that it stood on end. "It's just... teasing."

She'd never seen him so serious. So distressed. A bone-deep weariness clung to the area around his eyes, and the feeling struck her that she was seeing him for the first time. The real Luke.

"I'm so sorry," he said. "Please believe me when I say I've thought a lot of things about you, but stupid was never one of them. Not even close."

His words shone like a light, banishing the shadow of pain from her heart.

"I b-b-believe you."

A breath shuddered through him. "Thank you."

She licked her dry lips. "Wh-what other thoughts?"

A wrinkle puckered between his eyebrows.

"Y-you said you've had a lot of thoughts... about me. Wh-what other thoughts?"

With a sardonic smile, he dropped his head and studied the ground. "You don't want to know about those."

"I do." The words burst from her. "I really do."

His gaze heated while he searched her face. "They're bad thoughts."

"Bad thoughts?"

"Downright wicked."

A bevy of butterflies tickled her stomach. "Wicked?"

His eyelids grew heavy. "If I told you, you'd have more than enough reasons to hate me."

"Hate you?"

"Why are you repeating everything I say?"

She gave another shake of her head. "I d-don't know." The lie fell easily from her lips.

It was a habit. A trick she'd learned early on to help

her speak clear, stutter-free words, or to buy herself time when the words wouldn't come.

But she didn't want to talk about her childhood coping mechanisms. "I don't think I w-would hate you."

An odd mix of confusion and resolve played across his features. "I can't stop thinking about you—picturing you—" His throat worked as he swallowed. "Naked."

Heat swept through her. She searched his face for clues to any hidden meanings behind his words. "You're doing it now? Teasing m-me?"

His perfect features softened. "No, Emily, I'm not teasing you now." His fingertips brushed across her cheek. "I wish I were."

Molten liquid spread from the tips of his fingers on her skin to her belly.

His gaze skidded to her mouth. His lips parted.

She slanted toward his warmth. Large raindrops plopped on her face when she lifted her mouth up to his.

He bent his head low and her heart thrashed against her breastbone.

Then his lips brushed hers in a feather-light kiss.

She held herself still, unsure what to do. His tongue licked at the corner of her mouth and her world tilted with a dizzying swoop. To steady herself, she clutched his shoulders.

He nibbled her bottom lip, taking soft little tastes of her. His tongue gave a gentle nudge, and when she opened for him, he licked inside.

Before Luke, she'd kissed exactly one man. Those kisses, from her college boyfriend, Joshua, were soft and warm and neat. They were nice kisses, if a little awkward.

What Luke Nolan's mouth was doing to hers could not be described as nice. Or awkward. It was naughty, but tender. Part apology and part promise. A riptide of emotion whipped through her and conspired to drag her down.

She took her first, tentative taste of him with her tongue. A moan slipped from her at the delicious thrill of it.

The kiss changed and his mouth moved over hers with a possessiveness that wrenched her heart.

She didn't understand what was happening to her, or why Luke Nolan was even kissing her at all. He didn't like her, and truth be told, she didn't like him much either. Except she really, really liked what his mouth was doing to her.

She didn't understand how one simple kiss could make her forget everything that came before it. Or maybe she just didn't care. As long as he kept kissing her like he'd die without her, she'd be content if he hated her for all eternity.

His large hand on the curve of her hip inched higher and slipped beneath the hem of her blouse. His warm, calloused palm smoothed up her side. She arched toward his touch.

He made a sound at the back of his throat and his hand explored further. He cupped her breast and she nearly cried out—with what, she didn't know. Surprise and joy and a plea for more. The pad of his thumb skimmed across her nipple. Arousal spiraled through her and she pulled his tongue into her mouth, swallowing his moan.

Up to now, kissing, like sex, had confused her. Sometimes it was nice, but mostly it was awkward, and by the time it was all said and done, she was left wondering what all the hubbub was about.

She didn't wonder anymore. Hunger seared her and she grasped at him, wanting to crawl inside of him, or on top of him.

On a ragged gasp, he broke the kiss. He cupped her head in his hands and pressed his forehead to hers. They didn't speak, but only breathed together.

It was the most special kiss of her life. The most special, intimate moment with a man that she'd ever experienced.

So naturally, he had to ruin it.

He pulled back. Smug satisfaction chased the heat from his face. "So, how do you like me now?"

She blinked while the haze of arousal burned away. With a hard shove, she pushed away from him, only to stumble over the uneven ground. He caught her elbow.

She resisted the urge to shake off his touch and instead arranged her features into her best imitation of bored disinterest. "You're a pretty good kisser, I guess."

"I'm a great kisser." But his easy smile suffered a crack.

She shrugged one shoulder. "You're all right." She took a moment to enjoy his look of outrage. "Next time, try a little less sloppiness."

She brushed past him.

He turned with her. "I didn't hear you complaining."

"I couldn't speak with your tongue down my throat."

"That kiss was better than all right, Emily, and you know it."

She ignored how the way he said her name turned her insides to liquid. "If that's what you want to believe, I won't burst your bubble."

His mouth took a cruel twist and dread stole over her. "No vibrator is going to kiss you like that."

She bit down hard on the slash of pain. Her jaw clenched tight, she forced out words. Any words. "Your date must be wondering w-where you are."

Finally, his stupid smile wavered.

She left him staring after her, a fierce scowl on his too-beautiful face.

Chapter Seven

His name was Max Foley.

"M-M-Max Foley." Emily felt his name on her tongue. "M-Max. M-Max."

Her first guest, he'd reside in a tiny corner of her heart until the end of her days.

Also, he was the perfect distraction from the memory of Luke's hot mouth on hers, only three days ago. Or his hungry green gaze devouring her naked body.

As she readied the home's largest bedroom, which boasted a fireplace with a carved wood mantel and a balcony with a panoramic view of Lake Michigan, she continued to practice enunciating Max's name, and other phrases she'd likely need to speak to him.

She flung open the balcony doors to let in the summer air and performed a quick sweep of the bedroom to remove dust and provide fresh linens. In the garden off the kitchen, she'd gathered a bouquet of buttery yellow ranunculus and purple phlox, and arranged them in a white pitcher, which she left on the bedside table.

Downstairs, she removed a package of premade cookie dough from the refrigerator and arranged pieces on a cookie sheet while the oven preheated. Cookies baking, she moved to the living room at the front of the house.

"M-Max. Max. Max."

Sunlight streamed in through the oversized windows running across the front of the house. She fluffed the pillows on the overstuffed cotton sofa and coordinating armchairs, and kneeled before the whitewashed wooden coffee table to arrange the stack of Michigan-themed picture books she'd found in the home's library.

She'd bent to retrieve her dust rag when, with a thunderous crash, the front window exploded.

She dropped to her stomach on the floor and slung her arms over her head as a spray of glass rained down on her. Huddled on her knees, she peeked out from under her arms as a rock the size of a softball rolled to a stop a mere six inches from her face.

CB

A headache formed between Luke's eyes.

He'd been fighting for control of his thoughts all day. Now, he was too tired to fight off the images of her pert, pink nipples, and too depressed not to seek comfort in the memory of the taste of her bursting on his tongue.

He told himself it was just a kiss, but holy fuck, what a kiss. It was as if he'd been living with an eternal cold, which had rendered all food tasteless and odorless, and one small dose of Emily Cole had healed him.

He tugged a T-shirt over his head and zipped the fly of his blue jeans. Running late to meet up with Noah and

Shea, he shoved his police uniform into his bag and headed for the station's locker room exit.

At his computer, he logged out, capping off another red-letter day, highlighted by a domestic disturbance call at the Millers' residence. When Luke had arrived at the couple's home, the missus was en route to the hospital, having been beaten unconscious by the mister again. He arrested the husband, but hours later when the wife came to, she refused to press charges and he was forced to let the bastard go.

At his desk, Sloane held the phone to his ear. "What's the address?" He scribbled on a pad of paper.

Luke didn't like Justin Sloane. Hadn't liked him from the first moment he'd met him when he hired in to the island department a few months ago. Luke quickly learned Sloane, the son of a judge, wore the uniform more to bolster his fragile ego than to serve the ideals of justice and order. Didn't help he was hired to replace Anthony.

"We'll send someone over to take a look." Sloane banged the receiver into its cradle. "Sh-sh-shit, that was painful."

Luke stilled. "What's up?"

Sloane scratched his forehead with the eraser tip. "Just a broken-out window and a freaked-out homeowner." He reached for the dispatch radio. "I'm gonna put Newberry on it."

"You know what, I'll take this one." Luke kept his tone casual, in contrast to his thundering heart.

Sloane paused with his hand on the radio and regarded Luke with narrowed eyes. "Newberry can handle it."

"I worked a vandalism case last month." Luke rolled his shoulders. "Maybe there's a connection. I should check it out, just to be sure."

Sloane tore the sheet with Emily's address from the

notepad and handed it over. Luke snagged it and headed for the exit.

"Start with the neighbors," Sloane called after him. "I bet one of them has a ten-year-old missing his baseball."

Luke raised a hand. "I'll do that."

"H-h-have f-f-f-fun."

Luke came to an abrupt stop. His hands balled into fists. It'd feel good to hit the prick. Damn good.

Slowly, he turned. "You think that's funny?"

The greasy smile slid from Sloane's lips. "I didn't mean anything by it."

Luke's teeth ached with the effort to hold himself back.

What was he doing? He didn't have time for Sloane.

Emily needed him.

ଔ

Shards of broken glass sparkled in the sunlight as Emily dragged the broom across the hardwood floor and swept another pile of fragments into a dustpan. The sheer curtains danced in the breeze flowing freely through the fractured hole in the window.

A crunch of gravel carried to her from outside and she straightened to see the white SUV with dark green lettering roll to stop in front of the house. The engine fell quiet and Luke bounded from the vehicle.

Her heart did a backflip.

He rounded the vehicle, wearing ancient blue jeans and a black T-shirt, his attention riveted on the broken window.

She searched his face, wondering which Luke had come to her rescue. The easygoing charmer or the snarly grouch? She was still undecided when through the glass his focus shifted to her. His intense inspection of her face snatched the air from her lungs and she inhaled a slow, shaky breath.

He took the porch stairs two at a time and the sharp rap of the screen door snapping shut reached her ears a moment before he appeared beneath the living room archway.

His glittering green gaze touched over her and then swept through the room to take in the window, the spray of glass, and the rock at her feet.

"What happened here?" His casual tone belied the tension in his shoulders.

She pointed to the rock at her feet. "This came crashing through that window."

"You were home at the time?"

She nodded and took a half step to her left. "I was right here."

He crossed the room and inspected the area, his features carefully blanked.

"Did you see anything? A car in the driveway or someone on foot?"

"Nothing. M–my b–b–back was to the window and I ducked." A telltale quiver crept into her voice and she cleared her throat. "I didn't see a thing."

If she didn't know otherwise, she'd never guess his sea-green eyes had seen her naked or his pouty mouth had ravished hers. It was neither Luke the charmer, nor Luke the irascible grump standing in her living room.

It was Luke the cop.

She wasn't at all sure she liked this Luke, so impersonal and closed off.

"Are there any kids in the neighborhood?" he asked.

"What neighborhood? The closest house is the Cape Cod at the bottom of the hill." Nearly a half mile away.

"That's Ms. Beardsley. She celebrated her seventy-eighth birthday last month."

"Maybe her grandkids are visiting?"

"She never married or had any kids that I know of."

When he retraced his steps to the foyer, he didn't spare even a glance at her. She felt the loss like a lovesick puppy.

"I'll do a search of the premises and see if anything obvious turns up."

"Anything obvious? Like what?"

"Footprints, tire tracks. I'm not gonna lie, a photo ID would kick ass."

At the first hint of his smile, her heart took notice.

"Do ten-year-olds carry ID?"

"I can hope, can't I?" The gravity in his eyes betrayed him.

Her heart kicked up with her uneasiness. "You don't think it's a kid."

He scratched a spot on the back of his neck. "I don't know." His gaze trailed to the window and he appeared to wrestle with his next words. With a sigh, his eyes found hers. "Whoever threw that rock did it in broad daylight, with occupants in the house. And they came within a foot of hitting you. I have to consider someone meant to intimidate. That, or they're extremely careless. Either way, the situation just got a lot more dangerous." Then, likely in response to the way the blood drained from her head, he added, "Potentially more dangerous."

She rubbed at the ache in her temples.

"I'll ask around town." His tone gentled. "I'm sure someone knows of some kids visiting the island."

"That should do wonders for business," she muttered. If word got out the inn was unsafe, or the target of a rock-throwing serial killer, she'd be a failure before she even began.

Luke lifted his nose in the air and sniffed. "What's that?"

Just then, a piercing alarm shattered the quiet.

The cookies! Emily dashed from the room, through the foyer, around the oversized table in the dining room, and burst through the swinging door into the kitchen.

Smoke clouded the air and she stumbled toward the oven. The fire alarm's screeching wail rained down on her head as she stabbed the button to turn off the oven. She snatched a potholder off the counter and pulled open the oven door.

More smoke billowed into the room and mixed with the shrieking noise to forge a cocktail of chaos. Coughing, she yanked the cookie sheet from the oven and tossed the tray onto the stovetop. Several cookies were engulfed in flame. She backed away.

Luke appeared at her side. The epitome of calm, he raised a fire extinguisher, extracted the pin, and blasted the stove with a spray of pressurized air and foam. He discharged a second stream of foam into the oven's interior before he abandoned the extinguisher to the countertop and dragged a barstool away from the kitchen island. He positioned the stool beneath the smoke alarm, climbed on top, and stretching to his full height, silenced the blasted thing.

In the aftermath, the quiet was deafening. Smoke swirled before her eyes. A dollop of foam gathered at the edge of the stove and plopped onto the floor with a gooey splat.

"M-my first guest arrives today." She hated the hitch of defeat in her tone.

He slid the barstool back into place at the island and opened the back door. "What time are they expected?"

"Anytime between now and dinner."

"Why don't you go see if you can find someone to fix the window? I'll deal with this mess."

"You'd help me?" Disbelief snatched the words from her.

His features softened. "It's obvious you need me."

Unbelievably, she laughed. "I need a drink."

"That'll come later." He picked up a towel and moved

toward the oven.

"You don't have to do that." She jumped to take the towel from him. "You have work to—"

"I'm off duty." He took her by the shoulders and turned her away from the kitchen. "If there's time, I'll even make a fresh batch of cookies."

She twisted around. "You cook?"

His expression turned wry. "You sound shocked."

"I am."

"I'm offended." But his eyes sparked with humor. "I'm a thirty-two-year-old bachelor. Yes, I cook."

A bachelor? Not for the first time, she wondered about the blonde woman.

One hand on the kitchen door, she paused. "There's an unopened package of cookie dough in the fridge—"

He made a sound in the back of his throat. "I do not bake, nor do I eat, premade cookies. Fergodssake, woman, show some respect."

He pushed her the rest of the way through the kitchen door.

She pulled up abruptly, and he bumped into her from behind.

In the foyer, a young man stood beneath the oversize crystal chandelier, a black backpack slung over his shoulder. At their clumsy entrance, he turned.

He was younger than she'd expected. Probably in his early twenties, he was tall and lean with golden-brown hair and deep-set brown eyes.

She forced her feet to move.

Max. Max. Max. Max. "You m-m-must be M-Max."

At her stammer, his dark eyes grew alert. Then a surprisingly warm smile transformed his youthful face. "That's me. You must be Emily?"

She relaxed a little. "That's me," she repeated.

Chapter Eight

She lit up like a goddamned Christmas tree.

Luke's face ached with the severity of his scowl.

"This place is freaking awesome," the kid said. "How old is it?"

Luke recognized Max. Not the particular arrangement of his symmetrical features or the uniqueness of his light hair and dark eyes. But he recognized the lean, hungry look lurking in their dark depths. The desperation that clung to his too-thin, muscled body.

Yeah, Luke knew this kid. In his ten years as a cop, he'd met a hundred just like him.

Hell, Luke *was* him at that age.

"Over o-one hundred and fifty y-years old."

Max's gaze slid to Luke and the softness in his dark eyes shifted and hardened.

Luke folded his arms over his chest. "Hi."

Max tipped his chin. "Hey." He studied Luke with old eyes, and Luke allowed his assessment, sensing the kid's instant and absolute distrust had nothing to do with him personally.

Emily's hands twisted in front of her. "Uh... this is... uh... Luke. He's the... uh... he's the cook!"

"Chef," Luke corrected. "She pays me a fortune and I'm worth every penny."

Max's mouth moved in what Luke supposed was a smile, but with no flash of teeth or so much as a lip quiver.

"Can I show y-y-you to your room?" Emily scurried to one of the twin staircases and started to climb.

Behind her, Max set one foot on the bottom stair and stopped, his gaze snared by the rock and the hundred tiny fragments of broken glass.

"The neighbor kid did it," Emily burst out, her resemblance to Luke's four-year-old niece uncanny.

Max's brow wrinkled. "I didn't see any other houses around."

Feverish color painted her cheeks. "He's visiting."

Good God, but she was terrible liar. Luke didn't have to worry about this one deceiving him. A deep chuckle knocked loose from his chest and he followed them up the stairs.

Emily led them down a wide, well-lit hallway to the third door on the right. She motioned Max and Luke ahead of her.

Max flung his backpack onto the bed and continued to the French doors. When Luke stepped through the doorway, Emily's light scent tickled his senses.

He wanted to unwrap her. To see the smooth skin and delicious curves that lay beneath the shapeless, colorless loungewear she wore. She brought to mind hard candy with a surprise center, and he wanted to lick his way to the middle.

"Holy crap," Max breathed, looking out at the sweeping views. "There's no one out here."

Panic-filled brown eyes darted between Luke and the kid's back. "We-we're isolated, it's true, but the island is very safe."

Her voice sounded like sugar, and he knew she tasted the same.

Max tossed her an easy grin over his shoulder. "The isolation's what I like most about it."

Emily blinked. "It is?"

Luke coughed.

"I mean, great! That's great." She scooped up a manila folder off the nightstand and stuck out her arm.

Max lifted an eyebrow as he took it from her. "What's this?"

"Some information about the island. Local attractions and restaurants..." She trailed off when he tossed the folder into the armchair in the corner of the room.

"Cool, thanks." He turned back to the view.

Several beats of silence filled the room. Emily looked to Luke, and he shrugged.

Abruptly, Max turned away from the balcony door. "I have a proposition for you."

Luke straightened. "What kind of proposition?"

Max looked from Emily to Luke. "I want to rent out the entire house."

"The entire house?" Emily squeaked.

"Why?" Luke wanted to know at the same time.

For a moment, Max appeared confused about whom to address. He settled on Emily. "I'm making a movie and I want to film it here."

"What kind of movie?" Luke didn't bother with his usual charm offensive.

Max scratched an itch on his collarbone. "It's an indie film, small scale and low budget. Just an idea some film students at ESU and I came up with. We managed to raise $20,000 through a crowdfunding campaign."

"Wh-when w-would you start? And how long w-w-would you stay?"

Luke only just stifled an exasperated gasp. "You'll need a permit."

"Next month for a six-week shoot." Max addressed Emily before his gaze slipped to Luke. "We'll of course obtain all the necessary approvals."

Emily worried the pendant hanging around her neck. "The house is reserved for a w-w-wedding Halloween weekend."

Max's features pulled into a thoughtful frown. "To be honest, I need to work out the details of the schedule and line up my permits." He sent a nod in Luke's direction. "Maybe I can work around that weekend."

"How many p-people w-w-would be staying?"

"Not more than ten of us for sure." A calculating grin curled Max's lips. "More like five if I can figure out a way to pull it off."

"Five people?" Luke didn't bother to hide the skepticism in his tone. "What did you say this movie is about?"

The color heightened on Max's cheekbones. "It's a slasher flick." He returned his focus to Emily. "I promise we won't harm the house. If I want anything moved or even touched, I'll check with you first. You'd have veto power over everything we do."

A small smile turned up the corners of her kissable mouth.

Luke frowned. "What are you thinking?"

The whiskey color at the center of her eyes blazed. "It could bring some exposure to the inn."

"It could," Luke agreed. "If anyone bothers to watch the movie." He inclined his head at Max. "No offense."

"Tons taken."

Luke ignored the kid, distracted by the way Emily

worried her plump bottom lip.

"I could really use the b-business..."

A defeated sigh dragged from him. "If nothing else, you're at full capacity for four weeks during the off-season."

Her bright smile knocked him back.

Damn if she didn't turn it on Max.

"Okay."

Max smiled. "Okay?"

Emily nodded.

"Excellent." Max unzipped the front pocket of his backpack. "I'll contact the others."

"Do you n-need anything from m-me?"

A cell phone cradled in his hand, Max frowned. "Do you have anyplace we can store gear and equipment? Someplace out of the way but easy to access?"

"There's an attic space at the end of the hall. W-would that work?"

A light entered his eyes. "Sounds perfect."

"Anything else?"

"Yeah, can you keep that neighbor kid away from the windows?"

She blanched.

Max held up a hand. "I'm kidding. It's a joke."

She blushed an adorable shade of pink. Luke didn't meet many women who blushed.

"We really are very safe here," she said. "Plus, the island has a very... active police department."

Max let loose with a derisive smirk. "Aren't they all?"

With a guilty glance in his direction, Emily ate her smile. "They're very responsive."

A rusty laugh rattled around in Max's chest. "It's all good. The last thing I need are the cops hanging around this place."

СЗ

Luke turned on the stairs. "I was not interrogating him."

From her spot on the step above him, Emily peered into his eyes. "You demanded to read the script."

He twisted away and stomped down the steps. "Is that not a reasonable request?"

"No. It's high-handed and overreaching." A smile teased. "You're the cook, remember?"

"Chef," he snapped.

When they reached the bottom step, the fresh scent of sea air pulled her attention to the living room. Broken glass littered the floor, winking in the fading light.

Luke stiffened beside her. "I'm going to take a look around outside."

While he disappeared through the front door, she returned to the living room. She rescued the broom from the floor where she'd deserted it in her futile dash to save the cookies from their fiery death. As she dumped the last of the glass fragments into a trash bag, she heard the sound of Luke's voice through the broken glass.

"Hey, I'm not going to be able to make it tonight. There's been an incident at the inn..." His voice faded as he moved away from the window.

Was he talking to the exquisite blonde? The wrench of envy nauseated her. Somewhere during the nine years of her mom's slow death, she'd lost the taste for bemoaning her perceived misfortunes. In school, she'd devoted many long hours to wishing away her stutter, her unfortunate coloring, her awkwardness. All of herself, really. Then, her mom got sick and she learned what true misfortune was.

She scooped up the bag of glass and carried it to the trash can in the kitchen. The shiny, new, immaculate kitchen, now covered in a layer of foam and filth.

She plucked her cell phone off the countertop and sent Mina a text to ask if she recalled the name of the company that had replaced the home's custom windows last winter.

Then she filled the farmhouse sink with warm, sudsy water and set to work. Removing the slop proved tricky and she refilled the sink twice with clean water before she'd made noticeable progress.

As she turned back to the stove with a clean basin of water, the back door opened and Mina popped her head inside.

Her eyes grew huge when she saw the kitchen. "What happened?"

Emily sat back on her heels. She'd opened her mouth to try to explain the sequence of events that had led to the mess, when a loud pounding reverberated through the house.

She climbed to her feet. "What is that?"

"Noah and Luke are going to board up the window." Mina pulled open a drawer and picked out a dishcloth.

Emily filled Mina in on the rock, though she'd apparently already learned the whole story from Noah, who'd heard it from Luke. They cleaned the remainder of the kitchen, working side by side, just as they'd done the previous winter when Mina was putting the final touches on the house. Only a few weeks in all, but it'd given Emily a much-needed focus to her aimless life and helped ward off the crippling depression for a time.

Soon, the kitchen gleamed and they followed the sounds of erratic pounding to the living room, where Noah hammered a nail into the wide plank of plywood that Luke held over the window.

Emily sank into an armchair, her head tipped to one side and her gaze riveted by the sight of Luke. Specifically, the way his black T-shirt pulled tight across his back and shoulders and his muscles rippled beneath the fabric.

With one last hammering, the wood was secure.

Luke wiped an arm across his glistening forehead. Green eyes captured hers. "I think it's time for that drink."

Her spine snapped straight and a guilty flush warmed her cheeks. She lurched to her feet. "Anyone else?"

Noah opened his mouth, but didn't get a word out before Mina sprang up from the sofa. "I'll help!" Her voice pitched high and she nearly knocked Emily down when she bolted from the room.

Emily sent her cousin a curious look, which fell on Mina's back, as she was already halfway across the foyer.

Emily reached the kitchen as Mina knocked the refrigerator closed with her hip, two beers in either hand.

"Everything all right?" Emily pulled down two wineglasses from the cupboard.

Rummaging through the drawer of utensils, Mina nodded distractedly. "Everything's fine."

Emily stuck the bottle opener under her nose. "What's the matter?"

Worry disrupted Mina's blue eyes. "Let me get a beer in Noah, and then I'll explain."

Emily scooped up the bottle of wine and followed her cousin to the living room.

They rejoined the guys in the middle of a conversation.

"Are you and Mina staying for a while then?"

Mina stiffened midway to sitting, and then sank the rest of the way onto the sofa next to Noah.

"We're staying indefinitely." Noah sent Emily a kind smile as she reclaimed her spot in the armchair across the coffee table from Luke. "Emily's nice enough to let us freeload until we find something more permanent."

Mina shoved the beer into Noah's hand and snatched up the wine bottle. "Actually, we wanted to talk to you about possibly extending our stay."

Noah grew instantly alert. His smile vanished. "We

do?"

Mina filled her wine glass and sat back. She pushed a puff of air between her lips and faced Noah. "So here's the thing."

"Oh, boy," Noah muttered.

"I bought a house."

"Excuse me?"

Words poured out of Mina in a rush. "The city was going to demolish it in favor of green space and I couldn't let them do it. It's so pretty and old–it needs a little work, of course–but once we fix the foundation and repair the plumbing, and the electrical, and probably get a new roof, it'll be beautiful and we can move in. It's on the south side of the island and has an amazing view of the harbor."

Noah eased back on the couch. "So let me get this straight. You bought a house that we can't live in, can't resell, and can't rent out?"

Mina lifted her wineglass a notch higher. "It only cost a dollar."

"A bargain." Noah's tone dripped with sarcasm. "How'd you pull that off?"

"It was going to cost them $15,000 to demo it, so..."

"So you saved them the expense." Noah gave his head a soft shake. "Did it occur to you there might be a reason they'd be willing to drop that kind of money just to get rid of the place?"

A frown turned down the corners of her mouth. "They have no imagination."

"That may be true," he said easily. "But where are we going to live?"

"I thought we could live in the carriage house until the renovations are done." Her large eyes shimmered. "You're happy there, aren't you?"

Noah softened. "I'm happy anywhere you are." He reached for her hand and pressed a kiss to her palm. "But can't you just take in stray kittens or something?"

Luke's soft chuckle sloped through Emily, and Mina's soft smile when she leaned into Noah warmed the room. They sat snuggled on the couch and the conversation turned to other topics.

Noah and Luke talked about their niece and nephews, and schemed a way to force Shea, their eldest brother, to talk to his wife, a woman named Isobel whom Emily didn't know.

Emily found herself waiting for Luke to speak, curious what he might say. Curious about him and his life. When Mina and Noah talked about their time spent in Ireland, Emily wondered why Noah had a distinct Irish accent, but Luke, at best, had a faint lilt.

Their conversation took twists and turns, and by the time Emily finished her second glass of wine, she'd answered a few questions about Arizona and about her guest upstairs. She was shocked to realize she'd never experienced anything like it before: visiting with friends, in no hurry to get away from each other and in fact finding inconsequential things to say and ask for seemingly no other reason than to extend their time together.

How it hurt to realize what a sad, lonely life she'd lived. The closest she'd ever come was with her roommate in college, Haven. An outgoing, friendly girl, she'd had a knack for bringing Emily out of her shell.

When Noah and Mina retreated to the carriage house sometime later, the setting sun tilted soft light across the room.

From across the table, Luke watched her with hooded eyes.

She sat forward in the armchair. "I... uh..." Not knowing what to say, she trailed off.

She couldn't shake the feeling something had changed between them, something more than the kiss, or even the fact he'd seen her naked, but was unable to pinpoint when or what had caused the change exactly.

She made a motion with her hand to include the front window. "Thank you."

A smile pulled up one corner of his mouth. She braced herself for a flippant reply.

"You're welcome," he said softly, his eyes glittering in the dim light.

He stood, and so did she, prepared to walk him to the door. Except he didn't go to the door.

He sat on the sofa, flicked open a notepad, and tossed it onto the coffee table in front of him.

His cop face slammed into place. "Have a minute?"

Gooseflesh chased up her arms. "A minute for what?"

"If you don't want me asking questions around town, maybe I can ask you a few?"

Chapter Nine

"**W**h-what kind of questions?"

Luke shifted to the edge of the sofa and propped his elbows on his knees. "We need a list."

"A list of wh-what?"

"Suspects."

"Suspects?"

"People or persons who might wish you unwell. Nemeses, rivals, foes. Enemies."

"Enemies?"

A beat of silence followed while he blinked at her. "You're doing it again."

"Doing what?"

"Repeating everything I say."

Her throat tightened and she swallowed with difficulty. "I don't think I'll be m-much help to you."

"Shall we find out?"

"Wh-what do you want to know?"

"Any husbands, current or former?"

She shook her head.

"Boyfriends?"

He'd poked a sore spot. Insecurity over her lack of sophistication, or of any lasting meaningful sexual relationship, chafed like a shoe on a fresh blister.

She tossed up a flimsy smile. "So we're officially abandoning the misguided ten-year-old theory?"

"Best to be thorough, don't you think?"

She toyed with the end of her ponytail.

"So, about those ex-boyfriends…?"

"There are too many to detail, b-but none that are carrying a grudge."

His professional mask suffered a crack and she glimpsed a light spark in his eyes. "How about a flame?"

She'd met Joshua her junior year in college. For once, her crippling shyness didn't prove too large an obstacle to overcome and they'd begun dating. They'd even had sex a few times before Emily left school, but the fragile newness of their relationship combined with Emily's phobia of the phone and Audrey's illness conspired against them.

Five years after she'd dropped out of college, she'd run into Joshua at the hospital where Audrey had just been admitted and where Joshua worked. He was with a woman, whom he introduced to Emily as Becca, his fiancée.

Emily hadn't been aware they'd broken up. So caught up in the hell of death, she was shocked to realize years had passed, and that Joshua had moved on.

Without her.

Green eyes watched her intently.

She sighed dramatically. "I leave m-my lovers w-w-well pleased, but under no illusions."

His heated gaze landed on her mouth. "Is that so?"

She sipped from her wineglass so as not to give away her lie.

"How about a current boyfriend?"

With a flick of her ponytail, she snorted. "If I had a boyfriend, I w-wouldn't need BOB, would I?"

"Who the hell is Bob?"

Heat rushed into her face. "The vibrator."

One dark eyebrow inched upward. "You named him Bob?"

"I didn't name him. He's my Battery Operated Boyfriend." Eager for a change of topic, she tipped her chin toward the table. "Who's made your list?"

He drove a hand through his hair. "Nothing earth-shattering. Just a couple of delinquents and a competing business owner."

"Wh-what business owner? The motel downtown?"

"Hal doesn't pull in a lot of business. He's a known hothead, and from what I can tell, a slacker. I doubt he's ambitious enough to drive out here and terrorize you." His voice lowered. "Which leads me back to you, and any enemies that may have followed you to the island."

"I don't have any enemies. Sorry to disappoint." Growing more unsettled by the minute, she took another long drink of her wine. There was no one in her life, enemies or otherwise, worth mentioning.

Cradling his chin in his palm, he tapped the pen against the notepad. "Have you pissed anyone off since you arrived?"

"You mean other than the Thief Island Police Department?"

A muscle ticked in his jaw. "Yes, other than them."

"No one that I'm aware of, no."

His brows knitted together. "I imagine you haven't had a lot of interaction yet. Maybe someone thinks you're stuck-up."

A soft gasp slipped through her lips at the accusation,

one she'd heard a number of times in her life. "Or maybe one of your groupies saw you kissing me in a bar parking lot and is mad."

"I did more than kiss you." A conspiratorial husk came into his voice.

Her breathing hitched higher. So he did remember. Remembered, and was unaffected by it.

"I trust you can add the pertinent names to the list."

He shoved the notepad away. "So to recap, you've never maimed, harmed, or in any way neglected, insulted, or offended a single creature on the planet. That you are aware of."

"Is that sarcasm, Officer Nolan?"

"Not at all. I was just hoping you had a mortal enemy from childhood who I could charge with vandalism and wrap this case up tonight."

The clock on the mantel chimed nine o'clock. Rather than give up, Luke propped his feet on the coffee table and crossed his legs at the ankles.

Agitated and weary from the poking at her sad, lonely life, she scrambled to come up with a way to get rid of him.

"If I give you a name, will you go away?"

"Depends on the name, I suppose." His quick smile coaxed the dimples into his cheeks.

Her heart stuttered, but she held out against it. "There might be someone with reason to resent me."

His smug smile vanished.

"But it isn't likely," she rushed to add.

"I'll take anything you've got."

She let out a slow, shaky breath. "Wh-when my dad died, a large part of his estate was willed to my mom."

"Your dad? What was his name?"

"Harrison Cole."

He scribbled down the name in his notepad.

"His wife fought the will, claiming he meant to change

it before he died, but the court ruled in my mom's favor."

His head remained bent while his hand moved across the paper.

"But by the time the ruling came down, my m-m-mom had died, too."

"Your mom died last year?"

"In September." She took a sip of wine to dislodge the lump that formed in her throat.

"And your dad? When did he pass?"

"In the spring of that year."

His head came up. "You've had a rough go of it lately."

The gentleness in his voice surprised her, but she didn't want his misplaced pity. "Harrison wasn't a nice man."

The gentle tone evaporated. "Care to explain that?"

She lifted one shoulder. "There's nothing to explain. He was a corporate businessman and he didn't tolerate imperfection."

The pen poised between his fingertips as if he might break it in half. "Imperfection?"

She gave him a look.

His expression cleared. "You mean your stutter?"

"Not just the way I talk, but all of it."

"All of what?"

With his scrutiny, fierce heat rushed into her cheeks.

He sighed and looked down at the notepad. "When did Harrison remarry?"

"When I was nine, or maybe ten."

"So your parents divorced?"

She nodded. "When I was seven."

"Any idea what went wrong?"

"I assume there were a lot of things." Her fingers toyed with the stem of her wineglass. "Harrison was twenty-three years older than my mom, and he worked and traveled a lot."

He sat in silence, waiting.

Memories crowded forward. Of the time Emily ran home from school, tears streaming down her face after Angie Lawson humiliated her in front of the entire class again. She'd flung herself into Audrey's lap and soaked up her mom's comforting words and caresses.

"You coddle her," Harrison had said. "Why don't you ever give me that kind of attention?"

"She's a child." The bite in Audrey's tone had troubled Emily. "Not a grown man who should know how to take care of himself."

Harrison glowered down at them. "She's a dolt."

Emily hadn't known what that word meant. Not then, but she'd figured it out soon enough.

She shook off the memories. "I've always wondered if I was the cause of their strife. They disagreed on how to handle me."

The pen landed on the table with a clatter. "What does that mean? Handle you?"

"My dad thought I needed to be p-pushed. That I could correct my speech and become more outgoing if I only tried harder. He was w-w-wrong."

The room grew dark as night set in. She struggled to read his expression.

"What about the will?" he asked. "Do you think he meant to leave your mom in it?"

She stared into her empty wineglass, pondering his question. "It's possible. He would've heard about m-m-my mom's illness, and he probably knew we were drowning in bills. Maybe he meant the money to be used for her care. But I think his wife was right that he wouldn't have w-wanted it to come to me."

"How much money are we talking?"

"A million."

"That's a lot of money."

It was a lot of money, and Emily hated every stupid penny for the stress it'd caused her mom and for the constant, daily reminder that her mom was dead. Emily would happily give the money away for just one more day with her mom. So far, she'd spent well over half of it buying Mina's house and donating to research the disease that'd killed her mom.

"So it's possible your stepmom has motive enough to make you uneasy?" The low timbre of Luke's voice eased over her.

Emily shrugged. "It's possible. Or her kids might."

"You have siblings?"

"Two." The callused-over notch on her heart gave a little wrench. "I've never met them. It's possible they don't even know I exist. Or didn't, until Harrison's will was read."

"You've never met your siblings?" An edge crept into his tone.

"Once, in high school, I got the silly idea to contact them, but Harrison put a stop it before I met either of them."

"Any idea where they are now?"

"One goes to school in California. UCLA, I think. The other is married and lives in Denver."

"What are their names?" he asked, and wrote down the names she gave him.

"I seriously doubt any of this is relevant to the present situation. If I wanted a million dollars, I wouldn't think throwing a rock through a window might help me get it."

"You never know what motivates desperate people. I'm glad you told me." A disarming warmth wrapped around his words. "Thank you." His head turned toward the fireplace. "It's late."

He scooped up his notebook and pushed to his feet. She stood, and when he brushed past her, the warmth from his body arched through her. At the front door, she held it open and he stepped out into the night.

She was easing the door shut when he turned back.

Shadows cut across his face, but his voice reached out from the darkness to wrap itself around her.

"Goodnight, Emily."

ℭ♌

The pounding inside Emily's skull began as the first fingers of daylight peeked around the edge of the curtains. She drew the covers up over her head.

Get up.

Shut up.

After Luke had left, she'd locked up the house and crawled into bed. With the dredged-up memories, desolation spread through her. Like spilled paint seeping over white paper, it blotted out what little peace she'd recovered over the last few weeks.

It might be hours before she found the will to even attempt to get out of bed. She'd started to doze when a hammering jerked her back to wakefulness.

She lifted her head, listening. When the noise resumed, louder this time, she realized it originated from her back door. Who would be knocking on her back door—she squinted at the clock on her nightstand—at six thirty in the morning?

Her head dropped onto her pillow. It must be Mina. No one else would come around to the back of the house.

With a sigh, Emily climbed from the warm cocoon of her bed. Her limbs heavy, she dragged the quilt off the bed, wrapped it around her shoulders, and trudged through her suite to the kitchen.

In the mudroom, a trio of obnoxious thumps rattled the glass-paned door. Through the frosted window, she made out the figure of a man. Not Mina, but maybe Noah?

She yanked open the door and blinked into the morning light.

Bathed in a stream of golden sunlight, Luke's dark hair shone and his eyes sparkled like jewels. He wore blue jeans and a light blue T-shirt that conformed to his broad shoulders and lean-muscled frame. She grew a little light-headed.

A fierce scowl contorted his features. "Why aren't you up?"

"Why are you here?" Her scowl matched his. "Did you find who threw the rock?"

"No. I'm reporting for duty."

She gave a small shake of her head.

"I'm here to cook breakfast. Unless...?" He cut her with a look. "You weren't teasing me with that crack about me being your chef, were you?"

She gaped at him. "Yes. That's exactly what I was doing."

"We need to work on your delivery." He pushed past her.

She scrambled into the kitchen after him. "You don't have to make breakfast."

"I've seen what you can do to a cookie." He plunked a grocery tote onto the countertop. "I shudder to think what might happen to a poor, defenseless omelet."

She narrowed her eyes at him. "I *can* cook."

"That's debatable."

Well, she could learn. Any skill she might have had, had been geared toward preparing food her mom could swallow without choking.

He pulled open a cupboard door and then closed it. "Oh, and I should warn you, I'm not cheap."

"Is this about what Max said?"

He yanked the next cupboard door open, and closed it, too.

"Because I don't think he was serious when he made that remark."

"What remark?" With his head inside a cupboard, his

voice sounded muffled.

"You know what remark."

"Remind me."

"He said the last thing he needs is a cop hanging around."

Luke slammed a cupboard shut. "Tell me you have a skillet."

She flung the quilt onto the island and crossed to the stove. She retrieved a skillet from the bottom drawer and held it out to him.

He reached for it, but at the last second, she jerked it away. "Is this about Max?"

Rather than answer, his green gaze flared and dropped to her breasts. She ducked her chin to see what he saw. She wasn't wearing a bra and her nipples poked through the thin fabric of her nightshirt.

His gaze riveted to her breasts, his tongue slipped out to lick his full bottom lip.

Heat, both embarrassed and aroused, swept through her.

He snatched the pan from her grasp. "If a cop's the last thing he wants hanging around, that's exactly what he's gonna get."

"Do you really think that's necessary?"

"Probably not, but until I know for sure, you're stuck with me."

"What, like barnacles?"

He bared his teeth. "Cute."

"Thank you." She smiled, pleased with herself.

"See if you can toast a few slices without burning down the house." He tossed her a loaf of bread.

Caught off guard, she bobbled the loaf and it hit the floor with a thud.

When she'd recovered the loaf, she slid slices into the four-slot toaster while Luke cracked eggs into a ceramic bowl. He added a splash of milk and whipped the mix with a whisk before pouring the contents of the bowl into the skillet. Then he retrieved an onion and a green pepper from the grocery tote.

He selected a knife and she handed him a cutting board. His fingers worked expertly dicing the vegetables. She grew absorbed in watching him, the way the weariness faded from around his eyes while he worked, that she startled when the toast popped. Indeed, a little overdone.

Admitting defeat, she left him to it and went to grab a shower. She ran through her routine as quickly as possible, throwing on jeans, a clean bra, and a T-shirt before returning to the kitchen.

The aroma of freshly brewed coffee filled the room and he slid a fluffy omelet from the skillet onto one of her white platters.

Her stomach let loose an angry growl.

One of his dark eyebrows lifted.

"Sorry. It smells amazing." She carried a stack of plates and utensils to the dining room table and he followed with the omelets and toast.

"You might as well eat," he said.

She hesitated all of one second before scooping a healthy serving of omelet onto a plate and taking a warm, gooey bite.

A hand shot up to cover her mouth, stifling her moan of pleasure. "Omigosh, this is really good." She licked the corner of her mouth. "Like, really good."

A glimmer of light flickered in his eyes. "I'm glad you like it."

With her next bite, she couldn't quell her groan of ecstasy.

He coughed and his open expression slammed closed. "I've gotta get to work."

She set her plate on the table and followed him to the front door.

His hand on the doorknob, he stilled and gazed down at her, an odd expression on his face.

She ran a hand over her hair. "Wh-why are you looking at me like that?"

A flicker of baffled confusion played over his face. "I want to kiss you."

"Y-you do?"

His eyelids grew heavy and green flashed brilliant with the heat. "I really do."

So that's what a smoldering glance looked like.

A thrill rushed through her with dizzying speed. She told herself the light-headedness wasn't specific to Luke. After a lifetime of scarce male attention, any man would've caused her heart to race and her palms to sweat. Any man who looked at her with naked hunger would've made her insides turn all hot and liquid.

Any man would've made her yearn to get naked for him.

It just so happened, Luke was that man. The first to flirt with her in forever, and while she didn't yet understand the rules of the game they were playing, she suspected she'd suck at it when she did know.

He was a Harley Davidson when she needed training wheels, but she wouldn't let her ignorance rob her of the chance to ride such a supreme vehicle. Whatever game they played, she'd learn along the way, and what better way to learn than with a man like Luke?

She lifted her chin. "Then why don't you?"

The soles of his shoes scuffed against the marble-tiled floor as he closed the distance between them. "I'm all twisted up inside." He fondled a strand of her hair near her ear. "Afraid I can't compete with all your other lovers."

He was teasing her, and for once, she didn't mind. Indeed, she liked it. She liked that he caught her by surprise, and that he spent time thinking of ways to do so. She liked the intimacy of sharing a joke with him.

"Well, the only way to improve is with practice. Lots and lots of practice."

Surprise touched his features. "You're teasing me?"

She nodded. She couldn't explain it, except he made her bold.

"I'm so proud of you." His head bent low, until a mere whisper separated their mouths. "I should reward you."

Her heart slammed against her breastbone. She'd pleased him, and the thought excited her. Probably more than it should.

"Lucky for you, I respond well to praise."

His smile faded, chased away by the heat in his eyes.

He took a small nip of her mouth, and another. His lips nudged hers apart and his soft tongue explored her. Tasting, savoring. He tasted like lemon drops. Sugary and sweet, potent and tangy.

Their joke wasn't far from the truth, except Emily was the student learning from Luke, the pro. She mimicked his slow, erotic kisses. With her first tentative nibble, he moaned, and her world spun.

The kiss deepened and held, and his hands came up to cradle her head.

Then it was over.

His fingers lightly toyed with the hair at her temple. "Have you had a kiss better than that?"

"Tons," she breathed.

"Tons of kisses or tons better?"

"Hmm-mm," she purred.

His smile flashed only briefly. "Damn, I've got a lot to learn. Better get some more practice."

His head slanted over hers and his mouth came down with greedy possession. He suckled her bottom lip and a jolt of yearning spiraled through her to simmer low in her belly. A moan dragged from her and her hands sought out the warmth of his flesh. She smoothed her palms over the taut skin of his abdomen.

He tilted her chin, and with each slow lick of her mouth, liquid fire pulsed between her legs.

Her fingers danced along the waistband of his jeans.

On a gasp, he broke the kiss and pressed his forehead to hers. "God, Emily, you make it hard to breathe."

She held on to both of his wrists to keep herself from sinking to a puddle at his feet.

He gripped a fistful of her hair and nipped several more kisses.

When he pulled away, she nearly cried out with the loss of him.

He opened the door. "I have to go."

"Wh-why?" She didn't care that her desperation showed.

He snatched her to him once more. This time, he kissed her with several slow, lingering licks.

Releasing her, he backed away, but his heel caught and he tripped over the threshold. "Good-bye, Emily."

She scowled at his retreating back.

Chapter Ten

The early morning stillness hung over the island when Luke parked his SUV under the oak tree in Emily's driveway. He shouldn't have come back, but he couldn't stay away. Just as he couldn't stop himself last night from stroking out another climax with her name on it.

The occasional peep of a bird and the rustle of wind in the trees accompanied him as he rounded the side of the house.

He'd always enjoyed Thief Island, with its wild weather and the constant roar of wind and sea, but this spot, Emily's house, was particularly alluring. On the northernmost tip, her property sat up high and boasted one of the best views anywhere on the island. His pace quickened.

A split second before he reached the backyard, an unusual sound reached his ears and he lurched to a stop.

Struck by the sight and sound of her, he stood in the grass, his hands loose at his sides.

A garden hose in her hand, she moved around the patio, giving water to the flowers bursting out of the ground. All the while, she sang.

Her voice, though strong and sure, and without the slightest hint of a stutter, wouldn't overpower anyone. It was soft, sultry even, and heartfelt. Genuine and unassuming, like the woman. At the crescendo, a rasp came into her tone that grabbed him by the balls.

Her. He wanted her.

She sang of a long-ago lover, her song at once a celebration and a lament, a bittersweet mix of the joy and sorrow, and a flood of emotion—every emotion—rushed forth to drown him. Captured by her voice and her peaceful heart, he was unable to move toward her or run away.

He had to have her.

It didn't make any sense, why he wanted her so badly. He could have any woman. Yet none of the other women had managed to do what the shy, meek Emily Cole had managed to do.

Get him hard and keep him hard with wanting.

Just then, she started and spun in his direction. The spray of water from the hose shot across the patio and he lunged to avoid its frigid shower.

"Luke!"

He showed his palms. "Don't shoot."

She let go of the nozzle. The water stream collapsed and disappeared.

He bounded up the porch stairs.

"I already m-made breakfast," she called after him.

He turned slowly and narrowed his eyes at her. "What did you make?"

"I bought m-muffins and pastries."

His lip curled. "Store-bought muffins? Are you serious

right now?"

The screen door snapped shut behind him, his last glimpse of her tripping over the hose and scrambling after him.

He ate his smile, enjoying every moment he spent with her more than the last.

When she burst into the kitchen, he closed the refrigerator door, a carton of eggs in his hand.

"I'm perfectly capable of feeding a lone houseguest."

"There's a time and a place for processed junk food. Breakfast is not it."

She opened the cardboard box from the bakery in town and chose a cinnamon roll smothered in white frosting.

Her moan of pleasure when she bit into the bun tugged at his groin. "You're a cop. I thought baked goods were your weakness."

"I'm watching my figure."

Her gaze flitted down his frame and back up again. "Nice job."

His bark of laughter surprised him. God, she was fun. He enjoyed everything about her. Her animated features and frequent blushes, her sharp mind, and even the way she talked. Not the stutter necessarily, though he found it endearing, but her slow, deliberate speech intrigued him more and more all the time.

She didn't fight to be heard nor toss around careless thoughts or sentiments. Everything she said was specifically chosen for him, and he found himself hanging on each choice, awaiting the words she'd finally pick as worthy for his consideration.

His laughter died when her pink tongue darted out to lick a splotch of white frosting from her lower lip. The punch of lust stole his voice, and when she mentioned something about taking a shower, he grunted.

He focused on slicing a potato and tried to block out

the image of her under the warm spray, water sloughing over her smooth skin and beaded nipples, and his mouth closing over one pink areola.

He slammed his mind back to the potato wedges. He'd always been able to get lost in the mechanics of cooking. The mix of flavors, the aromas, the precise timing.

Today, it wasn't working.

She returned on a fresh-scented cloud that teased his nostrils. She'd dried her hair and pulled it into a ponytail that hung down her back in soft waves. As usual, she wore not a speck of makeup. A pair of blue jeans hugged her heart-shaped ass and a pale blue tank top exposed the ivory skin of her shoulders, still dewy with moisture.

He carried the dish of fried potatoes through the swinging door to the dining room. Her scent followed him.

When he returned to the kitchen, she tortured her swollen bottom lip. "M-Max still hasn't come down?"

"Nope." He plucked a leftover potato wedge from the pan and popped it into his mouth.

"He hasn't left his room in two days."

Luke swallowed. "He hasn't left at all?"

She shook her head and her bright hair shimmered about her shoulders. "Do y-y-you think—" Her throat worked. "Sh-should I knock?"

"You should knock."

She hesitated.

He turned her shoulders and gave her a little push toward the foyer. "At the very least, you have to make sure he isn't dead."

She blanched.

"I'm kidding." He hustled her toward the stairs. "We're going to have to work on your sense of humor."

"Later, okay?" With a resolved nod, she placed one foot on the first step, but then she whirled to face him. "I don't know what to say."

He folded his arms over his chest and blocked her retreat. "Say 'kitchen closes in ten minutes. If you want to eat, you need to do it now.'"

Her features pulled into an adorable frown. "That sounds rude."

"Say it however you like, but that's the general message you need to convey."

She plopped down hard on a step. Her expression twisted with such misery, he almost took pity on her.

Almost.

"You know, there are a few things I'd like to ask him." He started up the stairs. "Why don't I just–?"

"No!" Emily surged to her feet. "I'll do it. I'll do it right now."

She backed up several steps before she turned and started to climb. At the top, she snuck a glance back at him over his shoulder.

He gave her a stern look. "You can do it."

"I'm not very good at talking to p-p-people."

A pang wrenched his chest. "Visualize."

One eyebrow inched upward.

"Studies prove visualizing success increases the likelihood you'll succeed."

"It does?"

He had no freaking idea, but he heard a lot of such talk at the seminars Cynthia kept sending him to and he had to say something that might bring some color back into her cheeks.

"It's true if you make it so."

She didn't look convinced.

"Okay, listen to me. You're a piranha," he said. "A small fish with a big bite."

Her startled laugh knocked him in the chest.

Truth be told, he couldn't find a single humorous thing about the moment. Not the thundering beneath his breastbone, nor the white-hot lawlessness surging through his veins at the light, tinkling sound of her laughter.

When he'd started this, he'd wanted a distraction, and certainly he'd gotten that much. What he hadn't bet on was the desperate quality of his growing desire for her.

And as she turned from him, her terror palpable, something inside him shifted and forever changed what he saw when he looked at her.

Ϙ

A small smile touched her lips as she made her way down the hall.

He'd taken the time to figure her out, and he used his knowledge to challenge her, a fact that rendered her insanely giddy. Maybe she should've been upset that he'd manipulated her, but she wasn't. Not even a little bit.

Her mind turned to the task ahead of her. She visualized herself knocking on the bedroom door and informing Max that a scrumptious breakfast awaited him downstairs.

She lifted a hand and knocked two soft taps on Max's door. She waited. No noise reached her from within the bedroom. Was he asleep? Was he dead?

With an audible gulp, she knocked again, louder this time.

A crash and thump sounded on the other side of the door, and then a clatter of noise erupted. The thunder of footsteps shook the floor. Emily took a step back just as the door swung open and Max loomed before her.

He wore black running pants, but nothing else, and his dirty-blond hair stood on end. He peered at her with bloodshot eyes, red rimmed and heavy lidded. It appeared as though he hadn't slept in days.

"Are y-y-you hungry?"

"No." He pushed the door.

Her hand shot out and stopped it from closing. His gaze flew to her face, but words jammed in her throat.

He shoved both hands through his ruffled hair. "Look, I'm right in the middle of something–"

You're a piranha.

"I can b-b-bring y-you food. If y-y-you w-want. Do you w-w-want a tray of food?"

Annoyance melted from his expression. "That'd be great. Thanks. Just leave it in the hall." He turned, and with one foot, kicked the door shut in her face.

But not before she saw the deep, angry scar slashing across his back from his right shoulder to the top of his left hip.

☙

Luke balanced the skillet in the drying rack and let out the dirty dishwater. He was giving the countertop one final wipe down when she burst into the kitchen.

"I did it." Dark eyes shining, her cheeks flushed an attractive shade of pink. "Just like you said, and it worked. It actually worked."

Coaxed by her delight, a smile touched his lips. "Congratulations."

Her eyes shone. "Thank you so much."

"You did it all on your own. I just bullied you into it."

She flitted around him. "I'm going to take a tray to him."

"What's he doing up there anyway?"

Her hands stilled over the plate a moment. "I don't know." She resumed her task of loading down the tray with food. "Sleeping, I think."

"That's a lot of sleeping. You sure he isn't plotting world domination or something as nefarious?"

She paused for a split second, a crease wrinkling her brow, before her expression cleared and her smile returned. "You're too suspicious. Being a cop has jaded you."

He didn't argue.

She fussed with the arrangement of items she'd laid on the tray. "Finally, someone's going to enjoy all this amazing food."

"I didn't do it for him." Distracted by the whiskey-colored swirls in her brown eyes, the words fell from his lips.

His heart thrashed. What the hell was he doing, telling her that?

Startled brown eyes searched his face. "Wh-why did you do it?"

He threw up a seductive smile. "I'm hoping you'll feel beholden and offer to give me more kissing lessons."

Her eyes grew wide.

His balls tightened. "You have me feeling all inadequate and insecure, but maybe with a little more instruction from a professional like yourself, I'll be able to overcome my fears."

She licked her lips and her features tangled with an adorable mix of arousal and uncertainty. "I might be willing to tutor you."

She was the perfect woman. Perfect for him, that is. No drama. No deception. If he wanted to know her thoughts or feelings, all he had to do was look at her face. It was all there, for anyone to see. She fed his hunger yet presented zero risk of capturing his heart. His heart, the one thing he'd never surrender to a woman, was safe with Emily.

He sidled closer, twisting his fingers through the end of her ponytail. "Would you teach me how to please you?"

She looked at him with grave, lucid eyes. "Y-you want to please m-me?"

At the reappearance of her stutter, his heart pinched. "Very much so."

He smoothed a hand down the column of her slender neck and dipped his head to draw in her scent, stronger near the base of her earlobe. The hitch in her breathing stirred the rising ache between his legs.

He trailed his fingertips over the bare skin of her shoulder, and then pressed his lips to the spot. "If I do anything that pleases you, will you tell me?" With the tip of his tongue, he took a tiny taste of her skin.

"Th-that." Her breath rushed over his skin. "I like that."

Triumph tugged a smile from him. Her pleasure mattered to him more than he wanted. "What do you like? Tell me."

"I like the way you touch m-me."

His hands skimmed down the curves of her body to the exaggerated swell of her hips. "Where?"

"Anywhere. Everywhere."

His cock jerked painfully and he swooped down to claim her mouth. She opened for him easily, eagerly, and his heart lightened. His hands found their way beneath the hem of her shirt, the flat of his palms smoothing over her silky skin and narrow ribcage. A gasp tore from her when his thumbs brushed over her pebbled nipples.

Breaking away, he dropped his head and pulled one nipple into his mouth through the fabric of her tank top.

She arched into his touch.

Her. I want her.

Whatever this was between them, she wanted it as much as he did. With a desperation that bordered on needy, he wanted her. He wanted to feel. He wanted to feel her wet heat wrapped around his cock.

He popped the button of her jeans. The soft scrape of her zipper as he lowered it roared through him. His fingers pulled back the waistband of her panties and slipped beneath.

Her breathing stopped, and then redoubled with short, shallow pants. Large round eyes fixated on his hand in her pants, willing it.

He pushed his fingers through the soft fuzz of her bush to her wet, swollen core. Her startled yelp slid into a throaty moan that carried the brutality of desperation.

For a moment, he feared she would retreat. Their game had gotten out of hand and–

She shifted her stance, parting her thighs for his touch.

Her.

He had to have her. He *would* have her.

He stroked the folds of her sex, teasing and toying with her sensitive, puffy lips while she whimpered and rocked against his hand. Together, they drove toward something.

Climax, yes, but something more. Deeper.

His name was a moan falling from her lips, wrapped in a teardrop of uncertainty.

"What it is, sweetheart? Tell me." His voice, thick with some unnamed emotion, snagged on the words. "Tell me anything."

Tell me everything.

"I need you to–" She gasped with her arousal. "I need you–"

A wayward strand of hair fell across her forehead and he pushed it back. With a small wrinkle between her brows, she stared at him with eyes glazed with lust. Lost to the sensation, she clutched his shoulders and swirled her hips.

The torture of her expanding pleasure was exquisite and heartbreaking.

"You need me to what?" He was desperate to understand.

She shook her head. "I need you." Her head fell back and a moan vibrated in her throat. "That's all. I need you. Only you."

A moment of startled disbelief seared him, and then

he knew only heat and hunger. The fire consumed him, overwhelmed him. Overrode him. He undid his fly and his heavy shaft bobbed free.

Her mouth formed a tiny O of surprise when she gazed at his erection. His cock jumped and he snatched her to him to suckle her luscious lips.

She wriggled under him, working her blue jeans down over her hips, and soon stood fully exposed to his touch. With a groan, he smoothed his hands over the rounded globe of her bottom and lifted. Her arms came around his neck and she slid down his body, until the head of his cock pushed at her entrance.

He pressed her back to the wall. Eye to eye, he drowned in whiskey. He tilted his hips, but a fraction inside, he came up against her tight passage. She shifted and he slipped deeper.

Sweet Jesus.

With his hands on her hips, he eased himself inside her. The little sounds originating in the back of her throat as her body adjusted to him almost sent him over the edge. Still, he nudged further into her secret center until he reached home.

The glory of finally reaching her tight wet heat leached the strength from his body. His head dropped to her shoulder. God, she was tight. So tight.

Then he started to pump his hips, only three delicious slides before she cried out and her sweet pussy quivered.

Her. He had her. Now. Forever.

Her tight passage clamped around him and her cry of release broke his heart while he pounded up into her. With every thrust, his knowledge of her deepened.

Her. Her. Her.

He shattered.

The last talons of numbness suffocating him the past six months burned away with the pureness of her orgasm. His world was gray and tasteless no more.

Hadn't been since Emily Cole burst into his life with a heart-tugging stutter and a hot-pink vibrator, and yanked him back into the world of the living.

Except, he didn't want to be in the world again.

Anymore.

Ever.

He stumbled back.

He never lost control. Not like this. Not ever.

Certainly not over some woman.

His self-control was all he had. The only thing separating him from the delinquents and degenerates he faced every day.

The only thing that separated him from his dad.

"Luke? Are y-y-you okay?"

He couldn't think for the ache in his chest. Was he having a heart attack? "I... this..."

What had he done? He'd just fucked Emily Cole. Emily fucking Cole.

He tucked himself back into his jeans and yanked up the zipper.

The blood left his head in a rush. He'd just fucked Emily Cole...

Without a condom.

Oh, shit.

With a ruthless shove, he buried his hands in his hair. He hadn't done anything so reckless since he was thirteen years old and, at Noah's urging, bleached his dark hair platinum blond using lime, as the ancient Celtic warriors had, for authenticity's sake.

Now, he scooped Emily's discarded blue jeans up off the floor and thrust them at her. "This shouldn't have happened. I made a mistake."

She drew back, her wide eyes filling with pain.

He didn't care. He had to get away. Gulping for air, he shot out of her house like a convict from the Supermax.

He didn't look back. He didn't dare.

The right thing to do, and Luke always did the right thing, was to get away and stay away from her.

In his truck, he cranked the key in the ignition and the engine growled to life. He scrubbed a hand over his face, only to breathe in the intoxicating musk of her arousal, which lingered on his skin.

He balled his hand into a tight fist.

It was a momentary lapse in judgment. Nothing more. Just a mistake. A sweet mistake—the sweetest—but a mistake nonetheless.

But it wouldn't happen again. Not if he wanted to stay on the right side of rock bottom. It couldn't.

Chapter Eleven

She couldn't speak for his regret clogged in her throat, so rather than demand to know why he'd say something so cruel, she watched in mute frustration as he stormed from her house.

That night, she lay awake, replaying every detail of their lovemaking in her mind, trying to pinpoint exactly where it'd all gone wrong. Was it when they did it in her kitchen without any regard for being caught in the act by her houseguest, or cousin, or his brother? Or when they'd forgotten to use protection?

She may not have a lot of experience with men, but she had no excuse that might explain such an oversight. She had no one but herself to blame for that fact that such a special moment, her first orgasm with someone other than herself, had left her feeling rejected and dejected.

She flopped onto her side.

Had she really expected anything other than confusion and disappointment? Though oh-so-tempting, Luke Nolan was a billion light years out of her league. She'd known it the moment she laid eyes on his too-beautiful face a year ago. Pleasant to look at, but not for her.

Okay, pleasant was a bit of an understatement. Seriously, who looked like that? So perfectly perfect and symmetrical? She should've known not to dally with him. He shone bright like the sun, and lingering too long in his presence only guaranteed a blistering sunburn.

With a hearty kick, she thrashed onto her other side.

The most troubling part? She didn't care that he regretted it, she didn't. She couldn't regret the white-hot anarchy rioting through her veins with his touch, or the way he watched her when she came, with naked, unrepentant hunger.

He'd stolen her peace, and her sleep. Near dawn, she gave up and, throwing back the covers, climbed from bed. When she sat at the island stirring a heap of sugar into her mug, a noise at the door tipped her off to his arrival a moment before he burst back into her life.

Her heart hummed, the stupid thing, and so the words dropped out of her mouth unfiltered. "You're back."

His gaze didn't quite manage to connect with hers. "Good news. Ms. Beardsley had a friend visiting."

She blinked with bafflement, finding it difficult to think clearly with his presence suddenly filling the room.

A humorous tilt curved his mouth. "Her friend brought her grandson with her."

"Grandson?" A surge of hope stirred in Emily. "A ten-year-old?"

"Eleven." The tension in his shoulders eased a bit. "But he's our culprit. Confessed to the whole sordid affair."

Relief swept away her nervous tension.

Until green eyes locked on her face, his symmetrical features carefully blanked.

Dread prickled up her spine.

With the appearance of a man sentenced to a life term, he crossed to the counter opposite where she sat on the edge of her barstool, laid his palms flat on the countertop, and captured her gaze with his. "We need to talk about what happened."

Oh, no. Please, no.

"Emily, I'm sor—"

"Don't." The gash on her heart might never heal from all he'd said already.

He held her gaze while the moment stretched out, growing tight and thin.

Until she snapped. "It's m-my fault, really. I thought you were ready for an advanced lesson, but clearly I misjudged."

Relief swept over his face. "Em—"

"I forgot how inexperienced y-y-you are. I should've been upfront about what's going on between us."

A slow grin thawed the last of his cool expression. "What's going on between us?"

"We're just having fun." She meant for the ruse to deflect his apologies and regrets, but it twisted back around instead and pierced her heart with a poison-tipped reality dagger. She scowled. "Well, w-we *were* having fun, until you r-ruined it."

In truth, she had no clue what was going on between them, but she'd have taken as much or as little as he was willing to give her. She wasn't proud of the fact that, if given the choice between nothing or a kiss, or a touch, or one of those warm, lingering looks from him, she'd have chosen the latter without hesitation. No silly schoolgirl notion of promises and futures required.

If given a choice, she'd have chosen him.

If he'd only asked.

Which he didn't.

Instead, he lanced her with a look. "We need to talk about what happened."

The rush of heat burned her cheeks. "It's okay." She swallowed the tightening lump in her throat. "It's n-n-not the right time for me."

That was if, based on last night's panicky Internet research, she'd calculated her monthly cycle correctly, but the deep lines bracketing his eyes and mouth had eased with her words, so she buried her doubts.

"Are you okay?" he asked.

His gentle tone tugged at her insides, though she had no idea what he was really asking.

She changed the subject. "You don't need to cook breakfast. The muffins from yesterday are still good."

One of his dark eyebrows lifted. "Are you firing me?"

"Giving you the day off."

He pushed away from the counter and went to the refrigerator. "I'm already here."

She gritted her teeth. "He doesn't even eat your food."

"Yeah, but you do."

"Don't you have a real job terrorizing innocent people?"

"I'm on the night shift this week."

He'd been there by 7:00 a.m. the past two days. "Don't you sleep?"

He cracked open an egg and the runny guts dribbled into a bowl. "Not so much."

A weary pall stole over him while he stared into the bowl, lightly whipping the eggs.

"Wh-why not?"

A shadow seemed to settle around him. "Did you buy milk?'

She went to the fridge and retrieved the gallon. Handing it to him, she reached for the bread loaf and started to work the twist-tie. Two slices toasting, her mind poked at the fact he hadn't answered her.

At the stove, he poured the egg mixture into a skillet and raised the heat by turning the knob a notch higher.

"How long have y-you been a cop?"

He sliced an onion in half. "Ten years."

Nearly the same amount of time she'd been her mom's full-time caretaker. She wondered if his last ten years had been as trying as hers.

"Do y-you like it?"

"Parts of it." His knife hit the wooden cutting board with neat ticks.

"What parts?"

His mouth quirked. "The power."

She snorted. "Why doesn't that surprise me?"

A smile pulled at the corners of his mouth while he made more cuts through the heap of diced onion.

"You know, you're kind of a big deal around here."

"Am I?" A dangerous edge crept into his tone.

"Y-you know you are. They say you're a hero."

Lethal green eyes crashed into her. "The parents of a dead fifteen-year-old might disagree with you."

The words, delivered like ice, froze her heart, but the wounded anguish that slashed across his face devastated her. Like a lifetime of torment had piled into that singular, brief moment. With her words, she'd brought that moment to him, and she'd regret it until the end of her days.

Then, as quickly as it came, the pain evaporated. He tried to pull the charmer's mask back into place, but only managed a scowl.

The ticking of the toaster's timer filled the silence until, without a word or even a spare glance in her direction, he set the knife aside, turned his back and walked out of the house, letting the door bang shut behind him.

She stared after him while her heart constricted in her

chest and her mind raced to puzzle out what she had done to cause his reaction. His discomfort with the topic was evident, yet she'd pushed on, and had hurt him with her careless words.

Her stomach gave a sickening wrench.

Though she'd been doing it all her life, she despised disappointing people. Her dad. Her teachers. Her mom's doctors. In the end, she'd even let her mom down. She should be used to it by now.

The toast popped and she startled.

She scraped butter over the bread and laid it on a tray with a banana, a muffin, and a glass of orange juice.

At the top of the stairs, as she contemplated whether she should knock or leave the tray in the hall, Max's bedroom door swung open.

He strode into the hallway wearing jeans and the T-shirt of a rock band Emily didn't recognize.

She pulled up short. "Good m-m-morning…"

The greeting died on her lips when she saw the backpack slung over his shoulder.

"Y-you're leaving?"

He shoved a hand through his brown-blond hair. "Yeah, I gotta go. We're all set for next month?"

She nodded. "November second."

"Great." He moved past her.

She retreated down the steps behind him, but he'd reached the front door before she achieved the bottom step.

His hand on the doorknob, he twisted toward her. "Uh, thanks."

"Sure," she muttered as he disappeared into a ray of sunlight.

Suddenly alone, again, in the cavernous estate, the quiet menaced. In the living room, the antique clock's pendulum swing resonated with thunderous noise. She plopped down hard on a step and stared at the tray of food in her lap. With a heavy sigh, she picked up a slice of toast and bit into it.

She was wondering if Luke was okay and how her world had flipped on end so quickly, when an odd scent tickled her nose.

The eggs!

The screech of the smoke alarm punctured the air.

◌

Labor Day came and went, marking the official end of summer and, thus, tourist season. It also concluded Emily's first full month living on the island. Two weeks had passed since Luke walked out on her, and the image of his face, twisted with agony, haunted her still.

She'd had the window fixed only days before a cool north wind blew over the island. Nonetheless, that morning, she awoke with an ominous scratchiness at the back of her throat.

Still snuggled beneath the covers in bed, she sipped on ice water, the frigid liquid soothing her sore throat, and peered at the laptop balanced across her thighs. The inn's webpage was displayed on the screen and she fiddled with the positioning of the logo she'd created.

On the nightstand, her cell phone jingled with an incoming text. She opened the message from Mina.

Meet you out front in an hour?

Emily suppressed a groan. Over a week ago, she and Mina arranged to go to the bridal shop in town and pick out dresses for Mina's wedding next month. It was the last thing Emily wanted to do at that moment, but according to her Internet research, it was her job to make sure the bride was happy, even if that meant she must lie, cheat, or kill to achieve the feat.

An hour later, she met Mina in the driveway, a smile plastered on her face.

114

Tucked among the row of brick and mortar buildings lining Main Street, the bridal store boasted turn-of-the-century charm and connected to the chic clothing boutique next door.

A tinkling bell sounded when they passed through the entry. A pretty, dark-haired woman Mina appeared to know greeted them and showed them to a cream-colored room at the back of the store decorated with plush carpeting and brocade satin wallpaper.

The woman, Isobel, had smooth mocha skin, wide gray eyes, and a soft smile that put Emily at ease.

"I've pulled some gowns for you both to take a look at. Let me know what you like and what you don't like." She motioned to the white and ivory gowns on a rollaway rack.

Mina went in the other direction, to the rack with a rainbow array of dresses.

"I love this color." She held up the skirts of an emerald gown that reminded Emily of Luke's eyes. "What do you think?"

Emily offered her cousin a weak smile and nodded.

Mina selected several gowns and Isobel herded Emily behind the dressing curtain.

The first dress, a navy taffeta sheath, wouldn't fit over Emily's ample hips, and the second, in a deep burgundy silk, clashed with her bright hair. Isobel helped Emily into the emerald gown, a strapless A-line silhouette, and threw back the curtain.

Emily made her way in front of the mirrors. Beneath the store's harsh lighting, her skin appeared pale, pasty even, and dark shadows dwelled beneath her eyes. The dress, made of a soft crepe fabric, seemed to cling to her imperfections, and even brought to light a few she didn't know she had.

Just then, a petite brunette with a straight nose and catlike eyes swept into the room.

The air squeezed from Emily's lungs while she gaped at her aunt, Vivian. Her resemblance to Audrey was so strong that for just the briefest moment, Emily thought her mom had walked into that bridal shop.

"Mom, what are you doing here?" Mina spoke through clenched teeth. "All the way from Traverse City?"

Vivian blinked at her daughter. "When you told me you were coming, I had to be here. This is the biggest decision of your life."

"It's really not," Mina said. "Not even close."

Vivian's gaze turned to Emily.

"Mom, you remember Emily, don't you? We started with her dress."

Vivian's green-gold gaze lingered over Emily's face a moment, and then traveled lower. Her nose wrinkled. "That dress does nothing for you, dear."

She turned to the rack of dresses and in one brutal sweep, rejected half the gowns outright, and sent Emily to the dressing room with three more to try on. The first gown she declared gaudy, and the second she deemed too tawdry. Emily wasn't sure what the difference was between gaudy and tawdry, and in her opinion both gowns were pretty, but the last thing she wanted to do was engage with Mina's mom.

So she slunk behind the curtain to change into the next dress. Tension built between her temples and her head started to ache by the time she stood in front of the trio in a dusty-purple ball gown with a fitted bodice.

Vivian tipped her head to one side and studied her. "The color is flattering to your skin tone, but you look like a cupcake. I'm afraid this one won't work either."

Indeed, the puffy tulle skirt overwhelmed Emily's short frame. Disappointment twisted her face into a frown. She'd hoped this one might meet Vivian's approval, as the boning in the bodice pushed her boobs high and made her adequate cleavage appear downright abundant.

Isobel chewed her lip and pondered Emily's reflection in the mirror. "I wonder if we remove some of the layers of tulle, maybe you won't look so much like a cupcake."

She stuck her hands beneath the skirts and started to pull fabric toward the back of the gown. As Emily watched in the mirror, Isobel changed the shape of the dress from a bulbous ball gown to an elegant A-line.

"Oh, that's pretty." Mina fingered the tulle. "Do you like it?"

Emily considered her reflection. "I do."

Three pairs of eyes swiveled to Vivian.

With a firm nod, she approved the selection. "Now, let's make sure she doesn't overpower the bride."

Mina paled while Emily darted toward the curtain wall and out from under their scrutinizing gazes.

Vivian issued her directives to Isobel. "No mermaids and no ball gowns. They'll only make her look wider than she is. Lace or beading in small doses only, and under no circumstances should she wear anything strapless. She needs more support, and a sleeve will help conceal that little extra under the arms."

"This one's pretty." Dread filled Mina's voice.

"Oh, darling, no. You'll look like one of Rose's doilies. Besides, that shade of white washes you out."

When Emily emerged from behind the curtain, the trio was clustered around the rack, discussing the merits and drawbacks of each gown. Her limbs heavy with exhaustion, she sank into an armchair to wait.

She found her gaze drawn repeatedly to Vivian, so similar to her mom in appearance. So opposite her in personality. Sorrow squeezed like a painful knot inside her chest.

Only two gowns passed Vivian's inspection and Isobel quickly herded an increasingly dejected-looking Mina behind the curtain.

Vivian perched on the edge of an armchair next to Emily. "I'm not sure about this plan of yours to have dinner at the house," she called to Mina. "Shouldn't we find something nicer?"

"Noah and I are together because of the house." Mina's voice carried through the curtain. "We want to celebrate there."

Vivian heaved a martyred sigh into the air. "Maybe I'd better have a look. See if I can make it work."

A sneeze tickled the back of Emily's nose and erupted.

"Emily's taking care of everything," Mina called. "She planned the grand opening, and it was perfect."

Vivian's critical gaze swung to Emily.

Amidst a honking blow into a Kleenex, Emily froze.

Vivian turned her head back in the direction of the curtain. "What are you doing about flowers?"

"Emily's already picked them out." Mina's words sounded strained, as though she held her breath. "What are they called again, Em?"

"Ranunculus." Emily folded the tissue and tucked it into the pocket of her sweatshirt. "Wi-with brunia and seeded eucalyptus."

Vivian frowned.

"And wh-white lilies," Emily added.

The lines eased from Vivian's face. "Well, you have to let me do something."

With a whoosh, Isobel swept back the curtain and Mina appeared before them in a corseted A-line with delicate off-the-shoulder sleeves.

Vivian took one look at her and said, simply, "No."

Mina accepted the rejection without flinching. "You're helping me with my dress." She yanked the curtain closed. "You don't need to do anything more than that."

"I could use y-your help w-with the menu."

Vivian's injured expression turned calculating. "Stuffed baby artichokes and Tuscan salad. For the main course, smoked salmon with lemon, seasonal vegetables, and golden potato croquette. Either Pinot Grigio or Sauvignon Blanc for the wine. You can choose."

The curtain rustled and Mina stepped out from behind it.

Emily gasped while, for the first time since she entered the store, Vivian fell silent.

The dress conformed to Mina's curves with a standing shoulder collar and an elegant flare at the bottom. It contained no adornments, but was made of a buttery-smooth satin with a wide sash around her small waist. It reminded Emily of styles they might've worn in the forties, but with a sexier silhouette.

Vivian's head started to bob and her eyes filled with tears. "It's perfect."

Mina's eyes widened. "It is?" Her head bent as she tried to look at her body. "You don't think it's too tight? Or old-fashioned?"

Unable to speak, Vivian went to Mina and wrapped her in her arms.

A spasm of grief struck Emily near her heart as she witnessed the special moment. One of those rare instants in life when all the small pains melted away, or finally made sense, and good-byes only meant new beginnings.

It was a moment Emily would never share with her own mother. She told herself if she were fortunate to find a man she loved enough to marry, she wouldn't begrudge her fate, but her mom's absence from her life was like a big, gaping hole blown through the middle of her chest. It might callus over one day, but she would never be whole again.

Vivian sniffed. "It's timeless, and it shows off your curves. That's something every woman should do on her wedding day."

With Mina changed, the quartet made their way to the front of the store. Exhaustion clawed at Emily and she plopped onto a raised platform by the entrance where a mannequin posed while Mina and Isobel finalized the details of Mina's dress order.

Emily leaned back to gaze up at the faceless mannequin, outfitted in a taupe patterned blouse and a cream-colored corduroy blazer with dark-wash blue jeans and leopard-print ballet flats. She fingered the teardrop pearl earrings lying next to a chocolate-brown leather tote at the mannequin's feet.

It was a great outfit. The kind of outfit a smart, professional businesswoman might wear. Or a woman with a lover.

Vivian appeared at her elbow. Her throat worked when she swallowed. "I wish I'd known your mother was sick. I'd liked to have helped or... visited her."

Emily recoiled and her heart kicked painfully in her chest.

Vivian's voice wavered. "Did she suffer?"

Her throat closed and it took her many long moments to force out the words. "Y-yes, she did. Very much."

She knew it wasn't what Vivian wanted to hear, and maybe she should've censored her response for her aunt, but she couldn't do it. She couldn't downplay the hell Audrey had suffered.

Mina turned away from the sales counter and Emily stepped into her place. She barely listened while Isobel verified the size and color of her dress.

This month marked one year Emily's mom had been dead, and in that time, she'd moved across the country, opened her own business, and had regretful sex with a gorgeous man.

Isobel confirmed the total price, and Emily slid her credit card from her wallet. But before she handed it over, she pointed to the mannequin in the front window. "I'd like to b-b-buy the outfit on that mannequin as well."

Chapter Twelve

Sleep hadn't eased the exhaustion pulling at Emily's limbs, and by late afternoon the next day, she crawled to her bed and pulled the covers over her head. When she awoke near dinnertime, her head throbbed with the pressure in her stuffed sinus passages and her eyes burned.

In the bathroom, she rummaged through the cupboard in search of anything with enough strength to knock her out again, but her search turned up only a couple of allergy tablets and a bottle of multivitamins, and she discovered the nearly empty box of tissues on her nightstand was the only box in the house.

She counted the rolls of toilet paper and decided she could manage without more tissue. Then she swallowed and her throat screamed with raw aching. Her muscles sore and weak, she yanked a brush through her hair before she gave up on grooming and pulled on her sneakers.

Outside, clouds hovered overhead and blocked out any warmth from the setting sun. She didn't know if the temperature had dipped or if her body, with its weakened immune system, overestimated the chill, but she burrowed her nose in her sweatshirt and darted to her sedan.

At the store, she skipped the carts and searched out the health aisle. Her head as cloudy as the darkening sky, she loaded her arms with cough syrup and drops, throat spray, mentholated rub, and two boxes of ultra-soft tissue. En route to the checkout lanes, she added a jug of orange juice and a gallon of ice cream to her heap.

She tucked the ice cream under her chin and turned toward the front of the store. As she came around the end of the aisle, someone crashed into her. She registered only blonde hair and jiggly warmth before a box of Kleenex popped out from under her arm and landed on the ground with a crack of noise.

The pile in her arms shifted and started to slide. She bobbled the orange juice and a squeak leaked from her when the ice cream toppled toward the floor.

At the last second, two hands shot out and plucked the gallon from its freefall. Bright green eyes glinted up at her. Emily gulped back a curse, and winced with the sting of her inflamed throat.

"Nice catch." Her nose clogged with snot, she'd become a mouth breather.

Luke's dimples popped, and he straightened. "Cookie dough? Somehow I pegged you for a rocky road kind of girl."

She wished the cold hadn't destroyed her sense of smell. He probably smelled as good as he looked. A neat black suit hugged his lean frame and turned his bright eyes brilliant. The stunner at his side wore a gold shrink-wrapped dress, and held a bottle of wine nestled in the crook of her arm.

The butterflies banging around in Emily's stomach crash-landed somewhere around her naval.

He was on a date. They were on a date. Together.

"I'm allergic to n-nuts."

His gaze raked over her and his smile fell. "Are you sick?"

The blonde's perfect button nose crinkled and she drew back.

"It's just a cold." A menacing tickle built in her nose and erupted as a sneeze.

The other box of tissue hit the floor. She stooped as Luke bent over and her forehead bashed into his shoulder.

"You should get a shopping cart," the blonde said.

When Emily stood, the mucus clogging her sinuses shifted and the world tipped with a dizzying slant.

"Let me help you." Luke reached for the jug of orange juice.

Emily twisted away. "No, I've got it." Her gaze slipped to the woman found so often on his arm.

Luke seemed to startle. "Emily, this is Kate. Kate, Emily."

The women exchanged muttered hellos.

"Emily bought the old Winslow house and opened a bed-and-breakfast." The slide of his deep voice tried to pull her in, but she resisted its seductive lure.

Kate's mouth turned down at the corners. "Isn't it weird sleeping with strangers in your house?"

Emily preferred it to being by herself. With guests filling the empty house, she might be able to pretend she wasn't all alone in the world.

In the awkward silence that followed, Emily eased back. "Uh, h-h-have a nice n-n-night."

She spotted an empty checkout lane and dumped her

armload onto the belt. Moments later, she approached the storefront to find he had waited for her.

He plucked the grocery sacks from her hands and fell into step alongside her. "You sure you're all right?"

"I'm good." She attempted a cheeky grin. "I've got drugs now."

He didn't laugh, but only frowned down at her.

At her car, she opened the trunk and he set the groceries inside the dark interior.

"Let me give you my number. In case you need me—"

"All I need is sleep." She slammed the trunk closed. "Enjoy your date."

With Kate.

Emily didn't give Luke a chance to make excuses, think up a lie, or worse, not bother to do either, but went around to the driver-side door and ducked inside the car. She drove away while, in the rearview mirror, he scowled after her.

ᥫ

He ignored the voice inside his head screaming at him to get the hell out of there and pounded his fist on the back door at Emily's house.

This time, he'd keep his control in place. If he focused on her shortcomings, he'd forget about how pretty she was when she smiled, and how he desperately wanted to suckle her porn-star mouth again, and her pink nipples, and—

The muffled sound of a sneeze reached him through the heavy door.

"Emily, open up."

He heard a thump followed by a sharp curse.

The force of his smile surprised him. He leaned a shoulder against the house. "Take your time. I can wait."

A sliver of light filtered out to him when the door

cracked open a fraction of an inch.

One brown, red-rimmed eye appeared through the opening. "What do you want?"

He could hear the congestion in her voice, which managed to be husky and sexy rather than gross.

"You're not asleep, are you?"

"Not anymore."

"Good. Let me in."

"I'm in m-my pajamas."

"So?"

"So, go away."

He held up the bowl in his hand.

She eyed it. "What's that?"

"My special healing recipe. It'll clear your sinuses and feel good on your sore throat."

Naked longing swept across her face and he coughed with the force of lust that crashed into him.

Her small hand shot out through the crack. "The soup can come in, but you can't."

"We're a package deal." He held the bowl out of reach. "It's all or nothing."

A frown tugged at her mouth. "Where's your date?"

With one shoulder, he pushed his way inside the house.

A giant snowflake stretched across the chest of her dark blue nightgown. The twin peaks of her beaded nipples begged for his attention, and whatever words he might've said fled his mind with the blood rushing to his groin.

He set the soup on the counter and rummaged around her kitchen for a bowl and spoon. She sank onto a barstool at the island and slumped forward.

"Have you taken your meds?"

Another sneeze burst from her, and she moaned. "Uh-huh." She dabbed at her bright red nose with a crumpled tissue.

Soup warming in the microwave, he laid his hands on her shoulders. "C'mon then. Let's get you to bed."

She slid off the stool and he followed her into the mudroom, through a side door, and down a short hall.

"Man, you really are sick. You're not going to try to kick me out?"

In response, she released an exhausted sigh, and in a space set up like a typical living room, she trudged to the overstuffed sofa and dropped onto a pile of pillows.

He returned for the soup, and handing it to her, sat on the circular coffee table before the couch. She took a small taste and a soft moan slipped through her lips.

Heat rushed over his skin as she swallowed several more greedy nips.

Holding the bowl under her nose, she fixed him with a dark look. "You can leave now."

"I will. When I'm ready."

Her mouth pinched. "Wh-where's Kate?"

"I took her home."

She considered that. "You two—"

"Are friends."

"Well, I should hope so," she muttered.

"We're *just* friends."

She set the soup on an end table and burrowed deeper into the quilts. "If you say so."

"I do." With the pad of his thumb, he brushed over a callus on his palm. "I promised someone I'd look out for her and I am."

One eye cracked open to search his face. He allowed her assessment.

"I didn't come here to talk about Kate."

Both eyes popped open, and though they were heavy lidded with tiredness, he could still make out the whiskey swirls near the center.

He ran a hand down his thigh. "I owe you an apology."

"For what?" Her husky voice had a vulnerable hitch.

He shifted on the table, the right words suddenly difficult to find.

She grew impatient. "For insulting m-my cooking?"

"No."

"For nitpicking the way I drive?"

He shook his head. "No."

"For kissing m-me?"

He leveled her with a look. "Absolutely not."

"For not kissing m-me m-m-more?"

At the hopeful ring in her tone, a smile tugged at his mouth. "Maybe, but that's not where I'm going with this. I'm sorry for the way I left. You didn't deserve that."

Her cheeks turned a brighter shade of pink. "I said something to upset you. It's one of the reasons I try not to talk too much."

Guilt kicked in his chest. "No, it was nothing you said." He raked a hand through his hair. "It's all this hero bullshit. It's driving me crazy."

She studied him over the top of the quilt for a long moment. "You're so weird."

That startled a laugh from him. He opened his mouth to say more. Hell, he might've told her the whole shitty story if he hadn't caught himself in time.

For all he'd tried to forget the day a fifteen-year-old took his dad's gun to school and opened fire on his classmates, Luke found himself wanting to talk to Emily about it, if only so she'd understand what a load of bullshit this idea of him being a hero truly was.

Or maybe it was more than that. He couldn't shake the feeling, the hope, she'd understand the devastation he felt watching his fellow cop felled by that coward's bullet. How, when his friend slumped to the floor, he didn't think, didn't feel, but lifted his gun and fired. In cold blood.

Luke had been close enough that the kid's blood splattered on his face and clothes, marking him with the truth.

That though he'd built his entire life around being honorable and fighting for the good guys, he was no different than his dad. A cold-blooded murderer. A bad guy.

Her hand poked out from under the quilts and she knuckled one droopy eye.

"I'll let you rest." He scooped up her nearly empty bowl and turned to leave.

"Luke?"

He turned.

"Thanks for the soup."

"You're welcome." He closed the door to her suite behind him.

An odd disappointment spread through him and he rolled his shoulders, trying to shake it off. It was for the best he didn't tell her all of it. She was the one thing in his life not tainted by the stain of that day.

He rinsed out her bowl and laid it in the dishwasher. He should head out. There was still time to hit the gym if he wanted any chance of sleeping more than an hour or two that night.

Yep, that's what he should do.

Ɔʒ

She dreamed of him.

Of him with *her*.

Her white-gold hair cascaded across the pillow. Silken strands of spun gold. His mouth brushed over her milky smooth skin.

She laughed and rolled to face him. His large, tanned hand closed over her full breast.

Emily longed to kiss her skin, everywhere his mouth had touched, so that she might know the taste of his pleasure.

She stirred enough to know she dreamed before the blackness pulled her under once more.

Sometime later, she awakened to warmth and darkness, and the vague niggling of some far-off pain.

"Wake up, sweetheart." He wiped her cheeks with wet hands and she twisted away from him.

Light flickered against the beige walls and the silhouette of a man crouched before the fireplace. The glow of a fire cast him in warm lighting, illuminating his profile as he stared into the flame.

Her heart constricted. *Why does he have to be so beautiful?*

His head snapped up and he straightened to his full height.

The sofa dipped when he sat on the edge next to her. "How are you feeling?"

She blinked away sleep. Was he really there, beside her?

He held a cup of water under her nose. "Drink this."

The cool water slid down her parched throat. Her head pounded and she collapsed onto the cloud of pillows.

Sleep reached out to her, and a vision of Kate, naked and splayed for him, jolted her awake.

Emily didn't know if Luke was telling the truth that he and the beauty were only friends. She supposed it didn't matter. It changed nothing between them.

"You should go." The words cracked with the dryness in her throat.

"Can you take these? They're for the fever."

The pills scraped the walls of her swollen throat and she winced.

"Try to sleep," he told her. "I'm here."

But when she awoke the next morning, she was alone in her big old empty house.

Chapter Thirteen

The weeks passed in a flurry of cough syrup and antibiotic intake until Emily's sinuses dried out and her muscle aches eased. With her renewed energy, she completed the inn's website and designed an advertising campaign to begin in the next few months and slowly ramp up, peaking in the spring.

She'd also gotten her period.

At loose ends, she convinced Mina to let her take on more wedding-planning activities. She crafted handmade invitations and mailed all but one to the forty-person guest list comprised mostly of family members and colleagues from the university where Noah worked.

The last invite, to the Mayor of Thief Island, sparked a squabble between the couple, with Noah arguing Mina's ex-fiancé had no place at their wedding and Mina countering, gently, that despite their failed engagement, the Mayor had been a childhood friend to her.

Mina won the dispute.

Next, Emily delivered Vivian's menu to a caterer in town that would prepare the meal for the reception following the ceremony. She then selected a bakery and presented a sampling of three cakes—vanilla, red velvet, and chocolate—to the couple. Another heated discussion ensued with Mina favoring the red velvet and Noah arguing the cake, when cut, looked like roadkill.

Noah won the debate.

In that time, fall came to the island with a relentless chill and an explosion of color. Growing up in the desert, Emily was unprepared for the drama of the seasonal change. Deep red and vibrant orange torched the treetops, and a honey-yellow glow warmed the landscape.

One afternoon, she arrived at the cemetery to find her mom's oak tree had dropped a ring of fire on the ground, burying the tombstone with orange leaves, and for the first time, Emily experienced a sense of ease when standing beside her mom's grave.

Two weeks before the wedding, she sent Max an e-mail to verify his arrival the Monday after the wedding, which he confirmed.

Two days before the wedding, the order she'd placed for fresh-cut flowers arrived at the inn. She gutted twenty white pumpkins and stuffed them to bursting with deep purple ranunculus, cream-colored lilies, and greenery.

The day before the wedding, after she'd checked in with the vendors and fussed some more with the flower arrangements, she drove into town to pick up her dress from the bridal shop. On her way home, she spotted a sign hanging over one of the storefronts. With a muttered curse, she whipped into an empty parking space in front of the Curl Up and Dye Hair Salon.

Unable to recall the last time she'd had her hair cut, she didn't allow herself to think through her decision, knowing she'd only talk herself out of the long-overdue trim.

An electronic chime sounded when she entered the shop and a woman at the front desk looked up with a warm smile. The woman's smile crumpled.

Emily gasped. Her feet grew roots where she stood, or she'd have run. The psychologists had it wrong. Fight or flight might describe most people's instinctual response to attack, but not Emily's. No, for Emily, when a threat presented, the circuits of her brain went haywire, leaving her mute and motionless. It should be fight or flight or freeze, but they never mentioned the *or freeze*.

"Can I help you?" Kate managed a stiff smile.

"I n-n-need a haircut." Emily's voice sounded muffled through the whoosh of blood rushing past her ears.

Kate's cornflower blue eyes took in Emily's unkempt hair. She shoved to her feet. "Follow me."

Emily swallowed the bile rising in her throat and focused on not tripping over her feet as she followed Kate through the salon. Black leggings clung to her impossibly long legs, and her hips rocked with a womanly sway. She had everything a woman could want, Emily realized glumly. A killer face with unblemished skin, Luke Nolan, and a thigh gap.

"Just a trim today?" Kate swiveled a chair around.

Emily climbed in and Kate tossed a black cape over her.

Looking at her reflection next to Kate, Emily frowned. "Do wh-whatever you want to it."

Kate's blue eyes widened and her gaze locked with Emily's in the mirror.

"Wh-whatever you think wo-would look nice," Emily rushed to clarify.

With a comb, Kate started to pick at Emily's snarls.

"Have you ever considered layers?"

Emily shook her head.

"Layers would add some body. What about the length? Can I take it up a bit?"

Emily wrinkled her nose. Her hair was a kind of security blanket, providing her with a curtain to hide behind when she needed one. And she always needed one. "M-maybe a little, but I like to—"

"Pull it back in a ponytail." Kate finished Emily's sentence with a smile. An adorable dimple appeared in her left cheek. "Got it."

Kate led Emily to a row of wall-mounted sinks where she wet and shampooed Emily's hair. The conditioner's fruity scent floated with them when they returned to Kate's styling station.

After running the comb through Emily's now snarl-free hair, Kate picked up the scissors.

With the first snip, Emily squeezed her eyes shut.

"How long have you known Luke?"

One eye popped open. "Uh, n-not long. You?"

Kate's gaze remained fixed on the top of Emily's head and a frown pulled down the corners of her wide mouth. "We've known each other for years. He's been a good friend to me."

Relief swamped Emily, and with it, a smile brightened her face. Luke was telling the truth. He and Kate were just friends and Emily was not, in fact, the other woman.

Kate caught Emily's smile in the mirror and her frown deepened. "But we've been growing closer lately. It's only a matter of time before we make it official."

Emily's smile fell.

The scissors sliced and a hank of Emily's hair fell to the floor. "We're perfect for each other, really. I know we are..."

"But?"

"But... It's just... He's so..."

Annoying?

Bullying?

Kate sighed. "Perfect."

Emily deflated in the chair.

Another slash of scissors sent more hair falling. "Although, he does have this one little problem."

"What problem?"

In the mirror, Emily watched Kate hold up her index finger, straight and rigid. Then her finger drooped like a wilting flower.

Emily stared at her finger a moment before its meaning struck. "He's impotent?"

A frisson of panic swept over Kate's features. "I'm sure it'll pass, once we've gotten to know each other a bit better."

Emily recalled the firm press of Luke's erection poking against her thigh, and the feel of it sliding inside her.

"Promise you won't say anything. I'd feel terrible if he found out I told you."

Emily smoothed the shock from her expression. "Of course. I just can't believe it. He seems so...."

"Virile?" Kate offered.

Emily nodded. Yes, virile, and hot-blooded, and horny.

"He is. I'm just being picky. He's perfect, except for that one little thing."

Thinking to remove Luke's male member from the topic of conversation, Emily asked, "How long have you lived on the island?"

"I moved here five years ago. My husband grew up here."

Her husband?

The scissors trembled in Kate's hand before she steadied them and executed the brutal slash. "I need to stop calling him that. Anthony's been dead almost nine months now."

With the lost look on Kate's face, Emily experienced a

twist of misery. She knew that look. She observed the same expression on her own face most days since her mom died.

"My m-mom died last year."

The scissors froze above her head, a large swath of hair poised between the blades.

"She's still my m-m-mom," Emily said softly. "She'll always be m-my mom."

Kate's eyes glistened, but she blinked and ducked her chin. She cut the rest of Emily's hair in silence.

When a pile of strawberry-blonde hair lay at their feet, Kate spun Emily away from the mirror and attacked her head with a blow dryer and a round brush. Finally, the blow dryer fell quiet and she turned Emily to face the mirror.

Another blast of shock struck Emily at the way her hair shimmered about her shoulders.

"What do you think?"

"I think y-you're a miracle w-worker."

Kate even blushed prettily, her cheeks taking on a soft, rosy glow that wasn't at all splotchy.

"Do y-you think it will last until tomorrow? I'm in a wedding."

"Why don't you come by in the morning and I'll touch it up. What time is the wedding?"

"Three o'clock."

At the front desk, Kate pored over an appointment book. "Want to come by at nine?"

The next morning, Emily arrived as Kate was unlocking the front door. She wore her long blonde hair in an elegant ponytail and huge hoop earrings. Her blue jeans had more bling on the butt pockets than Emily had ever worn at any one time.

"I was wondering, what would you say to a little color?"

"What kind of color?" Emily asked and slid into the

chair.

Kate waved a comb through the air. "Nothing drastic. Just a touch of copper to bring out your red highlights."

The previous night, Emily had revisited her reflection in the mirror numerous times, and every time she marveled all over again at Kate's cut.

"Wh-whatever you think will look nice, I'll try it."

An hour later, with layers of tin foil sprouting out of her head, Emily regretted her impetuousness. "I didn't realize there was so much involved."

Kate just laughed and used the pointed end of her comb to separate another chunk of hair.

Soon, she set down her tools and pulled the apron off over her head. "We need to let the foil sit for a bit."

She bent to open the cabinet of her styling station and retrieved a large cloth bag from inside her oversized purse. With a yank on the zipper, she unfolded the bag and laid it open across the counter.

She stepped aside and smiled at Emily. "What do you think?"

Emily stared at the bag, stuffed to overflowing with makeup of every shape and shade. She'd never seen some of the utensils contained in multiple clear pouches.

She looked at Kate. "I don't w-wear makeup very often."

"Want me to show you how?"

Emily gulped. "Uh... okay?"

Kate squealed and dove for the bag.

For the next half hour, Emily submitted to Kate's attention in silence. She didn't even protest when Kate removed the tweezers from her little bag of torture devices and attacked Emily's eyebrows.

A brush in hand, she stepped back and studied Emily a moment. "This is too good. I'm going to turn you around and wait to show you the whole look when your hair is done."

After makeup, Kate took Emily to the sinks and yanked the foils from her head. The blow dryer and round hairbrush came out again, and then Kate tugged and twisted at her hair for some time before flitting around her wielding a curling iron.

Just when Emily had worked up the nerve to complain, Kate stepped back, a huge grin on her flawless face. "You ready?"

Emily's mouth went dry. With light hair, dark eyes, and pale, freckled skin, she was not an attractive woman. Objectively, she knew that. Certainly, she looked like a fool, having done so much to conceal her average appearance.

The chair whirled. For several long moments, Emily stared at the reflection in the mirror. Her reflection. Except, it didn't look like her. This girl, Emily didn't know.

This girl was pretty.

The makeup made her skin glow and highlighted the delicate lines of her nose and mouth. A smoky shadow and liner made her eyes appear large and almond-shaped, and coaxed a soft light from their dark centers.

The light blonde strands of her hair intermixed with the deep red undertones, like spun gold threaded through molten fire, which Kate had twisted into an intricate chignon at her nape.

Tears pushed to the surface. Most of her life, she'd wanted to be somebody else, anybody else, but in that moment, she wouldn't have traded places with anyone. She was just happy to be herself, a pretty girl blessed with unique coloring and well-sculpted features. Her tears pooled.

Kate paled. "Omigod, you hate it." She snatched three tissues from the box and lunged at Emily. "We can fix it. Don't cry. I'll just—"

Emily shrank back. "No, don't touch me!"

Kate froze with a wad of crumpled-up Kleenex in her

fist.

"Please," Emily whispered. "Don't ruin it. It's perfect."

The mirror ensnared Emily's gaze, and words she'd never once thought, not even privately, slipped out. "I'm so pretty."

∞

The stone church sat atop a gentle hill overlooking Lake Michigan. The day was cool, though a bright sun took the edge off the chill and a crisp freshness infused the air.

Emily and Mina settled in the small bridal room, but having already changed, when Vivian appeared to help Mina into her wedding dress Emily snuck out to make one last check of the church.

Sunlight streamed in through the deep-set stained glass windows and gleamed on the warm woodwork. She'd arrived early with the flowers, placing dark purple and ivory arrangements at the altar and hanging small bouquets with gossamer bows on the end of each pew.

When the first guests began to arrive, Emily headed for the brides' room, only to be cut off by a broad-shouldered man stepping into her path.

"Where's Mina?"

She pulled up at Noah's abrupt manner, and then because of the way the sleek black tuxedo he wore intensified his good looks.

Wow.

Deep lines of worry bracketed his mouth and eyes and set off alarm bells inside Emily's head. "She's here. She's getting dressed."

"Have you talked to her?" He glanced over his shoulder. "How is she?"

"She's fine," Emily said carefully. "Is something wrong?"

Noah's worry turned to irritation. "She won't let me in

your room."

"Well, you know what they say, bad luck and all that."

His teeth flashed in something like a smile. "Will you check on her for me? Make sure she's okay?"

"Sure. I'll be right back."

He caught her arm. "By the way, you look amazing."

The blush of pleasure still warmed her cheeks when Emily ducked into the brides' room. In her dress, Mina sat in a folding chair, her head in her hands.

A shiver of worry passed through Emily. She'd heard of brides getting cold feet on their wedding day, but she'd never understood it. Not the fact a woman would get so far as the church before speaking up–Emily could totally understand how that might happen. It baffled her, a girl with so few prospects, how a woman might throw aside a man perfectly willing to get married.

"Mina, are you all right?"

Her cousin's head came up, and at her pale complexion, Emily's worry turned to dread.

Mina rubbed her forehead and pushed a sharp puff of air between her lips. Then she dropped her head into her hands. "I'm okay. I just need a minute."

Emily licked her dry lips. "You're not... having doubts, are you?"

Mina's burst of bright bubbly laughter echoed around the small chamber. "No. Not even a little." She flung herself back in the chair, the smile lingering on her white lips. "It'll pass. I'm just nauseous."

"Nauseous? Are you nervous?"

Mina shook her head and her smile turned radiant. "I'm pregnant."

Emily sagged against the door. "Oh, thank God. I thought I was going to have to sneak you out the window. I'm not sure you noticed, but we're awfully high up."

"Stop, you're making me laugh." Mina wiped a tear of

mirth from the corner of her eye. "I have no idea how to redo my makeup."

"Have you told Noah?"

Mina's expression softened. "He knows."

"Good, because he's about to beat down the door trying to get in here to see you."

"Do not let him in."

"I promise. Can I get you anything?" Emily asked. "Some water or juice?"

Mina nodded. "Some juice might help. There's this awful taste in my mouth that won't go away. Do you have a breath mint?"

Emily pushed away from the door. "Be right back."

She slipped through the door and retraced her steps to the church vestibule. She scanned the crowd gathered in the church and spotted Luke standing at the altar with his brothers. The sight of four tall, great-looking men decked out in tuxedos caused Emily's brain to freeze.

Jack entertained the others with a vividly told tale while beside him, Shea, his white hair so at odds with his youthful face and lean, well-muscled physique, interjected with a point of clarification. Noah laughed and Luke, tall, dark, and tuxedoed, wore a mean scowl as he glared down the aisle.

At her.

Her heart kicked painfully in her chest as she strode down the aisle toward him.

Tipped off by his fierce regard, one by one the others turned as she approached.

Noah pounced. "How is she?"

"Giddy with joy. It's disgusting, really."

His smug smile teased a laugh from her.

Then she noticed the soles of two tiny shoes perched on Luke's shoulders. She tilted her head to one side to find the ring bearer hanging down his back.

"Crowd control?" She smiled.

Luke didn't. "What happened to your face?"

Fiery heat burned her cheeks.

"What the hell is wrong with you?" Noah snapped.

"Ignore him." Shea's brilliant blue eyes were soft with compassion. "He's an idiot and you're gorgeous."

She refused to let them see how much his words hurt. "Do p-p-people really think he's charming?"

"Truly, it's mind-boggling," Jack said, glaring at Luke.

She swallowed the knot in her throat and lifted her chin, though she couldn't quite bring herself to look him in the eye. "Do you have a p-p-piece of candy? It's n-not for me. It's for M-M-Mina."

He angled toward her. "Inside pocket."

After a moment's hesitation, she slipped her hand beneath the lapel of his tuxedo. His gaze fixated on something over her head while her fingers danced over the hard plane of his abdomen, seeking.

"*Breast* pocket."

"Oh." She registered only warmth and his spicy scent.

"Other side."

She found the pocket over his heart stuffed with hard candies.

"Unca Uke, let me down!"

Clutching a lemon drop in her fist, she risked one last peek at his dark expression before she retreated down the aisle.

With juice and candy, some of Mina's color returned. As Emily helped pin a cream magnolia into her auburn hair, Isobel poked her head inside the door to let them know it was time to begin the ceremony.

A small crowd of forty people gathered in the pews, their necks craned to see the procession. Before the altar, Noah and three of his brothers stood shoulder to shoulder. Joyous music cued Emily to begin the walk down the aisle.

As she progressed to the front of the church, Luke's

cold green eyes bored into her. Her hands trembled when she took her place across the aisle from him. She kept her focus on Mina until her cousin came to stand beside her.

Father John, an uncle and father figure to the brothers, presided over the ceremony. It took Emily a moment to catch the rhythm of his thick Irish accent, but once she did, she enjoyed both his eloquence and calming presence.

From her place at Mina's side, Emily watched Noah's face throughout the service. Unable to take his eyes off his bride, love and affection poured from him. An unexpected pang struck Emily beneath her breastbone.

When the time came to declare their devotion to one another, Mina's voice trembled and Noah's choked with emotion. They cried, and so did Emily.

The ceremony ended with joyous music and a beaming couple, who led the partygoers out of the church and into the cool fall air.

Before she climbed into Noah's car, Mina gripped Emily's arm. "Can you grab my bag for me? I left it in the bridal room."

Emily didn't wait to see the couple off, but scurried up the porch stairs, eager to retrieve Mina's belongings and stop on the way to the inn to pick up a bottle of nonalcoholic champagne.

But as she neared the doors, she slowed her steps.

Luke stood beneath the archway, blocking her path.

"Your hair is sparkling." He made it sound like an accusation.

"Kate did it for me." Emily watched for signs that it bothered him to know she'd spent time with Kate outside his presence, but saw none.

Instead, his gaze caressed her face, lingering on her mouth, before snapping back to her eyes. "What did she do to your face?"

Emily sucked in a sharp hiss of air. Then through clenched teeth, she said, "She fixed it."

She sidestepped him and ducked inside the church. When she reappeared a few minutes later, he was gone.

Chapter Fourteen

Fires blazed in the twin marble fireplaces located at either end of the inn's ballroom while soft light cascaded down from crystal chandeliers. A massive dining table with enough seating for forty or so people ran the length of the room. Flickering candles and white pumpkins stuffed with purple flowers decorated the tabletop.

When he'd first learned his brother planned to marry Mina on Halloween, he'd thought they were crazy. Now, if he weren't so annoyed, the clever pumpkins and warm ambience would've brought a smile to his face.

His gaze combed the dimly lit ballroom until he spotted her, propping up the far wall. He circled the room, careful not to let her catch sight of him.

What the hell had Kate done to her? He hardly recognized her. She'd turned Emily into a mini-Kate. Overdone to the point of obscuring everything special and different about her. The makeup blotted out her freckles. There was no movement to her hair. The dress was all right, a nice change from the pajamas she usually wore, he supposed, but so unlike Emily, he resented it, too.

Her transformation was both striking and complete, and he hated everything about it.

Still, he'd been an unmitigated ass to her at the church. He couldn't explain it, but the moment he saw her, a rage overcame him. Rage that a laid-back guy like him never experienced. Rage that the world wanted her changed.

He slipped along the wall to stand beside her. "Can I buy you a drink?"

She stiffened and snuck a glance at him from the corner of her eye. "The drinks are free."

"I know. That's why it's funny."

A frown tugged at the curves of her luscious mouth.

Her scent teased his nostrils and he frowned. She even smelled different. Perfume-y. Not at all like Emily.

"You know, some women would be flattered by that pickup line."

She snorted. "*That* was a pickup line?"

"You didn't like it?"

She tried to hide a smile.

He shrugged. "Okay, fine, I'll admit it. I'm out of practice. I don't pick up women at bars or weddings anymore."

"Reformed, are you?"

"Disillusioned. At our age, women tend to be either desperately insecure or shamelessly overconfident." He shuddered. "Not enticing."

"Gee, thanks. Which am I? Old and desperate or old and ridiculous?"

"You?" He sipped from his glass. "You're the exception."

An attractive blush stained her cheeks. "Okay, now *that's* a pickup line."

He smiled, pleased with himself. An easy silence fell between them.

Until a tiny black-haired woman crashed into their clandestine space. "There you are. Come quick. It's a disaster."

Emily's dark eyes filled with panic. "Wh-wh-what happened?"

"The salmon is too dry and the asparagus is undercooked and, oh my goodness, they want to serve a red wine. I don't know what we're going to do..."

Emily scurried after the miniature pit bull, and for the next half hour, Luke remained in her clever hiding place. Honestly, no one noticed him in the shadows, and he had a prime view of all the action. Though he didn't bother with most of it.

Instead, he tracked her movements as she played intermediary between the pit bull and the waitstaff, fussed with each and every stuffed-pumpkin flower arrangement, and tinkered with the overhead lighting until he suspected she would wear out the wall switches.

He might've laughed at her comical meticulousness, except he couldn't find the humor in her search for perfection. Around her, guests mingled, laughing and talking and soaking up the ambience she obsessively tended.

No one noticed her efforts, which only seemed to spur her on. She worked faster, harder, pursuing perfection where it already existed. As though, if she missed some irrelevant detail or overlooked some miniscule nicety, if she tripped up, or stuttered, they'd deem her unworthy.

Worthless.

His heart gave a sharp pinch.

When guests began to search out their seats, he strolled up one side of the table and located his place card between Jack and Isobel. Waitstaff appeared to deliver champagne flutes while across the room, Emily and Father John engaged in conversation.

Her arm swung out to motion toward the chair at the head of the table. She started to turn away, but John stopped her and, leaning close, made a brief comment before moving to take his seat.

Luke stilled. He'd never seen someone not in shock turn so ghostly pale as Emily did just then.

Noah and Mina took their seats in the center of the table across from Luke while Shea, as best man, filled the chair beside Noah. The seat next to Mina remained empty.

Emily hovered near the ballroom doors, as though she'd devised an escape plan and only awaited the exact right moment to execute it. More staff appeared, their trays overflowing with plates of food.

She was the last to sit, approaching that empty seat like a prisoner to the gallows.

With everyone settled, Father John stood and clanked his fork gently against the side of his crystal water glass. "Thank ye all for being here. My nephew and his bride are grateful to have ye here to celebrate the start o' their lives together as a married couple."

Luke appraised the contents of his plate, curious what was done about the dry salmon.

"You've heard enough from me today and so now I'd like to turn things over to the rest of you," Father John was saying. "First up, our gracious host and lovely maid of honor would like to say a few words. Emily, take it away, me dear."

Luke's head snapped up. She was going to speak? Had she requested to do so?

One look at her stricken features told him she most certainly had not. Her throat worked with a series of not-quite swallows, and then she lurched to her feet.

Her dark eyes darted back and forth in full panic. An apparent afterthought, she plucked her champagne flute off the table.

The palm of her hand landed hard on the tabletop.

"I w-w-w-want to w-w-w-w–"

His heart, lodged somewhere near his throat, suffered a gash at the tortuous stammer.

With a hard swallow, she began again. "To w-w-w-welcome y-y-y-you–"

A ripple of unease ran around the table.

"To the W-W-Winslow H-H-House and to–" Her voice broke.

The leg of his chair scraped on the floor when Luke stood abruptly. "And to introduce you to the groom's brother." He delivered a well-practiced, sheepish smile. "For those of you who don't know me, I'm Noah's younger, more handsome brother, Luke."

Soft laughter trickled around the table.

"And earlier this evening, I pulled our beautiful hostess aside and bullied her until she agreed to allow me to give this speech in her place."

Emily sank silently into her chair.

"You see, my brother, Noah, has spent the majority of our adult lives living overseas, and I wanted to take this opportunity to publically welcome him home and back into our lives."

A murmur of approval ran around the table.

"As you can see by his choice of a wife, Noah is an extremely bright man, and with his return, our family is made whole again. But not only do we have our brother back, he brought Mina into our lives as well. Mina, if your patience and compassion are half as true as your smile, I daresay my brother is the luckiest bastard on this island."

Amidst soft laughter and contented murmurs, Luke raised his champagne glass. "To Noah and Mina. May your love be the light to guide you when the twists and turns of fate darken your path."

"To Noah and Mina," the crowd enthused.

Luke drank and eased back down in his chair. With a smart-ass comment, Jack smacked him on the back. He risked a glance at Emily.

A small smile playing over her lips, she watched Noah and Mina. Then, as though she felt his gaze, she turned her head and soulful brown eyes tugged at his insides.

Her mouth moved. *Thank you.*

He inclined his head, and then turned aside when Isobel leaned close to speak in his ear.

The party lingered over dinner, only breaking up once the plates had been cleared away and two of Shea's bartenders started the free alcohol flowing at a makeshift bar set up in a corner of the room. In the opposite corner, a DJ increased the volume of the music.

Luke made his way to the bar.

"Hey, Matt," he greeted Shea's head bartender. "How's the new place?"

"It rocks. The boys love the yard." He held up a bottle of Guinness. "Are you looking for one of these?"

Just then, loud music kicked on and a corny song, at least three decades old, blared from the speakers.

"You know, I think I'm going to need something stronger," Luke said.

Matt laughed and held up pints of rum and whiskey.

"I'll take the rum. Mind if I steal the bottle and two glasses?"

Turning away from the bar, Luke spotted her immediately, sitting alone at one of the tall pub tables situated before the fireplace.

She looked at him with dark eyes shimmering in the firelight as he approached. He plunked down the bottle and slid onto the stool next to her.

"Is this my free drink?" She didn't quite manage to hide the chaos in her eyes.

"Impressed?" he asked, pouring two fingers of golden liquid into each glass.

"Only if your plan is to knock me out cold."

"Nah, I like the challenge of a conscious date." He lifted his glass. "Cheers."

They drank. A sharp hiss escaped her as the liquid burned a path down her throat.

"Feel better?"

"Not even a little." Though some of the color returned to her cheeks.

She licked a droplet of moisture from the corner of her mouth, and only the lost look in her eyes quelled the surge of lust.

He refilled their glasses. "I can't read your face in the dark. You okay?"

"Uh-uh, no. No confiding. I haven't had nearly enough alcohol yet."

"In that case." He tipped his glass at her and tossed back the contents. She joined him and they returned the tumblers to the table with simultaneous thuds.

She chewed her bottom lip while he feigned interest in the people embarrassing themselves on the dance floor.

"I, um... I'm... I..." She heaved a sigh of defeat. "Thank you."

"I don't know what you're talking about."

Her expression softened. "You do, but I'm willing to pretend if you are."

Heat from the fire in the fireplace warmed his back. "The truth is, I wanted to hear what you had to say."

Toffee-colored eyes searched his face.

"No, I'm not teasing you, Emily."

She snagged the bottle and poured a healthy splash of buttery liquid into both glasses. "I didn't have anything to say."

"Now I know that's not true."

Her gaze darted between him and her glass. "Nothing I wo-would've been able to get out." Her sigh held a lifetime of heartache. "I've tried everything. Breathing techniques, word avoidance, speech therapy, antidepressants. Nothing ever fixes m-m-me."

She tilted her head back and drank. He lifted his glass to his lips, a sliver of anger curling through him. He wanted to argue with her, but what the hell did he know about it? He had no idea what it'd been like for her.

He returned his tumbler to the tabletop. "I don't think you sound as bad as you think you sound. And I know having trouble coming up with the right words, on the spot, in a public setting, no less, does not mean you're broken or somehow need fixing."

"That's it. That's the problem, right there." Her face grew animated. "It's not that I can't find the words. It's that there's so much I want to say and I can't possibly say it all and-and-and the words jam and-and everything starts to pile up and-and—" She sagged back. "It's so... frustrating."

"You know, now that you mention it, I've noticed you sure have a lot to say."

She smiled and his heart lifted.

"You know what my favorite word is?"

"It's Luke, isn't it?"

She shook her head, laughing.

"Tell me," he said softly.

"Fuck."

The force of his laughter surprised him.

"It's the best word ever," she said. "I never stutter when I say it."

"Filth flows fluidly, does it?"

God, she was pretty when she laughed. He liked talking to her like this. It felt good to feel something other than bruised and weary when talking to a woman.

"Okay, I got it." He shifted on his stool. "The next time

you're struggling to get the words out, pretend you're talking to me and I've just pissed you off again. You don't have any trouble giving me a piece of your mind."

She brushed away his idea with a wave of her hand. "You're easy to talk to."

Warmth broke like the sun over the horizon in the center of his chest.

She mistook his smile. "But don't go thinking I've joined the ranks of your admirers. I am not, nor will I ever be, a Luke Nolan groupie."

A grimace pulled at his features. "I do not have groupies."

With a giggle, she laughed and slid her empty glass across the table until it knocked into his. "You really do."

Rum flowed as he refilled both glasses.

"Why don't you have an accent?" At his confusion, she pressed on. "It's just, I noticed Noah and Shea have accents and you and Jack don't have much of one, and I was curious why."

"We left Ireland when I was seven, and after living here for a few years, it sort of faded. Maybe because they were older when we moved, Noah and Shea never lost theirs." He dropped the timbre of his voice and with a thick brogue said, "Of course, I can turn it back on if ye'd like."

"Oh my, don't do that. Whew. That made me a little light-headed."

A chuckle shook his shoulders. They sipped their drinks in silence for a time.

"Do you miss it?"

"Miss what?" he asked. "Ireland or my accent?"

Amusement flickered in her eyes. "Ireland."

"I don't remember it all that much." A wish from childhood came flooding back. "I think about going back for a visit."

"You should."

"I will. Someday."

With the silence, they sipped.

"Wh-why did you leave?"

"My mom died and—"

Her soft gasp broke in. "You lost your mom when you were seven?"

"That's right." His voice sounded rough and he reached for the bottle. "My dad... he couldn't take care of us, so they sent us here, to live with John."

"Father John is your uncle, right?"

"Right. He's my mom's brother." He swallowed a healthy gulp.

"H-how did she die?"

"She had cancer."

"Luke, I'm so sorry." Her voice soft, she looked at him with softer eyes, filled with acknowledged pain.

One orphan to another.

"Thank you."

She slid the bottle back to her side of the table and added another splash to her glass. "Your dad... did you miss him?"

He snatched up his tumbler. "Nope." He threw back the contents of the glass and reached for the pint.

Smart woman that she was, she understood that door was closed.

"My dad used to come up with creative ways to try to make me quit stuttering. O-one time, he made me talk with a stone under my tongue for a wh-whole month. It didn't do any good, of course, but he was too stubborn to admit wh-when he was wrong."

Luke stared into his glass to hide his scowl. "Sure sounds creative, all right."

"He tried to take my name away." Her throat worked until finally she forced out the word. "Cole. I don't know what it was, but I couldn't say the name without a huge struggle. So he refused to let me say it or even write it for over a year, and every day he threatened to file the paperwork to permanently change it."

Though she kept her tone light, Luke could hear the ring of anguish in her voice.

A tiny hiccup escaped her. "Eventually he gave up and just hit–"

Luke's head snapped up.

She sucked her bottom lip between her teeth, as if to pull the words back.

His stomach gave a sickening wrench. "He hit you?"

She hesitated. "No. Not often. He had a temper and I... tried his patience."

"Don't do that." Fury caused his hands to shake. "Don't you dare blame yourself for his weaknesses."

Large, dark eyes stared up at him. Her throat worked. "You're right. That was silly of me."

Of its own volition, his hand reached out and he traced the fine bones of her face, from her fragile cheekbones to her small chin, imagining the damage a man's fist could yield.

"You aren't silly." He stroked her cheek with the pad of his thumb, where her freckles should be, but weren't.

She tilted her head, pressing her cheek into his palm. "Thank you for saying that."

With the rum sloping through his bloodstream, lazy warmth wrapped around him. She slid off her barstool and came to stand between his thighs. His cock took immediate notice, even as her fragrant perfumed scent filled his senses and a pang of frustration kicked in his chest.

Warm whiskey swirls pulled him in, until her tongue darted out to lick her lips and his gaze riveted on her mouth.

"You're so cool," she whispered.

A soft laugh rumbled through him. "You're drunk."

"A little." Her soft breath rushed over his skin. "And

you have the most kissable lips."

"Maybe you should prove it."

Her body pressed against his and she touched his lips with hers. He held himself still while she explored his mouth with tiny tastes and tentative nibbles. A soft, slow lick.

Heat seared him.

She pulled back and gazed into his eyes for a long moment, as though searching for some clue.

He tossed up a smile, the one that charmed everybody, while his mind puzzled out the most efficient means of getting her naked. The bare bones of a plan formed, but before he could set it in motion, her expression shifted, growing serious, and her brown eyes turned all soft and slippery.

Unease stole over him.

Her voice trembled when she spoke. "You're so beautiful."

The smile froze on his face. Her fingers touched the side of his cheek and he only just managed to stifle a flinch.

"Not just here," she said, and then she pressed the flat of her palm to his chest. Above his heart. "But here."

The air sucked from his lungs. He couldn't draw breath, and his heart started to pound. Vines wrapped around his ankles to hold him rooted to the spot, unable to run while she gazed upon him.

The real him.

It was the first time in as long as he could recall anyone bothering to look beyond his pretty face, past the mask of charm he kept in place.

Now, for the first time, someone looked. And she found him beautiful.

Her name broke over his lips.

Then her plump mouth pulled down at the corners. "Except, of course, when you're being a jerk."

A song ended and through the speakers, the DJ invited Noah and Mina to take to the dance floor. Emily pulled away. His hands shot out to grip her waist.

He tugged and she fell softly against him. "Don't go."

Her heat soothed the aches his body had carried for all time. He was drowning in her softness.

Chapter Fifteen

"**D**ance with me." He spoke low in her ear.

Gooseflesh chased up her arms. "I'm supposed to dance with Shea."

Indeed, the oldest Nolan brother wove his way through the crowd toward them.

"Take my hand."

As if of its own volition, her hand settled inside his. The warmth of his skin sloped through her as he led her toward the dance area.

Slipping an arm around her waist, he pulled her close.

Her pulse thundered in her ears and she fixed her gaze on his chest, sneaking the occasional peek at the strong column of his neck.

Her body hummed with awareness of him.

"There it is." His lips brushed her earlobe.

She turned her head. "What?"

He executed a small move to turn her toward the dance floor. "Shea and his wife are dancing."

Emily spotted Luke's brother a few couples away with Isobel wrapped in his arms. "They're married?"

"They've got it into their heads that they don't want to be together anymore." The flat of Luke's palm smoothed up her back.

Sensation ricocheted through her and she squeezed her eyes shut.

"They separated last year, yet they're madly in love with each other." His hand found the curve of her hip. "They're driving everyone crazy."

It was too much, his heady scent and heated touch. His electric, lingering gaze. She started to tremble. From beneath her eyelashes, she snuck a glance at his face.

Maybe it was the rum, but his beauty hurt to look at. His square jaw and pink lips. His eyes that shone like jewels against his tanned skin.

"Don't look at me like that."

At the bite in his tone, she ducked her chin. "S-sorry."

His grip on her hip tightened. "Because if you keep looking at me like that, I'm not going to be able to stop myself from doing something about it."

She bit down on her lower lip to hide the hitch in her breathing.

"I'll find us a nice, quiet place, and do all the things I've been wanting to do to you for the past two months now."

Her tongue slipped out to lick her dry lips. "Wh-what things?"

His fingertips danced over the bare skin of her shoulder. "I'll touch you." He dipped his head and his lips followed the path his fingertips had blazed. "Taste you."

She shivered.

His mouth nuzzled her ear. "Tease you until you can't endure anymore. And then...."

"Wh-wh-what? And then wh-what?"

"And then, I'm going to fuck you."

The swift, fierce shock of arousal zinged through her.

"Is that what you want, Emily?" With an easy nudge, he entwined his fingers with hers. "Do you want me to fuck you?"

More than she wanted her next breath, except, "I thought... you said it w-was a mistake. That I w-was a mistake."

On a curse, his large hand clamped around hers. He hauled her away from the dance floor and hustled her through the ballroom doors. In the hall, she stumbled along behind him until he pulled her with him into the library and swept shut the door, plunging them into darkness.

The lock turned over, followed by the muffled sound of his footsteps on the Persian rug. A thump, another curse, and dim light from a lamp threw a warm glow over the room.

"You think I rejected you." Emotion rode the top of his voice.

"You called m-me a mistake." Hadn't he?

"No, not you." He detached from the shadows. "It's me. I... I can't give you what you want."

"You don't know wh-what I want. You never asked m-me."

His taut features softened. "What do you want, Emily?"

"You." She rushed forward with the words, close enough to feel the warmth from his body. "I want you."

"I can't do long-term. Not right now." His voice was rough, as though he was being pulled apart. "Maybe never."

"I don't want y-your promises. Or your heart." It wasn't a lie. Not exactly. She wanted whatever would make her feel less alone.

His thumb dragged across her bottom lip with a

ruthless stroke, rubbing lipstick from her mouth.

She jerked her head back. "Stop, you'll mess it up."

"Damn straight, I will."

She backed away. "I get it. You don't like it."

"You're right, I don't like it. I don't like it at all." Heat from his body invaded hers when he came to stand behind her. "You look hot as hell and I'm out of my mind with wanting you."

Her heart slammed against her breastbone. "I can't tell if y-you're teasing me."

His palm closed around her bare shoulder. His hand slid up the column of her throat, beneath Kate's artful chignon. Emily protested, but his fingers tangled roughly through her hair and the heavy curtain fell over her shoulders.

"I want you back." He kneaded her scalp. "The real you. Without the sparkles and the paint." His lips brushed her shoulder. "Without the dress."

He buried his hands in her tulle skirts and, slowly, inched the fabric up her thighs.

Through the walls drifted the muffled drone of music and partygoers. A snatch of someone's laughter rose above the din. Her gaze darted to the large picture window behind the mahogany desk.

Then cool air kissed the skin of her thighs, and her bare bottom. Her thoughts scattered.

A soft curse slipped from Luke and his calloused palms smoothed over the smooth globes of her buttocks, left exposed by the thong underwear she wore.

Arousal spiraled through her to settle low in her belly.

He rubbed her lower back in slow, tight circles. Seeking stability, she pressed her palms to the smooth wood desktop.

One of his large shoe-clad feet pushed between her high heels and nudged, gently, until she stood with her feet shoulder-width apart.

She trembled in anticipation of his touch.

Beneath the tiny string of her thong, his hand stole lower, between her legs, until his fingers feathered along her slit. Her sharp gasp morphed into a needy moan.

He explored her, circling and massaging, but not touching, never touching, the place where she most ached.

She arched her back and wiggled her hips in a slow circle, chasing his touch while his hot mouth suckled the side of her neck. Her moans grew desperate and he soothed her by whispering soft nonsense into her ear.

Still, he evaded her swollen core.

His hardness pressed into her bottom and she wriggled to fit herself more snugly against him.

"I can't," he croaked. "I don't have a condom."

"I'm on the pill." Relief rushed through her that she'd made the brash decision to ask the doctor for a prescription. "And I haven't been w-with anyone else in a long time."

Turning her, he cupped her face with both of his hands. Green eyes pierced her. "Neither have I." His mouth brushed over hers in a soft, lingering kiss. "Thank you."

A tangle of emotions surged and clogged in the back of her throat. In that moment, the thought came to her that she could love him forever.

Cool wood struck her bare bottom when he lifted her onto the desk.

He eased her down. Standing between her parted thighs, he watched her with suddenly hooded eyes as he gently pushed her skirts above her waist.

His palm pressed to the soft swell of her abdomen. With his other hand, he hooked a finger around the crotch of her panties and tugged them aside. The tip of his finger stroked her.

Sensation pulsated between her legs. She threw her

head back. Color burst behind her eyes when the heavy slide of his fingers coaxed the first ripples of her orgasm.

She felt his hands between their bodies as he freed himself. His solid warmth brushed her opening and she whimpered with wonder. It was really going to happen. Luke Nolan was going to make love to her.

This time, he wouldn't regret it.

Thoughts splintered when his shaft teased at her entrance. He dropped his head to her shoulder when he pushed inside her and her awareness narrowed to the slide of pleasure his body wrought from hers.

"Jesus, Em, you're so tight." He gripped her hips and pressed deeper.

Her body swallowed more of him, and his fingers stroked a sensitive spot. A cry tore from her throat.

Cast out to sea, she clutched at him while he pumped into her with long, languid strokes. In the quiet room, the sound of her slick wetness mingled with their labored breathing.

The world fell away. There were no people on the other side of the door. No large windows through which they might be discovered. No spiral notebook poking into her backside.

There was only Luke, and the exquisite, excruciating pleasure of his touch.

"I'm sorry. I can't wait—"

His muscles bunched beneath her hands and he thrust into her with fierce desperation. With his release, he groaned her name into the side of her neck. His teeth scraped over her hypersensitive skin. Her orgasm screamed through her, beautiful and dangerous, like a comet streaking across the night sky.

After, she listened to the sound of his pounding heart while faint tremors eddied through her body.

Rising up on his elbows, he peered down into her face. He brushed a strand of her hair off her temple. "You okay?"

She nodded.

"What are you thinking?"

Thoughts. She should have some, but as she gazed up into his flawless face, only a lone, inappropriate thought crystallized. "When can we do that again?"

A surprised, helpless laugh rattled in his chest and he pressed his forehead to hers. "The second I can go again." His lips brushed hers. "I promise."

Oh, my. She would definitely love him forever.

A soft knock sounded on the library door.

He pushed off her and she bolted upright. Still standing between her legs, he smoothed her skirt down over her thighs and fastened his tuxedo pants, but he didn't retreat.

His hand slipped beneath her hair and he pulled her to him. His mouth met hers in a whisper-soft kiss. He dawdled, taking small nips at the corner of her mouth, as if no one waited on the other side of the door.

Finally, he left her and crossed the room. He opened the door a tiny fraction of a crack.

"Is Emily with you?" She recognized Noah's voice.

"She is." The possessive edge in Luke's tone sent a shiver rippling through her.

"Now that she's family, I have to ask—do I have any reason to kick your ass?"

Luke held his body rigid. "Not one."

"Oh, good." Noah's tone lightened. "Then there's someone here looking for a room. She says she has a reservation."

Emily placed a hand on Luke's elbow and he stepped back to allow her to pass.

Noah took one look at her and shot Luke an exasperated look. The color heightened on Luke's cheeks, though his expression turned roguish rather than remorseful.

"All the rooms are reserved for the night with w-wedding guests." Emily entered the hall. "Is she one of the guests?"

"She's not one of the guests." Noah motioned to the end of the hall, where a woman stood waiting in the foyer.

While Noah headed back to the ballroom, Emily moved toward her. Luke followed a step behind.

"M-may I help you?"

The woman wore her dark hair pulled back in an unruly ponytail and heavy horn-rimmed glasses obscured her dark eyes. "I hope so. I'm here to check in." She had a subtle southern accent, as one who'd grown up in the Deep South but hadn't returned home in many years.

"I'm sorry. I don't have any rooms available tonight."

The woman frowned. "Are you sure? Max Foley was supposed to book a room for me."

Emily stepped aside as the Mayor of Thief Island passed through the foyer on his way to the front door.

"M-Max? Are you with the film crew?"

"That's right. I'm Honey Breedlove."

Drew slid to a stop and pivoted. His pale gaze lighted on Honey. "Excuse me, did you say Honey Breedlove?"

Honey eyed him.

"You aren't supposed to be here for two days. M-Max said M-Monday."

Drew took Honey's hand and, lifting it to his mouth, pressed a soft kiss to her knuckles. "To what do we owe the honor of your presence on our little island?"

At her side, Emily sensed Luke's rigid alertness.

"Well, aren't you a sexy ass-kisser," Honey cooed.

"I've been known to kiss women in all sorts of interesting places."

Honey rolled her eyes and pulled her hand from Drew's grasp. She turned back to Emily. "Is there any chance you can make room for me tonight? I'll sleep on a couch or the floor. Anything's better than my car."

Emily hesitated. She couldn't kick her out with no place to stay in a strange town. The last ferry had run for the night. "Of course. I'm sure I can find something...."

Honey's smile was bright and warm. "Thanks. I owe you." Then she turned on Drew, her gaze sliding over him with such heat Emily felt the blast of radiation. "I'm going to go grab my bag. You'll be here when I get back?"

A slow smile curled Drew's lips. "I'll be here."

Honey disappeared through the front door and Drew leaned into the doorjamb, watching her retreat.

Then he regarded Emily with glinting light eyes. "So tell me, why is a porn star staying at your inn?"

Chapter Sixteen

A strenuous swallow worked Emily's throat, but just then, the ballroom door banged open, depriving Luke of her reply.

Mina and Noah tripped down the hall toward them.

"That's it, we're done." Mina leaned into Noah's side. "I'm dead on my feet."

"We're leaving you to deal with the rabble-rousers back there," Noah said. "You throw a hell of a party."

Honey returned with her suitcase in tow. "I'm ready for my couch."

Emily's hand touched the pendant around her neck. "M-Max said y-y-you're filming a horror movie...?" Her question hung in the air.

"That's our agreement." A hint of defiance slid through Honey's tone.

Not the ringing endorsement Luke was hoping to

hear. "The script didn't convince you?"

"I'm still waiting to read the script," Honey said. "Max hasn't sent it to me yet."

Drew sidled close to Honey. "How exciting. A slice of Hollywood here on our little island."

Emily twisted her hands in front of her. "I'll find you a room. Can you give me just a minute?"

Drew stuck out his elbow. "I'll be glad to show Ms. Breedlove around while she waits."

Honey slipped her hand under his arm. "What are you going to show me?"

"I'll show you anything you want to see," Drew said as he led Honey toward the ballroom. "And probably a few things you don't want to see."

"Trust me, I've already seen it all," Honey said.

"That sounds like a challenge."

"Who is that?" Noah whispered.

"A famous actress," Luke whispered back. "She's here for the film."

"Two days early." Emily's hushed tone managed to ring with panic.

"Aren't all the rooms taken with wedding guests?" Mina hissed. "Where are you going to put her?"

Emily lifted her shoulders. "I'll put her in my room."

"Where will you sleep?"

"Why are we still whispering?" Luke slid a hand to the small of Emily's back. "She's staying at my place."

Mina's eyes grew wide and Emily turned an unnatural shade of pink.

"We wouldn't want to put you out," Noah said smoothly.

"It's no hardship." Luke tugged Emily back toward the library. "Enjoy your wedding night."

When he'd closed the door behind them, she whirled on him. "Was that really necessary?"

He didn't know if it was necessary, but it was

unavoidable.

He'd tried to stay away from her, but that was no longer an option. Having blown past the point of no return, his priority now was to find a way back to the hot, secret place between her thighs.

He lowered his voice to a conspiratorial, intimate purr. "I'm ready."

A fiery blush blotted her peaches-and-cream skin. He wanted to lick every inch of it.

Now that he'd made his intentions clear to her, there was nothing holding him back. It was just sex. Fulfillment of a biological need. Release.

With no fear of hurting her, and no chance of suffering a fate like the one that ruined his dad, his desire for her rushed forward to consume him.

"I want you in my bed, Emily. I don't want to wait."

"I can't leave." A flash of disappointment flitted across her face. "I have a houseful of people."

"I'll have you back first thing in the morning."

She wavered and her hand motioned to the couch. "This couch has a pull-out bed. We could, uh, sleep here."

The ferocity of his desire for her unsettled him. "What do we have to do to get rid of all these people?"

They devised a quick and dirty plan, which had Luke pulling Matt aside while Emily talked with the DJ. Soon the flow of alcohol slowed to a trickle and the parade of upbeat pop songs downshifted into ballads with slow, melancholy tempos.

It was another hour, however, before the last guests wandered up to their rooms for the night and they closed the doors on Mina and Noah's wedding party.

Emily, her arms loaded down with bed linens and pillows, slipped into the library and he swung the heavy wooden doors closed behind her.

The puffy expanse of her skirt sprang up and he shoved it down to avoid catching the delicate fabric in the door.

"That dress is ridiculous," he said.

She deposited her armload on one end of the sofa and faced him. The corners of her puffy mouth turned down. "I think it's p-pretty."

"It is. Take it off."

The pulse point at the base of her throat thumped wildly.

His erection throbbed.

Her small, oval face clouded with uncertainty.

A nugget of unease wedged beneath his breastbone. The same sensation occurred earlier, when he was inside, except he couldn't think with her hot sex clamped around him.

He circled wide around an armchair and meandered closer to her. The hollow of her neck filled with shadows and he trailed the tips of his fingers along her collarbone.

Her breath hitched.

"You said it's been a while since you've been with anyone. How long has it been?"

He didn't miss the frisson of alarm that chased across her face, but she quickly tamped it down.

He watched her mind working the problem a moment, and then she made her decision.

A predatory smile curved her lips. She placed a hand on his chest and shoved.

He collapsed onto the sofa.

"Don't worry." She reached behind her. "It's like riding a bike."

A laugh burst from him.

Then, with the scrape of her dress's zipper as she dragged it down, his laughter died. The bodice of her dress sagged, and then fell into a heap of purple at her feet.

She stood before him in high heels, a bra, and—he swallowed the painful lump in his throat—the flimsy Gstring.

A seductress.

Except for the insecure curve of her shoulders and the teardrop of uncertainty shimmering in her eyes.

Her eyelashes swept down, shutting him out, and her trembling fingers fumbled with the clasp of her corset thingy. Soon her pert breasts bounded free and the bra joined the pool on the floor. Her breasts were not the biggest, but they were perfectly round and plump enough to fill his palms.

His cock came agonizingly erect, its throbbing beat echoing the one in his heart.

Her hands skimmed down her body to push the tiny scrap of her underwear over the exaggerated swell of her hips. The string caught on the edge of her heel. With a panicked kick that pierced his heart, she jiggled the thong loose.

In nothing but the heels, she climbed onto his lap.

He smoothed his palms over the silky skin of her hips, down her thighs and over her calves. He gripped her ankles while her fingers worked the buttons of his dress shirt. She shoved the fabric aside and her small hands skittered over his bare chest. They roamed lower, to the fastening of his tuxedo pants.

His erection bobbed with its release and an appreciative growl vibrated in the back of her throat.

Blood rushed to his groin. He craved her as he craved his favorite whiskey. Would she taste as lovely, between her thighs? The golden jewel tones in her eyes beckoned to him.

The soft fuzz of her bush teased his cock when she rubbed herself against him. Then all he knew was heat and softness, and the bliss of her swollen pussy swallowing his cock and his soul.

God, she was tight.

He pushed deeper.

So fucking tight.

Uneasiness prickled–

But she rolled her hips and he was lost.

He clutched her lush ass and his head dropped to the sofa back. So tight. Tight and hot and wet.

"Luke, tell me wh-what to do. I w-want to please you."

The fog of his lust burned away. In the library, he'd been too far gone, too quickly, to understand, but now, as her tight pussy sucked him, the truth slammed into him.

Reaching up, he took her head in his hands. "You're a fraud, Emily Cole."

Terror shimmered in her dark eyes and he soothed her with a small kiss on her mouth.

"How many men have you been with? Tell me the truth."

"What, like, in the last year?"

"How many men ever?"

"O-one. Before you."

A soft curse slipped from him.

Her inexperience was far beyond what he'd imagined. Far beyond what she'd let on.

He felt a moment's regret that he'd taken her the way he had, against the wall in a mad rush. On the library desk. In a mad rush.

His heart softened. "How long ago?"

Her throat worked and her gaze slid away. "Oh, it's been a while."

He brushed back her hair, which had fallen forward to hide the upper swells of her breasts. "How long?"

"Ten y-years."

He stilled.

"Don't freak o-out. It's not a big deal."

"It's kind of a big deal. Why didn't you tell me?"

She chewed her bottom lip a moment. "There wasn't really time, before the first time, and then... I thought, if y-you found out, y-you'd find me less... attractive."

He pulled her head down and sucked her plump bottom lip between his teeth. "Not possible."

In between his soft nibbles, she whispered against his mouth, "I'm sorry."

"Don't ever apologize for being who you are."

She melted into him with a soft moan. Her hands on his chest, she rolled her hips.

A sharp hiss of air sucked between his teeth. He gripped her hips. "Emily..."

She threw her head back and rode him. Her bright hair fell about her shoulders like cascading fire, and matched the fuzz between her legs where her body swallowed his cock. Her slick moisture eased his passage, and before his heavy-lidded gaze, her breasts bounced. His mouth clamped on a pink nipple.

Her greedy moans wrenched everything from him. Caught in whiskey-colored swirls, he pounded, pounded, pounded up into her until her moans of pleasure slanted toward orgasmic cries. His balls squeezed. The tight walls of her sweet pussy clenched around him. Shoving deep and holding there, he emptied his seed inside her.

While their breathing slowed, he smoothed a hand up her back. Gripping her nape, he pulled her face down to his.

"Don't ever lie to me again, Emily. That's the one thing I cannot tolerate."

A ripple of worry disturbed the liquid softness in her eyes. She shifted and, with a reluctant kiss of regret, her body released his.

He held her waist, keeping her on his lap. "What is it?"

"There's something I should pr-probably tell you."

He didn't understand the slash of disappointment that sliced through him.

"It's about BOB," she said.

His lust-addled brain seized.

"Remember, the vibrator? From the airport?"

"I remember," he snapped. "What about it?"

"It's not mine."

There was nothing to do about it. He laughed at her.

She frowned. "Wh-why is that funny?"

"You scared the piss out me. Jesus, from the look on your face, I thought you were gonna lead me to a dead body or give me the details of your smuggling ring." When his body stopped shaking with laughter, he smoothed his hands over the swell of her hips. "Though this does put a damper on one or two of my more intriguing sexual fantasies."

"It was m-my mom's," she blurted. "No, not like that!"

A relieved breath burst from him.

"She didn't die of cancer. She had a disease that caused her muscles to w-weaken and, eventually, stop w-working. I don't know why I don't tell people what killed her. It was such a horrible disease. I used the vibrator to help break up the congestion in her lungs as her muscles grew weaker and couldn't do the w-work anymore."

Like that, the tongue-tied stray kitten silenced the silver-tongued charmer. What she described, the painfulness of a certain slow and steady death, struck him as familiar. He couldn't speak for the chaos rioting through him.

"They say it's painless, but I don't think that's true."

"Oh, Em. I'm so sorry." His mouth found hers and he drank in her sweetness.

"I won't lie to you ever again, Luke. I promise."

Her hips shifted and the soft fuzz of her red bush tickled his cock.

He became semi-erect.

Her eyes flashed, but he couldn't go again so soon. Not just yet. His fingers slid through her soft curls.

She moaned and her head fell back.

❧

Luke lay awake, the sound of the wood crackling in the fireplace the only noise in the quiet house. Tucked up against his body, Emily slept.

Naked. Her pale skin appeared pure in the firelight and the round swells of her peachy ass beckoned to him. The ridiculous makeup had worn away and her hair was in hopeless disarray. A satisfied smile tugged one corner of his mouth. That was how she should be.

He smoothed a hand up her thigh to cup one butt cheek, his darker skin a stark contrast to her paleness. Like a black stain spilling over a pristine canvas. Regret twisted through him, even as his cock grew thick and heavy.

His smile faded as one corner of his heart fractured. The blasted thing just crumbled and broke off like a chipped tooth or brittle bone. He could never have her. Not fully. He knew that.

But he could indulge, for a little while at least. Just until he no longer needed the distraction and had buried himself inside her sweet pussy a few more times. She was his winter break, a vacation from the cold and the bleakness.

He might enjoy his visit, but he couldn't buy real estate.

Though what would it hurt to lie next to her in the dark, and breathe and sleep with her?

❧

Emily cracked open one eye to the soft halo of daylight leaking into the darkened room at the edges of the curtains. A delicious soreness in unmentionable places teased a smile to her lips.

Beside her, Luke's warmth reached out to her. The long sweep of his lashes kissed his cheekbones and his full mouth fell slightly ajar. The sight of him in peaceful slumber poked holes at the protective wall around her heart.

She slipped from the bed and padded around the room, naked, collecting the scattered articles of her clothing. Her hair hung in hopeless tangles about her shoulders and she knew Kate's makeup must be smudged beneath her eyes. She struggled into her dress and tiptoed to the door, sparing one last look for the gorgeous man she'd left sleeping–

He sat up in the bed, watching her. Shirtless and droopy-eyed, his dark hair stood up in all directions.

At the sight, her heart sprouted wings and soared.

"I'm going to start br-breakfast."

He tossed back the covers and climbed from the bed. She gulped, witnessing him in his naked glory.

"You don't have to get up. I bought a box of pastries and some fresh fruit. I just need to make the coffee."

With a stern scowl at her, he pulled his tuxedo pants over his lean hips. No words were necessary to convey his opinion on the matter.

He yanked the white undershirt over his head and crossed to her.

Hand on the door, she gave a light flick of her puffy tulle skirt. "Hope no one's awake yet."

"Wait." He took her face in his hands, and tipping her chin, took full possession of her mouth.

The kiss managed to be both urgent and languid. A dizzying thrill jolted through her and she grasped his forearms.

He moaned against her mouth. "You taste so good." He pulled back and peered down into her face. "Now, shall we find out why there's a porn star in this movie?"

He flung open the doors. The house was quiet as they

padded down the hall and into the foyer. Emily went to the front door and pulled it open. Sunlight streamed into the house when she stooped to pick up the newspaper.

"People still read those?" Luke asked as she shut the door and followed him into the dining room.

"I think so. Don't they?"

She laid the paper on the dining table and pushed open the kitchen swing door.

Voices bombarded them.

"Did you guys see the beach? Holy shit. Max, man, tell me there are going to be lots of beach scenes."

Bodies packed around the kitchen table, the box of doughnuts opened between them and already half-empty.

Luke gave her a small shove in the back and she tumbled forward into the room.

At her entrance, Max turned. "Guys, this is Emily. She owns the house. And this is Luke." A light came into his dark eyes. "The cook, was it?"

Luke bared his teeth. "Chef."

"Right." Max gestured to the group seated at the table.

"H-how did y-you get in?"

"Honey let us in."

"Only because you called my cell phone at 6 a.m."

"This is the crew. Ian and Jared handle the camera and lighting. Will, here, is in the lead role, along with Honey, who I hear you've already met." Max's brow wrinkled when he considered Drew sitting beside Honey. "I have no idea who this guy is."

Honey's mouth lifted in a coy smile. "Don't worry about him. He's mine."

"You're, uh, early," Emily said.

Max's brow pulled into a frown. "Am I?"

She nodded. "I wasn't expecting you until tomorrow."

Color touched his cheekbones and he shifted his weight to one foot. "Details are a little lost on me sometimes. Hope it's okay."

"The rooms aren't ready. I need some time..."

"That's cool. We've got enough to keep us busy for a while." He passed a stack of papers around the table. "Here's the first scene. We shoot tomorrow morning at 8:00 a.m. sharp."

"Sure would have been nice to get these sooner." Honey sipped coffee. "Hard to memorize your lines in twenty-four hours."

"I'm working on it." A hard edge crept into Max's tone.

Honey's dark eyes studied his face. "You haven't finished writing it yet, have you?"

A scruffy guy with a man bun—was he Ian or Jared?—rocked back in his chair. "Is she shitting us, Max?"

Max rubbed his nape. "Don't worry about the script. I got it under control."

"Those pesky details," Honey murmured.

"Wait, does that mean I didn't have to memorize those pages you sent?" Will asked around a mouthful of doughnut.

"Yes, you did."

Will's despondency was short-lived. "As long as it's a beach scene, I don't care." He flipped through the pages Max had set in front of him.

"Not gonna happen," Max said. "The permit won't allow it. I'm appealing, but for now, it's a no-go."

"How about we have a look at that permit?"

All eyes in the room turned to Luke.

Max straightened and eased back in his chair. "It's a painfully dull document, I can assure you."

"Nonetheless, I'll take a look at it."

"What exactly are you looking for?"

Luke lifted a shoulder. "I just want to verify everything's in order. Thief Island has some interesting ordinances that most other places don't have. Isn't that right, Mayor?"

Drew raised his coffee cup. "We're a bastion of quirks and oddities, it's true."

Max's eyes narrowed to slits. "You know an awful lot about ordinances."

Luke shifted his weight from one foot to the other. "Emily pays me to keep her out of trouble."

"A chef and a bodyguard?" Max's dark eyes shimmered. "You're a handy guy to have around."

"I try to be."

With a swift movement, Luke turned to Emily. "Why don't you go check and see if any of the guests have started to stir while I make breakfast." He spoke in a low voice and the conversation around the table resumed without them.

"You sure you're okay in here by yourself?"

"I'll be on my best behavior."

"I'm officially worried."

After a quick change out of her bridesmaid dress and into a pair of blue jeans and a sweatshirt, Emily wandered upstairs where guests had in fact begun to rouse. She made sure they all knew food awaited them in the dining room and then she rushed back downstairs to help Luke in the kitchen.

He put her to work manning the toaster and the coffee station—he didn't trust her with anything else—while he kept platters of eggs and pancakes replenished.

When the food consumption slowed, she headed upstairs to strip beds and remake them with clean linens.

She dumped the used sheets and towels down the laundry chute to collect beside the washer and dryer in the mudroom. As she passed through the dining room, Luke stood poised before the rapt audience seated around the table, endeavoring to juggle a spatula, an orange, and a teacup.

Vivian's tinkling laughter rose above the merriment and exposed her as yet another victim to Luke's charm.

Emily was still smiling when she closed the lid to the washing machine and pushed the button to start the items washing.

She didn't hear him sneak up behind her. He captured her around the waist and hauled her in to his side. "When can you meet me in the library?"

He eased her back against the wall and she tilted her face up to his. His mouth brushed over hers in a whisper-soft kiss. One hand came up to touch the side of her face while he savored her mouth.

He pulled up abruptly. "What was that?"

She blinked away the languid warmth settling over her. "What was what?"

A loud thump sounded when something hit the other side of the wall at her back. They stilled.

Heavy panting carried to her. "I've never met a woman quite like you," Drew said thickly.

Honey's soft laugh carried a hard edge. "I'm a little different from the spoiled rich girls I'm sure you're used to."

"Sweetheart, you're as different as different can possibly be."

"Is that so?" A ring of disappointment tinged Honey's voice.

"For one thing, you're smarter. The smartest, I'd wager."

A beat of silence followed before Honey asked, "And easier?"

"You turned me down last night."

"Maybe I'm not the whore you've imagined me to be?"

"I know a whore when I see one," Drew said. "That's not you."

The soft slippery sounds of their kiss went on for some time, until finally, they gasped for air.

"You're going to be bad for reelection," Drew said, his voice thick.

A few more thumps on the wall, and the door to her suite closed.

"Y-you don't think they're going to have sex in my bed, do y-you?"

Luke shrugged. "At least someone gets to."

She smacked his arm and slipped out from the prison of his arms. He pinched her butt as she darted away.

Whenever she was near him, her heart lifted, becoming light and buoyant.

After a decade-long enslavement to creeping death, when she'd known only the panic of helplessness and the despair of hopelessness, she hadn't recognized the light, airy feeling for what it was.

Happiness.

Chapter Seventeen

A few days into filming, Emily contracted a flu bug. She barricaded herself in her suite and stayed in bed for two days. On the third day, she woke with a throbbing in her head, but no queasiness.

With a groan, she rolled to her side. Her cell phone blinked with a waiting message and she opened the text from Luke.

At work. Call or text my cell if you need me.

He'd checked in on her both days she lay in bed, managing to find ways to make her smile even through her misery.

She typed a reply. *Feeling better today.*

His response came immediately. *Excellent! Let me know if you're up for dinner later. I'll cook. For both our sakes.*

She slept on and off throughout the morning. In the

afternoon, she soaked in a warm bath and as dinnertime neared, the first rumblings of hunger stirred in her belly. Excited flurries joined the mix when she sent Luke a text about dinner. His reply came right away. He was delayed at work, and if she didn't mind waiting, he could swing by to pick her up in an hour so they could head to the pub for a quick dinner.

She told him she could wait.

Though exhaustion dragged at her body, she put on the skinny jeans and corduroy blazer outfit she'd purchased at the boutique downtown. Before the mirror, she tried to mimic Kate's eye makeup application, but it came out looking more smudgy than smoky and didn't conceal the dark circles under her eyes. With a blow dryer and a round brush, she worked at detangling her hair for a time, but eventually gave up and fastened the strawberry-blonde mass in a ponytail at the back of her head.

When she padded into the foyer to collect her coat, a loud voice carried to her from the front room.

"Will, you're supposed to look afraid, not aroused." Barely constrained anger polluted Max's tone.

"I can't help it. Honey's nipples are poking me in the arm."

Emily peered into the room to see Will before the front window. Honey, wearing a thin cotton tank top, stood at his elbow.

"Honey," Max barked. "Dim the headlights."

"It's, like, twenty degrees in here." Honey sounded bored. "Unless you let me put on an actual shirt, there's nothing I can do about it."

The cloying scent of men's cologne hung in the air and Emily's stomach gave an ominous wrench.

Just then, the beam of headlights moved across the wall. Her heart jumped.

Luke.

She snatched her coat off the newel post and scurried to the front door. Not thrilled by her visceral response to him, Emily reminded herself it was just a fling between them, but she hadn't seen him in days and her body craved the nearness of his.

She flung open the door. A small gasp slipped through her lips.

Large snowflakes fell lazily from the sky and a mantle of pristine white blanketed the earth. Snow clung to the trees and brightened the darkening sky.

Closeted away in her suite with the curtains drawn the past two days, she hadn't been aware of the heavy snowfall.

Luke climbed the porch stairs, all dark beauty against the backdrop of pure soft white.

She stepped onto the stoop and pulled the door closed behind her. "It's so beautiful."

A faint smile teased at the corners of his pink lips. "Have you ever seen so much snow?"

She shook her head.

He bent, and scooping up a handful of snow, packed it into a tight ball in his hands. Green eyes flashed bright above the standing collar of his black wool coat. "So you've never been in a snowball fight?"

She eyed the snowball in his hands. "You wouldn't dare."

He tossed the white ball in the air and caught it. "Wouldn't I?"

She shuffled down the porch stairs. "W-we should go. It's freezing out here."

The snowball hit her in the butt.

With a gasp, she packed a ball of snow as he had and let it fly. More snowballs whipped through the air between them, until she collapsed in the fluffy powder in the front yard, breathing hard from exertion and laughter.

Luke dropped down on the ground beside her. "Let me know when you're ready for your next lesson."

Her deep breaths formed puffy clouds over her face. "I need to rest."

"You don't have to get up." He started waving his arms and legs.

Laughing, she mimicked him. She liked herself better when she laughed.

There hadn't been much to laugh about when her mom grew sick. Then, when she got really sick, Emily thought she'd never so much as smile again.

Luke stood over her and pulled her to her feet. She looked down at the two angel impressions in the snow.

He packed another snowball and, laying it on the ground, started to roll. He pushed the ball around the front yard until it'd grown to ten times its original size. He rolled it to a stop in front of her. "Last lesson for today."

She arched an eyebrow. "A giant snowball fight?"

"How to build a proper snowman."

Delighted laughter spilled out of her. Under his tutelage, she rolled a torso and a head. Luke snapped two twigs from an oak tree and inserted them into the snowman's sides as arms, while Emily dug up two rocks from the driveway for eyes.

They stepped back to survey their creation.

"Not bad for my first time, is it?"

"You're a quick study." His voice sounded gruff and sexy. "Guess I should reward you."

Heat zigzagged through her when he leaned close. One hand snuck around and cupped her bottom. His mouth brushed over hers.

Fog mingled in the air between their mouths when she asked, "Will there be more rewards with my next lesson?"

"Lots of rewards." His grip tightened. "We're supposed

to get five more inches this weekend."

"I'd say more like seven or eight."

A growl rumbled in the back of his throat. "Let's skip dinner."

She pulled away. "No way. I haven't eaten in two days. I'm starving."

Bodies packed the pub when they arrived at Lucky's. The Friday night crowd was lively, and judging by the amplified music and abundant flirtations, they were well into their after-dinner drinks.

Luke's palm smoothed over her lower back as he shouldered a path for them through the crowd to two empty stools at the bar. They squeezed in as the bartender slid a pint of Guinness in front of Luke.

Emily ordered a soda and opened a menu, but her queasy stomach couldn't settle on an acceptable choice and she closed it again. When the bartender returned, Luke ordered soup and a baked potato. Her stomach let loose with a wimpy growl, so she ordered the same.

"It's important to eat a warm meal after being out in the snow." He took a sip of his pint.

"Wh-what else do I have to learn before I'm considered an educated Michiganian?"

"I'm pretty sure it's Michigander."

"It is?"

"Consider that a bonus lesson." The soft lights caught the strands of copper threaded through his dark hair. "Let's see, there's sledding and snow forts, and of course we have the snow sports to consider: snowmobiling, snowboarding, and skiing."

Her nose wrinkled. "Cross country or downhill?"

"Both."

"I'm not exactly athletic."

"You'll be fine."

"Anything else?"

"Before it's over, you'll be able to name ten different

types of snow."

"There are different types?"

He shook his head. "So, so much to learn."

A woman's voice cut into Emily's laughter.

"Hey, stranger, where have you been?" She slipped her arms around Luke from behind and her smooth dark hair fell over his arm.

A cloud of uneasiness settled around Luke. "Hey, Jenna. How are you?"

"Lonely." She slid around to stand in front of him, giving her back to Emily.

She had long, slender legs, a tight butt, and—damn it all—thigh gap. What was it with the women on this island? Maybe it was the skiing?

Jenna squeezed between them and Luke scowled at Emily over Jenna's head.

Emily hid behind her glass. Even in her dark-wash jeans and ivory blazer, next to Jenna's sparkle, she felt dull and dowdy.

"Where's Kate?" Jenna asked.

"I'm not here with Kate." He pulled Jenna's hands from around his waist. "Jenna, this is Emily. My date."

Fizzy bubbles caught in Emily's throat and she coughed when Jenna's head whipped around. The woman took all of two seconds to size Emily up.

And declare her a non-threat.

She smiled brightly. "Nice to meet you, Emma."

Emily grunted.

Jenna turned her full wattage back to Luke. "You gonna sing for us later?"

"Not tonight." His voice sounded strained. "See you around."

Jenna's wounded look turned shrewd when her gaze slipped back to Emily. "Yeah, see you around." She slipped into the crowd.

"So, you and Kate are friends?"

He hesitated, measuring her for a moment. "That's right."

She hoped her smile appeared easygoing. "Because it kinda seems like everyone thinks you're a couple."

"It was a front."

She blinked. "Wh-what?"

"The whole thing was an act." He rolled his shoulders, as if shrugging off an uncomfortable burden. "She was grieving and I wasn't interested in a relationship. If people thought we were a couple, we didn't have to deal with the constant barrage from the opposite sex."

Emily grimaced, though given the way her heart leapt when he referred to her as his date, she should probably be thankful for the reminder of his temporary interest. "A barrage, huh? How awful for you."

His eyes narrowed. "It was just easier that way."

Their food came, and just as Luke lifted a spoonful of soup to his mouth, a young man with blurry eyes smacked him on the back.

"If it isn't my favorite doughnut muncher. How the hell you been, man?"

"Hey, Jacob. I'm good. How are you?"

Luke and Jacob talked sports for a bit, and soon two other men joined them. Their conversation wove in and out, touching on each of their lives, before the men drifted away, but before Luke could resume his meal, more people rushed in to fill the space around and between them.

They regaled him with stories and he listened intently to each and every one, interjecting once in a while with a thoughtful comment or an enthusiastic question. For that, they loved him.

Feeling awkward, she shifted uneasily on her barstool.

It was like dating the star quarterback. Unlike other high school girls she'd known, Emily never once dreamed of dating or even becoming friends with the popular kids.

From her vantage point, the popular kids were cursed to have everyone's eyes on them, dissecting their words and scrutinizing the clothes they wore.

But Luke didn't seem to mind, and indeed, it almost seemed as if he liked being around people.

If she were honest with herself, part of what had attracted her to him was his beauty and charm. Same as every other woman. Hell, even the men were attracted to him, and dogs, most likely.

Her chest twisted with jealousy. He interacted with others so easily and authentically. He didn't have insecurities—what was there for him to be insecure about?

Although, as she observed him, she noticed that the fine lines around his eyes began to deepen with exhaustion. No one else seemed to notice. Instead, they bought him drinks and badgered him to sing until he gave in to their relentless requests.

When Luke climbed onto the tiny stage in a corner at the front of the pub, a cheer rippled through the crowd. He sat on a barstool with a guitar, and when he strummed the first chords of his song, an immediate quiet fell over the room.

He performed a mix of Irish ballads and pub tunes. In between songs, he exchanged quips with the male audience members and won over every female with his smile and suddenly thick Irish brogue.

Soon, he declared the next song his last for the evening.

A groan of disappointment greeted his announcement.

The chords of a trendy pop melody drifted from his guitar. "I came here to eat, not to subject myself to your ridicule."

Then he started to sing. His voice, as beautiful as his face, whipped and whirred something inside Emily. He sang to no one and to everyone, of nothing and everything. She began to tremble.

He closed his eyes and his fingers tenderly plucked the guitar strings while pain twisted his features as he gave voice to all the anger and sorrow of loss and grief locked up inside her.

It was all there, the story of her life, in that inane pop song.

She sat helpless and shaking on the barstool while he bared his soul. To an entire room full of people. It was something she could never do. Not ever.

Had there ever been two people more unalike? It was as if they were exact polar opposites.

A vise clamped around her heart. Whatever this thing was between them, Emily hadn't deluded herself that it had anything resembling forever written on it. But seeing him up there, dazzling a room full of people with nothing more than a smile and a song, she realized just how farfetched the idea of them as a couple truly was.

It was nothing short of ridiculous.

Luke reached the crescendo, and a heart-wrenching softness tinged his voice. He held the note and her heart lodged in her throat. Tears swam before her eyes.

The crowd's eruption of applause jolted her. She turned away from the stage, devastated. Though she should be grateful she'd realized now how impossible a future would be for them, before she did something stupid like fall in love with him.

The green-eyed man who knew her heart.

His large, warm hand slipped to her waist and his low voice sent shivers up her spine when he spoke in her ear. "You wanna get out of here?"

She nodded because she couldn't speak and, clutching her purse, shot from the barstool, frantic to be away.

He held the door for her and they burst into the chilly night air. She resisted the urge to melt into his warmth and solidness at her side, to disappear inside him and become a part of his soul.

No, good thing she didn't love him.

At his SUV, he opened the passenger-side door for her. She climbed into the vehicle.

He stood in the door with a sheepish smile. "I'm really sorry about that."

"You didn't do anything wrong. You can't help it that everyone loves you."

He frowned. "They don't love me."

"Yes, they do." She reached for the door handle, but his grip on the car door remained firm.

"They don't love me." A thread of vulnerability disturbed the calm pools of green. "They don't even know me." He shut the door on that statement.

As he came around the hood of the car, he turned his head to peer at something in the shadows. He continued to the driver-side door and a blast of cold air swept into the cab with him.

"I'm sorry, but I need to check on something." He started the car and cranked the heat to full blast. "Can you give me another minute? I swear I'll be quick."

"Take y-your time."

He pulled his cell phone from his coat pocket as he bounded back out into the cold. The phone pressed to his ear, he backtracked down the sidewalk. He tucked the phone away and approached the figure of a man huddled on the ground in the mouth of the alleyway between buildings.

Buried under a heavy winter coat and stocking hat, his bare feet poked out from his too-short pants, exposed to the biting wind.

Emily's heart constricted. She hadn't noticed the man huddled there. Was he unwell?

Luke crouched beside him and, gripping his shoulder, gave him a firm shake. Slowly, the man lifted his head.

They talked a moment. Luke gestured toward her in the warm car, as though offering him a ride somewhere.

The man shook his head and his chin dropped to his chest.

Luke roused him once more. As he spoke, he pointed at something in the distance.

The man nodded.

Luke strode to the street corner and crossed the road. In her side mirror, Emily watched him disappear inside the convenience store. She debated going to help, but minutes later, Luke emerged from the store carrying something bulky in one hand. He returned to the sidewalk and stepped into the stream of light from the street lamps.

He crouched before the man again, working the laces on a pair of winter boots.

The man's head came up when Luke slid a bulky ski sock onto one of his bare feet, and grew more alert as Luke worked the boot onto his foot and tied the laces. Together, they dressed the other bare foot.

Snowdrifts gusted and blew across the sidewalk while they talked another few minutes. A minivan pulled into a parking spot, catching them in the headlights' beam. A young woman scurried to them. With Luke's help, she guided the man to his feet and inside the minivan's passenger-side door.

After a brief exchange, the woman ducked inside the van and Luke made his way back to her.

He fell behind the steering wheel. "Sorry." Cold radiated off him when he put the car in gear and backed out. "Sorry, that took a little longer than I expected."

Emily couldn't speak past the emotion clogging her throat, so she shook her head and turned her face to the glass.

It was many long moments before she found her voice. "Y-you offered him a ride?"

He rolled his shoulders, as if to throw off the heaviness trying to cling to him. "He refused me. He always does."

"You know him?"

"He's sort of the town drunk." Green eyes touched her face and then darted back to the windshield. "Like my dad was, when he was alive."

The car's headlights touched snowcapped sand dunes alongside the road as they passed by.

"That's why they all love y-you, and they're right to do so."

His Adam's apple bobbed and her eyes moved to the strong column of his throat.

She wanted to lay her head on his shoulder and hug him. To touch warm skin and breathe in his spicy scent, which teased her senses even now.

She wanted to love him.

She *did* love him.

Another wave of nausea rolled through her.

Chapter Eighteen

Luke yanked open the station door and tore through the glass-walled vestibule.

He was late. Again. For no reason, other than he couldn't muster the will to leave Emily's bed.

He pushed aside the thoughts troubling him about the sallowness of her peaches-and-cream skin tone more than a week after she'd recovered from the flu bug, and headed straight for the conference room.

Chief Brown sat in her usual seat at the head of the long conference table while Sloane's focus was riveted to his cell phone.

"Nice of you to join us, Detective Nolan."

Luke didn't insult her with a half-assed excuse as he slid into a chair across the table from Sloane.

"Let's start with the disturbance call at City Hall last week. Officer Sloane, you want to give the summation?"

Sloane flipped open a manila file folder. "The call came in at 11:15 p.m. when a dispute over payment of the DJ broke out at a work retirement party. I arrived at City Hall at 11:29 p.m. to find a crowd of approximately thirty people gathered on the front lawn. I placed a call for backup; Detective Nolan arrived at 11:49 p.m. The dispute was between the DJ and the employee in charge of organizing the event, with several individuals in attendance joining in. Detective Nolan and I calmed the crowd, and when we ran licenses, the DJ's came back with an outstanding warrant for arrest. I took the suspect into custody without incident. At this time, the case has been turned over to the prosecutor's office and arraignment is set for next Wednesday."

Luke listened in silence to Sloane's account of events.

"Anything to add, Detective Nolan?" Chief asked.

"No, nothing. Officer Sloane's summary is complete."

All except for one tiny detail. A detail no one but Luke knew.

When Luke and Sloane approached the milling crowd, several men shouted insults at one another, and a sudden flash of movement had caught Luke's eye. The instinct that'd saved his ass too many times to count in his ten-year career screamed at him and he'd whirled in the direction of the disturbance.

His body reacted to visual confirmation of the gun before his mind fully assessed the situation. He would draw his weapon first and neutralize the threat before it struck. He almost did it, too, but for the slightest hesitation wherein his mind caught up with his instinct.

Not a man, but a child.

Not a gun, but a replica.

A motherfucking toy, cradled in the tiny hands of a young boy.

Luke stood with his hand on his weapon while waves of horror and shame poured over him. Drowning him.

He'd been a heartbeat from shooting a child. An unarmed boy.

The report didn't include his break of focus, his misstep in procedure, nor his nearly fatal mistake.

In the days since, he'd tried talking himself out of a downward spiral of self-loathing. It was a heated dispute. Near midnight. Why was a child even there, wide awake and running around playing pretend? Nothing about the situation made sense, so how could his reaction to it?

"While I have you both here..." Chief Brown broke into his thoughts. "I want to let you know we're finally able to move forward with filling the position."

The ball of dread in the pit of Luke's stomach gave a hard wrench. He hadn't minded the delay to the job search while the county argued over funding for the department.

Cynthia placed her hands on the table in front of her. "We've reviewed applications and will be contacting both of you to schedule interviews in the next couple of weeks. I look forward to discussing the position with each of you."

He forced a plastic smile onto his face and pushed to his feet. "Thank you for the opportunity."

He didn't acknowledge Sloane's peevish scowl when he left the conference room. He didn't give a shit about the job just then. Though maybe he'd earned the chance to broaden his role in the island's force, he couldn't spend time thinking about a new position. He needed to stay focused on the moment before him, and not give in to the worry of more assignments, more responsibility, more doubt and despair and death.

Always death.

All he wanted was to get through the damned day and return to the inn.

To her.

☃

Emily collapsed onto Luke's couch.

His studio apartment, housed in an old warehouse, had exposed brick walls and a warm wood floor and ceiling. It was wide-open, with a small kitchen at one end, followed by a dining table, a living area, and at the far end, a bed rested before the patio doors. Outside, his beachfront property offered a breathtaking view of the harbor.

She closed her eyes. She couldn't recall ever being so exhausted. The sound of running water from the bathroom where Luke was taking a shower lulled her.

He'd stopped at the inn on his way home from work just as Max and the gang were set to shoot a scene in the foyer. A disagreement about lighting quickly broke out between Max and Honey. They fought like mortal enemies, or as Luke described it, siblings.

So Luke and Emily decided to escape to his loft for a few hours.

The bathroom door swung open and Luke appeared in a cloud of steam from the shower. A towel was wrapped around his lean waist, and his hair stood on end from a hasty rub. He disappeared in the walk-in closet at the far end of the loft and emerged dressed in a sky-blue T-shirt and dark blue jeans.

"You hungry?" he asked. "I'm going to make some dinner."

Her stomach let loose an angry growl. "I'm starving."

She dragged her weary body off the sofa and settled on a stool at the kitchen counter.

A soft smile teased over his lips. "You sound surprised."

"I am. This is the first time I've felt hungry in a while." Though two weeks had passed since the flu bug hit, her queasiness had lingered.

He set a skillet on the stove and turned the heat on low. Then he retrieved a cutting board from the drawer and attacked an onion with expert skill.

"Thanks for letting me stay again tonight," she said. "It's chaos at m-my house."

"How is the film going?" He diced the onion into tiny bits. "Any zombies popped out at you yet?"

She rolled her eyes. "Sort of. Yesterday, I walked right through the middle of a scene. I thought they were taking a lunch break, but I guess they're using different foods for blood and internal organs."

"Sounds appetizing." He sliced into a green pepper. "I see Max and Honey are still going at it."

At times, it got to be too much for Emily. Max had a short temper and when he went off, the urge to hide, as she had whenever Harrison started to yell, overwhelmed. After the yelling, came the hitting.

"I could do with less fighting, and I could do without Will's cologne. The smell makes me want to gag."

An odd expression chased across his features, but he said nothing.

Later that night, after they'd returned to the inn to sleep, she dreamed of charred meat and mayonnaise. Her stomach gave a sickening wrench that roused her from sleep. Luke lay by her side, his broad, bare chest facing her. By the deep, even rhythm of his breathing, she knew he slept. Her stomach roiled and sweat beaded on her forehead.

Shaken and disoriented, she closed her eyes.

Another wave of nausea hit her. She kicked off the covers and lurched from the bed. In the darkness, she stumbled to the bathroom off her bedroom. She closed the door behind her and dropped to her knees before the toilet, ill.

After, she flushed and sat back on the cold tile floor. She laid her head on her trembling arms and dragged air into her lungs while tears streamed down her face.

There was a soft, cursory knock on the bathroom door before it opened and Luke stepped into the small space. He knelt beside her on the floor and ran a hand over the crown of her head.

"Sorry to w-wake you."

"Don't be." Without turning on the bathroom light, he retrieved a washcloth from the cupboard, wet it in the pedestal sink, and lay it over the heated skin on the back of her neck. Tendrils of her hair stuck to her damp skin. He sat on the edge of the bathtub and rubbed a hand up and down her spine.

When she was certain the nausea had passed, she sat back on her heels. "I think I'm okay now." She removed the cloth from her neck and wiped her tear-stained face. "I thought I'd finally kicked this flu bug."

He tucked a loose strand of hair behind her ear and peered into her face. He was sleep-rumpled, but alert. Concern etched his features.

"Do you want to come back to bed?"

She nodded. He took her hand and helped her to stand.

At the cabinet, he withdrew the mouthwash and poured a capful. She used it, and then followed him to the bed on weak legs. He pulled back the covers and she crawled in. When he stretched out beside her, she turned toward him and buried her face in the hollow where his shoulder met neck, like a sick child seeking comfort.

His cheek rested against her forehead and his fingers toyed with the hair at her temples.

Soon, exhaustion reached out to claim her once more.

"Hey, Em?"

"Hmm?"

"Is there any chance you're pregnant?"

Her eyes shot open in the dark.

Chapter Nineteen

She'd been locked in the bathroom for a long time. Too long.

Luke flicked away a heap of wet snow and set his coffee mug on the patio table she'd neglected to store inside the garage for the winter. He shoved his hands into the pockets of his fleece and ducked his chin inside the collar to shield against the chilly breeze coming off the lake.

At first light, she'd slipped from the bed and snuck out of the inn. She'd returned twenty minutes later with coffee and muffins from the bakery in town and then faked her way through a stilted conversation with him about the driving conditions of the roads before she disappeared into the bathroom with her purse.

As if he didn't know what she was up to.

A smile played on his lips. He shot a glance over his

shoulder, through the patio doors and across her bedroom. The bathroom door remained shut.

He knew she was taking a pregnancy test.

He also knew what it would say.

Despite the life-altering ramifications, or maybe because of it, his smile cracked open and he had to wipe it away.

With a last look at the whitecaps churning toward shore, he turned away from the landscape and stepped into the warmth. Silence greeted him.

He crossed to the bathroom door and knocked. "Em, are you all right?"

Nothing.

He tried the knob and the door gave way.

She sat on the toilet lid, staring down at the white stick in her hand.

He eased into the small space and perched on the edge of the bathtub.

Huge brown eyes clamped on his face. "I'm s-s-so sorry."

He reached for her hand and laced his fingers through hers. "This isn't your fault. Not solely."

"I don't understand how this happened." She tossed the stick in the trash. "I'm on the pill. We used condoms."

"Not every time."

"Because I'm on the pill." With each word, her voice pitched higher.

"Maybe you forgot to take one?" he asked gently.

"No, never." She shook her head. "I take it every night wh-wh-when I br-brush my-my-my teeth. I've never m-m-missed."

He grasped the back of her neck and kneaded the tight muscles. "I don't know, Em. Maybe when you were sick with the flu—"

The color leeched from her face.

He pushed her head between her knees. "Breathe."

She sucked sharp inhalations in through her nose and pushed out short puffs of air through her lips.

"Good girl." He relaxed his hold.

She bolted upright. "I can't have a b-baby. I don't know anything about b-babies."

"No one knows anything about babies until they're responsible for one."

"I've never been responsible for one. Wh-what if I hurt it or-or-or break it." A broken sob tore from her. "I don't know how to take care of a b-baby."

He shoved her head back down. "You've got to breathe, sweetheart."

Air wheezed in and out.

"Taking care of the baby is the easy part." He eased his hold on her neck. "It's rough at first, but once you figure them out, it's not so bad."

She shot up. "How do you know that? Do you have kids?"

"Don't you think I would've mentioned if I had kids? I'm an uncle, and I lived with my brother and his wife until their firstborn was five years old."

"Oh." But the panic had taken hold of her. Her eyes glistened. "I can't do this. I was a caretaker for nine years. I'm not ready to do it again."

He pushed her head between her legs again. "Keep breathing."

"I *can't* go through that again."

"It's not the same thing."

She bolted upright. "It is—"

He took her hands between his and tugged so that she met his gaze. "No. Watching a baby grow bigger, stronger, brighter every day is not the same thing as watching someone you love die. It just isn't."

Tears welled. "I don't think I can do this."

Her panic didn't bother him. Indeed, he was happy to see it. It meant she'd be a good mom.

"You can," he said. "You will. It's going to be okay."

"How do you know that?" Her voice broke over the words.

"It's a baby, and a baby is never a bad thing."

That pierced the fog of her panic. "Wh-what's the hard part?"

He wrestled with her question a moment.

"You said the b-baby's the easy part. Wh-what's the hard part?"

A shiver of unease rippled through him. He shrugged. "Us."

She blinked at him and he could see the gears of her mind working. "Omigod, we're stuck with each other. For the rest of our lives. We'll never be rid of one another."

"That's not exactly what I—"

"We'll always have to know each other. We'll have to see each other, like, every day."

A satisfied calm spread through him. "Yes, we will."

"We'll have to watch each other date other people. M-marry other people. Have b-babies with other people."

His good mood vanished.

"Why aren't you freaking out about this?" Her shrill voice echoed around the small space.

He gripped her hand again. "Because we got this. Trust me."

"I broke the egg." She bit her lip on the outburst.

"You what?"

"The egg. In high school. You know, the class where they make you carry it around for a week? I broke it."

He gaped at her a moment. "That's... I mean, it's an egg—"

"Omigod, I'm going to kill our baby." She bent over, tucking her head between her own legs.

He smoothed a hand over her back. "You're not going to kill our baby."

She jerked upright. "How do you know that?" Her

voice reached shrill heights.

"Because I won't let you. We'll do it together."

Her eyes gripped his, as if he were her only life raft in a raging sea.

She swallowed with difficulty. "Luke?"

"What is it, sweetheart?"

"I think I'm going to be sick."

ଔ

Sleep eluded him. Tucked into his side, Emily slept, her soft snores tickling over the bare skin under his arm.

Restless, he left her bed and padded into the dark kitchen. At the off chance she'd stashed a bottle of whiskey somewhere, he searched her cupboards. He let a cupboard door fall shut and turned.

And startled.

Noah and Mina sat at the kitchen island, twin bowls on the counter before them.

Noah finished chewing and swallowed. "Lose something?"

Luke's gaze slipped to the box of cereal between them on the counter. "My Cocoa Puffs." He filched a bowl and a spoon from the cupboard and plopped onto a stool. He snatched the box away and filled his bowl.

Mina slid the milk jug across to him. "Is Emily, um, sleeping?"

"Yep." He crunched on a spoonful of chocolate balls.

He could practically feel her mind gnawing on a thought thread. The cousins had much in common. Loud minds and faces that gave away their every thought and emotion.

She tried to catch Noah's eye.

Noah ignored her.

She set down her spoon and clasped her hands together. "So, Luke, you and Emily–"

"Are getting married." The words slipped from him like smooth whiskey.

"*What?*" Dual expressions of incredulity gaped at him.

Luke didn't bother to take offense.

"She didn't say anything to me," Mina said, her mouth screwing into a frown.

Noah was less tactful. "Did she actually agree to marry you?"

Luke sniffed. "I haven't told her yet." She needed a little time to adjust before he moved forward with his plan.

"*Told* her?" Mina's jaw hung open. "What if she says no?"

His heart hammered against his breastbone. "She won't."

Luke's gaze slid to Noah. Explanations floated through his mind, but nothing emerged that didn't sound barbaric. The brothers stared.

The fact was, Luke wouldn't leave Emily on her own to raise their child. Nor would he leave the parenting of his child up to whatever man she decided to marry one day in the future. Statistics had a lot to say about stepdads and their stepchildren. He wouldn't risk her moving out of town, out of state, out of the fucking country, and taking his kid with her.

And he sure as shit wouldn't leave his child to face the cruelties of this godforsaken world alone, without their dad around to defend them.

Not. Fucking. Happening.

Besides, he wanted to marry Emily. He didn't deserve her, yet, but he would one day. When he got his shit together, or found the strength to power through the darkness. To make the nightmares that were actually memories stop. Then he'd be the guy he was before That Day, and *that* guy, he knew, could make her happy. He just needed a little more time. He could do it. He *would* do it. For her.

For them.

Until then, if Emily were his wife, at the very least he'd be there, for the rest of their lives, to make sure no man's fist ever harmed her again.

"You're sure about this?" Noah asked quietly.

Mina gasped. "Noah, I don't think—"

"I'm sure," Luke said, and he was.

For once, doing the right thing was also the easy thing.

Noah leaned back and a broad smile split his face. "All right then. When's the party?"

"Noah!"

"Who am I to interfere with true love?"

"I'm not saying we should interfere, but marriage? Marriage is so..." Mina's hand moved in front of her face, as if she might pluck the word out of the air. "Permanent."

Noah's mouth twisted with a wry smile. "You say that like it's a bad thing."

Stammering, Mina blushed an attractive shade of pink. "Of course not, it's just..."

Noah planted a kiss on her mouth. "We can't do a thing about it, baby. He's determined."

A broad grin split Luke's face. "Thank you, brother."

Mina scowled. "I'm not done arguing about this."

Noah lifted his shoulders. "How can I deny him wedded bliss? It's the best thing that's ever happened to me."

She visibly melted. "That's not fair."

Noah grinned and shot Luke a glittering glance. "Are you taking notes?"

"I taught you everything you know," Luke said around a mouthful of cereal.

Mina's serious round eyes swung to Luke. "Don't take this the wrong way, but I think we ought to wait until

Emily is, uh, informed of her impending engagement before we book the church. If she doesn't agree–"

A cold dread started in Luke's chest and snaked through his veins like a dark taint. "She will."

"You may be right," she said. "But if she says no–"

His heart banged around in his chest and he stood abruptly. At the sink, he rinsed his bowl. "She won't say no."

He planned to make her an offer she couldn't refuse.

Ↄ

Emily's chest ached from the battering of her heart against her breastbone. While Luke slept, she lay wide awake in the darkened room as the 3:00 a.m. hour ticked away.

A baby.

A week since she'd taken that pregnancy test, she still couldn't wrap her brain around this new reality.

She'd never done anything so big, so critically important, as bear full responsibility for a tiny, helpless person. With certainty, she knew she would mess it up, as she knew absolutely nothing about how to be a mom.

She reached for her phone to call her mom, only to remember her mom was dead.

She had to do this by herself. A bead of sweat broke out on her brow and her hand trembled when she returned her phone to the bedside table.

Panic choked the breath from her lungs and the peace from her heart, as if she were trapped on a roller coaster and could do nothing to change her fate except hold on and pray for the ride to end.

Light from the stained-glass lamp by the front door threw a soft glow into the room and allowed her to make out Luke's features. His mouth was slack and his hair rumpled, his bare chest rising and falling with his deep, even breaths. She couldn't recall ever before seeing him sleep. The notch on her heart ached.

Luke's baby.

Would they have a boy or a girl? Would he or she be awkward like her mother, or charming and generous like her dad? Would she stutter?

Beneath the bruise on her heart, a tiny seed of wonder sprouted.

A baby. Someone she'd love forever and always, with the whole of her heart. A family.

She'd never been one of those girls to pine for a baby. The mere thought struck terror in her. But after living so long with impending death, the hope of new life was irresistible.

Luke stirred and his hand smoothed over her stomach. "What's wrong? You all right?"

She squeezed his forearm. "I'm all right. Just restless."

"Want me to distract you?" His voice was groggy with sleep and suggestiveness.

"Your distractions get us into trouble."

"Can't really get into any more trouble than we already are, now can we?"

The laughter that came so easily around him trickled from her.

They let the quiet fall between them.

Until he pressed two fingers to the spot between her eyebrows. "What's this?"

She wanted to fall into his arms and let his warmth melt away all her worries. It was a ludicrous thought, so she rubbed her forehead, as though she might erase the lines of worry there.

"How did y-you know?"

Green eyes landed on her face, searching out the meaning of her question.

He lifted one shoulder. "You'd been sick for a while, and I remember when Isobel was pregnant, she had strange aversions. Strong smells would set her off, and there was this one song that made her ill every time she heard it."

Biting her lip, she ducked her chin. "I made a doctors' appointment."

He propped up on his elbow and peered down at her. "That's good."

She folded and unfolded one corner of the sheet. "It's not until next month, if you want to come... But y-you don't have to come if you don't w-want to," she rushed to add. "I don't think anything too exciting will be happening. Yet."

"I'll be there," he said softly.

In the troubled silence, he reached out to toy with a strand of hair at her temple. "I think we should get married."

She sucked in a sharp hiss of air and whipped her head around. The soft light threw shadows across his face, obstructing her study of his features.

"W-would y-y-you be serious? I'm trying to talk to you."

"I am serious." He rolled away, yanked open the top drawer of the nightstand, and twisting back around, he set a small black box on her stomach.

Over the thundering of her heart, she heard herself ask, "Wh-what is that?"

"It's a ring."

She sprang from the bed, sending the little box tumbling through the sheets. "B-b-but w-why?"

He pushed himself upright, flipped on the bedside lamp, and reclined against the headboard. "Because I just asked you to marry me and it's customary to offer a ring as a testament of my devotion."

Her heart, lacking logic as it did, started to soar. She ruthlessly squashed it back down. "Okay, you got me. That was a good one."

"Emily, I'm not joking."

She gaped at him. "You want to marry me?"

"Yes."

"Because I'm pregnant."

"No." His denial came quick and he pushed up off the bed. "That's part of it, of course, but not all of it. I like you. I like us. I want to marry you, Emily."

She liked them, too, but– Wait, he *liked* her?

The painful slash at her heart sparked an ember of anger. "You know what? Let's do it. Let's get married."

He eyed her skeptically.

"What do you say to St. Patty's Day? It's a little sudden, I know, but just think about it–I'll wear a gold dress and you can wear a green tuxedo, but instead of walking down the aisle on a red carpet, I'll slide down a rainbow-colored one."

He folded his arms over his chest. "Are you finished?"

"You don't like that idea, I can tell. How about Valentine's Day? It's a little predictable, sure, and I should warn you, I do not look good in red. It totally clashes with my hair."

He settled on the arm of a club chair and crossed his legs at the ankles. "Valentine's Day is a little over two months away."

Only her misery curtailed her smug satisfaction.

Startling green eyes captured hers. "I don't see any reason to wait that long, do you?"

"You don't see any reason...?" She trailed off as her racing thoughts slowed and thickened to tree sap.

"We could get married next weekend."

"This weekend?"

"But if you're willing to hold off, we could do it the week before Christmas. Jack will be home, and Leo's supposed to make an appearance. I'd like it if they could be there."

The breath she'd been holding erupted from her like

the air from a burst balloon. "We're talking about getting *married*. Not taking a weekend road trip or trying a new hairstyle. We barely know each other."

"I know enough."

She stumbled back. "We can't. It would never work. We're too different."

"We're not that different."

Somehow, he managed to say that with a straight face.

"You're gorgeous and charming and-and-and everyone likes you and I'm..."

His features darkened. "You're what?"

She lifted her shoulders. "I'm not any of those things. I'm the opposite of those things."

"You know what they say, opposites attract, and all that."

"Or someone ends up murdered in their sleep," she muttered.

"I promise not to murder you." He crossed to her and slipped his hand beneath the curtain of her hair. "Marry me."

"People will think—"

Storm clouds gathered on his face. "Do you honestly believe I give a fuck what anyone thinks?" Just as quickly as the clouds had gathered, they scattered like mist at dawn. "You're smart and sweet, and I can't wait to watch you become a mom." He scraped the pad of his thumb over her bottom lip. "And I'm more than convinced you and this mouth will keep me quite contented until the end of my days."

The lure of him was so incredibly seductive. She couldn't stop her heart from imagining what it'd be like to marry him. If she'd allowed herself, she'd have dreamed this dream a thousand times already. Instead, she experienced the thrill of all her secret longings at once.

She swayed slightly.

She wouldn't have to be alone anymore. No more fear.

No more soul-crushing loneliness.

He doesn't love you.

He dropped a light kiss on the tip of her nose. "Marry me."

In all her life, she'd never wanted to say yes to anyone for anything more than she did in that moment. Maybe one day, he'd grow to love her.

Except, other than her mom, no one who knew her had ever grown to love her. Not even her own father.

She opened her mouth to deny him, but he spoke first.

"I can make you happy, Em, I know I can. Give me a chance."

Tears tightened her throat. He cradled her head in both his hands.

"Say it," he whispered.

The hole near her heart filled to overflowing. She made the mistake of looking into his eyes, which glittered with some unnamable emotion.

"Marry me, Emily, and let me give you a last name you can be proud of. One that nobody can deny you."

Chapter Twenty

She said yes.

It'd taken his full power of persuasion, and a touch of manipulation, but he'd won.

The smug smile still lingered on his lips when he entered the station the next morning.

He made her say it again, and again, and spent several long, languid moments tasting the flavor of the yeses on her tongue. Then he'd gone to the bed for the little black box and tossed it to her.

Caught by surprise, she batted the box around a few times before reeling it in. She cracked it open.

Her head bent, he couldn't read her reaction. She didn't speak, or smile, or sigh dreamily, or even reach out to finger the delicate ring.

He'd grown self-conscious. Maybe he should've spent more than ten minutes picking out the round-cut solitaire with white-gold banding, but as soon as he saw it, he knew it was her ring. Flawless and unpretentious. Simply beautiful, like her.

He'd scratched a phantom itch on his shoulder. "In a couple of years, I'll be able to upgrade to something a little bigger."

She'd pressed the box to the center of her chest, over her heart, and her eyes shone when she looked up at him. "I love it. I'll never wear another."

The gut punch knocked the breath from his body.

He reached for her, and soon lost himself in her soft, warm body. His release building, emotions he couldn't name rioted though him. He wouldn't regret his decision to marry her. She made him happy.

Now all he had to do was settle in for a life of easy, wedded bliss. No drama. No disasters. No despair. Oh, and make sure he didn't fall in love with her.

No love. Just happiness.

At his desk, he pulled up the day's log, already counting the minutes before he could get his soon-to-be wife naked again, touching and teasing her until they both collapsed in contented exhaustion.

The figure of a man appeared before him and Luke looked up into Captain Davison's grizzled face. Behind him, Chief Brown came into view.

"Good morning, Detective," she said. "We're ready for you."

Shit.

In the chaos of the last few days, he'd forgotten about the interview. Dread crystallized into a heavy ball in the pit of his stomach as he followed his bosses into the conference room.

The interview started well, with Captain Davison posing a couple of questions about Luke's educational background and experience, which he answered with ease.

Then Chief took a turn asking questions. "It's no secret there is an enormous amount of stress in our jobs. How do you handle stress and avoid burnout?"

Luke's mind blanked. He blinked at her while his mouth filled with sand.

But the Chief and Captain were staring at him, waiting, so he started to talk. "You're absolutely right, Chief. In my career, I've experienced stressful periods and have had to find various ways to decompress."

Wrong.

Unless heavy drinking and insomnia counted.

"I spend time with my friends and family, particularly my niece and nephews."

Wrong.

Since the shooting, he'd avoided close contact with any of them, his niece and nephews in particular, afraid he'd be unable to keep it together in their presence.

"I enjoy several hobbies, including music and playing in a hockey league."

Wrong.

He'd dropped out of the league this year and never played music, except when others forced him to do so.

"Finally, I guess I'd say I find comfort in talking to my colleagues and those close to me about my job and its challenges. Their understanding and support is an invaluable gift."

Wrong and wrong.

He had a sharp distaste for Sloane and, by design, no relationship with the rookie, Newberry. Neither of them would ever replace Anthony.

He flashed his charmer's smile. "Oops, I lied. I have one more."

Chief and Davison smiled, perfectly at ease.

"This department has been on the forefront of providing assistance and access to mental health professionals, which has been both a surprise and a blessing."

Not entirely wrong. At least the seminars he'd been pushed to attend helped him come up with all the bullshit he was now spewing.

The remainder of the interview progressed without incident. Until the last question.

"Where do you see yourself in five years?"

Not working here.

He muttered some bullshit answer and soon the interview ended.

On the drive to Emily's at the end of the day, a clear winter sunset painted the horizon in lavender and pink. A chilly wind blew a blinding white canvas of fresh snow across the island.

Dusk in winter. It brought to mind memories of That Day. Like parasites, crawling and wiggling under his skin, they harassed. He turned up her driveway and pulled to stop in front of the house.

Lost in his inner battle, he failed to notice the threat until it was upon him.

Red blood splattered over pure white snow. Dark, nasty, brutal.

A massacre.

He stumbled back. The screaming inside his skull drowned out his ability to think, to assess, or to search out options. His vision narrowed.

Emily's snowman lay in scattered pieces. His head severed from his body. His torso hacked into tiny bits.

Blackness closed in on him. He was underwater, the surface fading away. He gasped for air, an instinct his body couldn't let die. Hope faded. It was too heavy, this burden.

Wet snow seeped through his blue jeans.

Get up, you piece of shit. Get up right now!

At the water's surface, huge brown eyes stared down at him. She lifted her hand under her nose. "It's ketchup.

They're filming a scene."

"I killed him."

Her dainty features pulled into a frown. "Who?"

"The fifteen-year-old." Horror rushed through his veins along with the self-hatred. "I fucking killed him."

The words broke over his sobs with the dread and hopelessness crashing into him, dragging him down, down. All was lost.

A weight pressed down on his chest, pinning him to the ground beneath a large object. He clenched her small hand. His grip clamped so tight around her fine bones, it had to hurt her.

But he didn't let go, and she didn't complain.

"I think about it every day. Every goddamn day I relive that moment I pulled the trigger."

The pad of her thumb stroked back and forth over his palm.

"If just one thing had happened differently, maybe I wouldn't have killed him." Wetness smeared his cheeks. "If just one fucking thing had gone differently—if the kid's friend hadn't said something shitty on Facebook. If his mom didn't get on him about his attitude that morning. If they hadn't left the gun safe unlocked. If it'd been sunny instead of cloudy for the fourth day in a row. If he hadn't been called on in class. If only the kid had forgotten his Kevlar and gave up his insane plan, or his gun had jammed, or he'd turned just a little to the right rather than the left, my bullet would've caught his arm instead of his chest cavity. Anything could've made the difference. He didn't have to die. None of them had to die."

But they did die.

Tears fell from her cheeks and plopped onto his hand. "You had to s-stop him from killing those other children. It was the only choice."

"Maybe, but that doesn't help me sleep at night."

Nothing did.

"How many other children are alive because of what you did? How many other parents didn't have to mourn their babies?"

"You want to know the worst part?" He could see she didn't, but he couldn't hold the words back any longer. "Fuck him."

"Wh-what?"

"The fifteen-year-old. Fuck him. He killed eight people that day. And I murdered him, a fucking child. He killed my friend and I fucking hate him." His voice trembled with his soul's seething. "Do you hear me? I *hate* him."

She shivered in the cold. "I know. It's okay."

She didn't say another word. She didn't ask him why, or what she could do to help. She didn't try to soothe or placate him. She just sat beside him in the snow, tolerating his death grip around her fingers, until he slowly came back to himself.

He hadn't had a flashback in months, and he'd let himself believe he was over it. Or moving past it, or... whatever.

Shit.

He wasn't over it. Not even close.

He'd clawed and scratched his way to the top of the mountain, leaving blood and guts and all sense of self to rot on the cold, hard ground, only to realize he'd simply scaled the first foothill. An entire mountain range lay beyond.

After this, she probably wouldn't want to marry him.

It was for the best, he supposed. He should be relieved. He'd let himself get a little cocky, thinking he could build a life with her without the taint.

Even now, he could feel her heart reaching out to him, trying to wrap itself around him, and he was tempted, so goddamned tempted, to let it happen.

But if he did, he'd be one step closer to turning into

his father.

No, it was a good thing she'd caught a glimpse of the real him. So she could leave him.

Once he let go of her hand.

☙

He was avoiding her.

Three days had passed since she found him on his knees in the snow, a thousand-yard stare in his stricken eyes. Three days since she had sat beside him, wishing she might somehow pick the scattered pieces of him out of the snow and hold them in her hands. Hold him together.

Three days since she had last laid eyes on him.

In her pajamas, Emily sat at the kitchen island and tried to focus on the brochure she was creating for the inn. As the hour approached midnight, hope he'd come to her when his shift ended began to fade.

An old familiar vise squeezed her heart. For nine years, she'd lived with the misery of watching someone she loved suffer while knowing of no way to ease their pain.

A noise sounded at the back door and she sucked in a sharp breath. Her heart galloped.

Until Noah appeared beneath the archway to the mudroom. "Hey, Em."

At the refrigerator, Noah yanked open the door and disappeared behind it. His head popped up. "Is there any of that lasagna Luke made the other night?"

She noticed then the lines bracketing his eyes and mouth. He looked tired. Drained.

"It's in the back behind the m-milk. I was hiding it."

He rummaged around for a moment.

"Aha." He kicked the refrigerator door closed with the heel of his foot, a Pyrex dish in hand. "Mind if I steal a couple of pieces?"

She waved her hand. "Have it all."

The lines smoothed. "Thanks, I owe you one."

He turned to leave, and she bolted to her feet. "Can I ask y-you something?"

He twisted back around. "Sure. What's up?"

"Have you, uh, talked to Luke in the last couple of days?"

His brows slammed into a frown. "No. Why? Is something wrong?"

Disappointment slashed through her. "No, nothing's wrong..."

Just then, his head turned toward more rustling at the back door.

"Did you find it?" Emily recognized Mina's voice.

Noah lifted the dish in his hands. "Got it. I was just talking to Emily."

Mina appeared in the doorway. "Oh, hey, Em. He didn't wake you, did he?"

Emily startled at her cousin's appearance. There was a blanket wrapped around her shoulders, and her face appeared sunken and pale.

Emily shook her head. "I was still up."

Mina ran a hand through her tousled hair. She and Noah shared a long look, one that carried an entire conversation and ended when Noah gave a small tilt of his head in Emily's direction.

Mina took a tiny step into the room. "You have a minute?"

Denials screamed in Emily's mind, much like the way they did whenever her mom's doctors had approached her with an update on Audrey's condition. She didn't know what Mina had to say, but she knew she didn't want to hear the words.

She swallowed with difficulty and found her voice. "Sure."

A long, shuddering breath rattled through Mina. "I

miscarried."

"Oh, shit." Emily clamped both hands over her mouth. "Mina, I'm so sorry. Are you okay?"

She winced at the stupid question. Her cousin had just lost her baby. How could she be okay? Emily pressed a fist to her abdomen and sank back onto the stool.

"I'm okay," Mina said, though the devastation was there to see on both their faces. "I was still early and they say I'll be fine."

Mina turned her face to Noah, who reached out and pulled her in to his side. He dropped a kiss on the top of her head.

She sagged against him. "In a little bit, I think we'll try again."

"Trying is my favorite." Noah's lips moved against her hair.

Heat washed over Emily's face and neck at the intimate display, so unguarded and tender. She had to look away.

A soft light came into Mina's eyes. "But I hear you might have some good news for us?"

Emily cringed inwardly. "Oh, yeah, I was going to tell you…"

"Is this what you want?" Mina prodded gently.

Emily's heart lurched. "Yes. Very much so."

Both Noah and Mina visibly relaxed.

"We'll be in-laws twice over." Noah smiled, and for a moment, he looked so like Luke, Emily stared. "That bond will be nearly unbreakable. Looks like you're stuck with me."

Her heart cracked open with his words. By marrying Luke, she'd be gaining four brothers. For an orphaned only child, it was a heady proposition, and just one of the many gifts Luke had given her.

"Have you settled on a date?" Mina eased further into the room.

Emily shifted on the stool. "Uh, in a few weeks, actually. The weekend before Christmas."

To her credit, Mina hid her shock well. "That's so soon."

Emily couldn't tell them she was pregnant. With their grief so palpable and raw, the words simply refused to come.

"We didn't want to w-wait." The half-truth tasted sour in her mouth and she pursed her lips closed.

Noah's astute gaze searched her face. "Ah, new love. Fun, isn't it?"

Luke could feel her watching him.

He was six hours removed from a grueling eighteen-hour shift, which concluded only when they'd pulled the body of a sixteen-year-old kid from the icy waters of Lake Michigan.

Unable to look away, he'd stared into the kid's childlike, colorless face, devoid of life. He'd listened to the agonized screams of the mother, feeling her child's death as his own.

Now, he looked at Emily. So sweet and beautiful and... alive.

She needed him, but the numbness hung around his shoulders wouldn't let him love her. He couldn't give her what she wanted. Not in that moment. So he slammed the mask into place. She'd be happier not knowing what lay beneath the charm.

Though he might not be able to give her his heart just then, but he'd damned if he'd allow that worried frown to mar her delicate features any longer. She'd experienced enough death and despair for one lifetime and he wouldn't add to it. Not for anything.

He swallowed the last bite of tasteless casserole on his

plate. "Do you want to get married at the church or City Hall?"

She laid down her fork. "I'm not Catholic."

"No problem." He flashed a quick smile. "Neither is Father John."

"Really?"

"Really. He used to be a priest, but resigned years ago. If you ask him about it, he'll tell more than you could ever want to know."

"So it's not a Catholic church? Is that why the sign changed?"

"It'd been a struggling congregation for years, and largely seasonal with the population dropping by nearly half every winter. The diocese finally pulled out last year. When the church went up for sale, John bought it and now holds non-denominational services."

"It's such a lovely place, and my mom's there..."

His heart wedged somewhere near his throat. "The church it is then." He started to stand.

She sat forward. "I w-wondered if w-we could talk for a minute."

Though she hadn't eaten the last of her casserole, he swiped her plate out from under her and carried it along with his to the kitchen.

At the sink, he flipped on the faucet. "Tell you what," he said over the running water. "I'll book the church if you handle everything else. You have a talent and I wouldn't dare to interfere with such artistry."

A blush of pleasure touched her cheeks. "Is there anyone you'd like to invite?"

"I already told my brothers." He turned off the spray of water. "How about you?"

She shook her head.

"No one?" He saw no sadness on her face and that only made the pinch in his chest squeeze tighter. He returned to his chair at the table. "Who would you invite if you knew they could come?"

"Well, there was a friend from college, but..."

"Who?"

"My roommate." Her features softened and she toyed with her napkin.

"You should invite her."

"W-we haven't talked in years, and it's such short notice."

"So you won't be disappointed if she can't make it." He cut off her protest. "Invite her. People love to be invited to parties, even if they can't attend. It makes them feel good, and besides, you have nothing to lose."

She pondered that a moment. "You're right. I'll invite her." Then her dark, serious eyes clamped on his face. "But I didn't want to talk about the wedding."

He shoved to his feet and crossed to the stereo. "No? What did you want to talk about?"

"The other day—"

A song kicked on over the speakers and he treated her to his finest, most charming smile.

Her slender brow remained furrowed and he abandoned the charm offensive. Hell, it wasn't as if it'd ever worked on her anyway. Only when he wasn't trying did he ever breach her defenses.

He began to move his shoulders in time to the beat and crooked a finger at her. "Come here."

Her sudden smile knocked him back. "Why?"

Soon, his hips were involved. "Come here, Emily."

A giggle escaped her. "I want to talk first."

"You don't like talking." He lifted her hand and brushed his lips over her knuckles.

A shiver passed through her. "Luke—"

"One dance. Then we'll talk."

"But—"

"I can't believe I have to say this to you." He tugged on her hand and she fell against him. "Shut up and dance with me."

He held her body tight against his and she melted into him. The fragrant scent of her hair teased his senses and he bent his head to inhale deeply of her.

They began to move.

When the music changed, she pulled away, but he grasped her hand and whirled her under his arm.

Her light, lyrical laughter rang out. He didn't stop until she was breathless from laughing. Then he dipped her low, cradling her in his arm, and stole a taste of her over-plump mouth. When he broke the kiss, a contented smile glowed from her small face.

And she'd forgotten all about asking her silly little questions.

Chapter Twenty-One

The bell over the door chimed when Emily stepped into the boutique on Main Street.

A voice called out a greeting, and then Isobel's head popped out from behind a rack of winter coats.

"Emily." She lurched forward with an armful of wool. "Luke told me the news. I'm so happy for you both."

Emily found herself engulfed in wool and Isobel's flowery scent. The tension in her shoulders eased somewhat. "Thank you. Actually, I'm here for a dress."

"Wonderful." Isobel heaved her armload onto the front counter. "The bridal boutique is next door."

Emily remained planted to her spot. "I don't w-want to shop over there, if that's all right? It's going to be a small ceremony and I'd like to w-wear something... simple."

"Oh, okay." Isobel frowned. "Our stock is a little low

right now. Do you have a color in mind?"

Emily bit down hard on her lip and shook her head. "No. Whatever you have."

Isobel blinked at her. "You're not like our other brides."

Emily didn't doubt that for a second. Her wedding, hastily thrown together in a couple of weeks, probably wasn't like most of their other brides' weddings either.

At least Luke had stopped avoiding her. Though he worked long hours and she saw him only rarely, each morning he made an elaborate breakfast and left it for her to eat when she woke. Throughout the day, he bombarded her with text messages, asking her how she was feeling, how she had slept, if she had eaten, was hungry, had a craving, if she needed anything, anything at all?

Once more, she'd asked him to talk to her about what had happened that day in the snow. In answer, he'd taken her to bed, and she went because the vulnerability swirling behind his eyes wouldn't let her refuse him.

"Our dresses are back here." Isobel showed her to a small corner at the back of the store with several racks of dresses. "Would you like help?"

"I think I'll just look around a little first."

Isobel eased away. "I'll just be up front if you need anything."

Emily browsed the racks for a few minutes, but quickly grew discouraged. Exactly two dresses belonged on the white-to-ivory spectrum. She tried them both on, but the first dress wouldn't fit over her hips and her smaller breasts couldn't support the strapless style of the second one.

She dug up a dark blue dress she thought might complement her coloring, but again, the fabric pulled tight across her hips and abdomen. Though her belly hadn't begun to round, she'd swear her hips had widened.

That or she'd simply gained weight, which she could probably attribute to Luke's genius for pasta dishes and sweet treats.

Back at the racks, discouragement turned to frustration.

A sharp longing wrenched her heart. She wanted her mom.

Audrey had a knack for finding styles that complemented Emily's unique assets and bright hair. More than that, Audrey had a way of melting Emily's doubts and insecurities. They laughed and talked about interesting things and there just wasn't time to focus on her shortcomings.

The same as when she was with Luke.

As she gazed into the mirror at the too-tight dress that made her skin appear sallow, her vision blurred. She was fat, and pregnant, and so damned lonely she'd agreed to marry a man who quite possible only wanted to marry her because she was pregnant.

He shared his bed with her, but not his heart.

Isobel peeked around the corner "How's it going?" She took one look at Emily's face and abandoned her armful of clothing. "Oh, sweetie, what's wrong?"

Words piled in Emily's throat.

Isobel dug in her pocket. "Best thing about having two little kids—I come prepared." She handed Emily a rumpled tissue. "It's clean, I promise."

Emily took the tissue and wiped her nose.

"Wedding dress shopping is emotional." Isobel motioned her to a plush bench in the fitting room. "Is there anyone you can bring along to help you?"

Emily didn't wish to put Mina out with everything going on. Her tears pushed to the surface. "M-my m-mom is gone."

Isobel dug out another Kleenex and plopped onto the bench next to Emily. "This isn't right. We can't both cry."

A watery laugh escaped Emily. "I'm sorry."

Isobel waved off her apology. "I lost my mom when I was sixteen. Which is probably why I jumped into marriage."

"With Shea?"

A hard swallow worked Isobel's throat and she nodded. "We got married the day I turned eighteen."

Emily thought back to her eighteen-year-old self, before college and her mom's illness. "So young."

"Way too young. And naïve." Isobel dabbed at the corners of her eyes. "It didn't help I was pregnant. Nothing like an unplanned pregnancy to put a strain on a new relationship."

The blood left Emily's head.

Isobel twisted on the bench. "I have a dress I want you to look at. It's a wedding dress, but it's ivory, not white, and it's in stock. I think it would fit you nicely. Want to try it?"

Peering at Isobel's pretty, hope-filled face, Emily didn't have the heart to tell her no. She shrugged. "Sure."

Isobel returned with an armful of deep ivory lace and tulle. She hung the dress on a hook in Emily's dressing room and shuffled her through the door.

"It comes in two pieces." She removed the gown from the hanger, but the tulle stayed behind. "You can wear the dress alone or with the tulle overlay. Want to start with the dress and see what you think?"

In the dressing room, Emily shucked the ugly blue dress and stepped into the lace-embroidered, long-sleeved jacket dress, which fit her hips and ended mid-thigh. The dark ivory color turned her skin bronze and picked out the gold in her hair. Her dark eyes shimmered.

For just a moment, she almost looked like a woman a man like Luke might marry.

She opened the dressing room door.

Isobel's face lit up and she rushed forward. "I can take

a couple of tucks here at your waist." She pinned a spot at Emily's lower back. "Do you want to try the tulle skirt?"

Speechless, Emily nodded.

Inch by inch, Isobel moved around her, hooking the tulle onto hidden hook-and-eye closures around the waist of the dress. The gossamer layers floated about Emily, dropping well below her knees.

Isobel stepped away. "What do you think?"

Emily touched the lace bodice, interwoven with gold thread and adorned with tiny crystals that caught the light. "I think it's the most b-beautiful dress I've ever seen."

Radiant joy swept across Isobel's face. "If you want it, I can cut you a deal."

"That isn't necessary." Emily pulled her gaze away from her own reflection. "Well, I guess I should ask how much it is before I say that."

Husky laughter trickled out of Isobel. "We'll find a price you can live with."

Emily opened her mouth to explain she wasn't worried about the price when Isobel continued.

"You'll be doing me a favor."

"How so?"

"Free advertising." A blush stained Isobel's cheeks. "I'm thinking about opening my own store, with my own designs. This is my first dress."

"You made this? Oh, Isobel, it's amazing." Emily ran her hands over the bodice. "I insist on paying for it."

Isobel tilted her head to one side, studying Emily. "It's so perfect on you."

The dress was perfect, and her marriage to Luke would be perfect, too. She might not take his breath away, or mend his wounded heart, but she could give him comfort.

A new start.

A family.

Her heart, even if he didn't ask for it.

Isobel crept forward. "Those are happy tears, right?"

"Right," Emily whispered.

☙

She returned home feeling battered and bruised. In the foyer, the sound of voices drifted down the hall and Emily shuffled toward them. She poked her head around the library doorframe to peek inside the room.

Honey stood with her back to the door. "I'm here to see Alistair Thane. Are you him?"

Will glanced up from the chair behind the desk. "Who's asking?"

"I am. He's purchased something valuable and I'm here to deliver."

Will's head bent over the paperwork on the desk. "What are you delivering?"

Honey unzipped her hoodie and let it drop to the floor. She stood before Will in a thin tank top. "Me."

"Cut!" Max shot from the shadows. "Honey, lose the bra."

A warning alarm screeched inside Emily's head.

"I knew it!" The plush rug swallowed the sound when Honey stomped her sneaker-clad foot. "I'm the bimbo that gets killed after an obligatory tit shot, aren't I? Dammit, Max, I told you I wanted to do some actual acting in this movie. I'm trying to go legit here, but so far, all my character has done is make stupid decisions, including her choice of teeny-tiny T-shirts."

Max held up a hand. "Forget the zombie-slasher thing. We're going in a different direction."

A collective groan went around the room.

Honey folded her arms over her stomach. "And what direction would that be?"

"The chemistry between you two is ridiculous," Max

230

said. "Besides, I've been thinking we need to take advantage of current trends."

"Current trends, huh?" Honey's voice dripped with sarcasm. "Which trends?"

"S-s-superheroes?" With her outburst, five pairs of eyes swung toward Emily. "S-superheroes are popular."

Honey turned to Max, her head tilted to one side. "Are there gonna be any superheroes in this movie, Max?"

The desk chair creaked when Will rocked back. "That'd be sick."

Max shifted his dark gaze from Honey to Emily. "Not that trend. Look, one of the biggest movies in years was an erotic novel adaptation. There's a large, hungry market for adult romantic dramas."

Bile rose in Emily's throat.

Ian's head stuck out from behind the camera. "Max, man, it's a little late to start back at the beginning."

"I can use a lot of the footage we've already filmed."

A skeptical arch lifted Ian's brow. "You can use cuts from a zombie flick in your, what is it, erotic romantic drama?"

Max's dark eyes glinted. "The magic of editing."

Honey was shaking her head. "I didn't sign up for this."

"You're too talented to kill off." Max's tone held a hint of impatience. "Not to mention, you're a million times more believable as a desperate virgin co-ed than an idiot murder victim."

Honey's eyes grew huge. "That's so sweet."

His upper lip curled. "That's incredibly sad you think so. It's also the truth. I may not like you, but I'm not going to lie to you."

"Well, that's a relief," Honey muttered.

Max's well-formed features hardened. "This is business, and we're all here to make money. Anything else is a waste of time."

Honey sniffed. "If we're going to do this, I want a

raise."

Emily crept forward. "If we're going to do wh-what?"

"Ten percent," Max said.

"Twenty-five," Honey countered.

"Done."

A flash of surprise swept over Honey's face. "And I want a makeup artist."

"No." Max retreated to his chair in the corner.

"If you want me naked, I get a makeup artist. It's not negotiable."

"N-Naked?"

"I just gave you a twenty-five percent raise," Max bellowed. "Hire your own damn makeup artist."

Instinct screamed at Emily to take cover.

"Think of it as an investment." An impudent smile curved Honey's wide mouth. "A few hours of makeup will add value to the final product. You'll make back ten times what it cost, trust me on this."

Max's jaw clenched. "Fine." He headed for his corner. "Lose the bra."

Pain stabbed Emily's temples. "Uh, M-Max? Aren't you supposed to be done filming next week?"

His brows pulled together. "We're gonna need a little more time."

"How m-m-much time?"

"Can you give me two weeks?"

She fixed Max with an even stare. "I need p-payment upfront."

"No problem." He started to turn.

"And o-o-one more thing."

She caught the flicker of unease in his dark brown eyes before it was gone. "What's that?"

"Promise me you're not violating any laws." She rushed forward with the words piling in her throat. "O-or ordinances. Or p-permits."

"Easy." His quick smile made him appear surprisingly

boyish. "I promise I'm not violating any laws."

ℝ

The day before her wedding, Emily learned a new snow word: lake effect.

She and Luke had agreed to meet at his place for dinner, and she set off early so that she'd have time to stop at the grocery store on the way to pick up supplies for their meal. But while she was inside the store, the storm worsened.

Winds lashed at her skin with a biting cold, and thick, sticky snowflakes dropped from the sky in a frenzied blur. In her newly leased sedan, her knuckles turned white on the steering wheel as her visibility through the windshield shrunk to a few feet in front of the car's nose. The roads grew treacherous and, as a girl from the desert, she struggled to handle the car in such conditions.

At Luke's apartment, she saw no signs of his SUV. She sent him a text, and he quickly responded. He'd been held up at work dealing with a surge of road spin-offs and other weather-related crises. He directed her to the loft's spare key.

For the next few hours, she watched the snow piling up.

Her cell phone buzzed and she moved away from the slider to retrieve it off the dining table. Luke's number lit up her display screen and she accepted his call.

He gave her a quick update of the conditions. "Did Haven's flight make it?"

"Her flight is delayed. She's stuck at the airport in Chicago."

"We're supposed to get six more inches tonight, but it should slow down near midnight. You hunkered down there for a while?"

"I am. Mina's going to keep an eye on the inn for me." No way would she attempt the drive home tonight. "What about you?"

"It's gonna be another few hours before I can get away. Don't wait up."

She stirred when he slipped into the bed, and started to get up, but he clamped an arm around her and pulled her back down. He buried his face in her neck and soon the soft, rhythmic sound of his breathing lulled her back to sleep.

When she next opened her eyes, the storm had passed, and through the patio doors, sunlight danced over the mantle of snow, setting off a twinkling display of diamond flecks amidst the snowdrifts.

She turned when Luke moved over her. The sunlight caught in his green eyes, turning them brilliant, and the playful messiness of his dark hair pinched her heart.

"Maybe we should w-wait until we're married," she teased.

In answer, he shoved her T-shirt up around her waist and dropped a kiss on her stomach, near her belly button. She pulled the shirt over her head and his hungry gaze devoured her body. While she reveled in his open admiration of her, his mouth brushed over her ribcage, and then, moved lower. The tip of his finger trailed along her slit and liquid warmth sloped through her.

His mouth pressed against her core and he tasted her with his tongue. She gasped with the shot of sensation and her awareness narrowed to the exquisite torture each lick of his tongue lashed.

She rocked against his mouth, moaning, while waves of arousal whipped through her. She dug her hands into his hair and held him to her, greedily taking all he gave.

A noise sounded in the far-off distance, but she was too far gone to the feel of his hot mouth to take heed.

His hands gripped her waist, rendering her hips

immobile while his tongue massaged and teased. Each soft slide coaxed more sensation, more whimpers.

Just then, a woman's voice punctured the quiet. "Honey, I'm home."

Emily's eyes flew open.

A curse shot from Luke, and in one fluid motion, he rolled off Emily and tossed the sheets over her naked body.

Emily thrashed to a sitting position to find a beautiful woman standing in the doorway of Luke's loft.

"What in the hell are you doing here?" Luke yanked a pair of boxers over his hips.

The woman's chestnut hair shimmered about her shoulders when she flipped it. "I couldn't miss the big day. My invitation must've been lost."

A man appeared in the doorway and stepped past the woman.

Luke drew up. "*You* did this?" His voice held an edge of barely contained fury.

Even in her frantic state, Emily pegged the newcomer as a Nolan. The youngest brother, Leo, maybe? Though his dark hair was cut short to his scalp, his deep-set, thickly lashed eyes, straight nose, and swarthy skin gave him a marked resemblance to the brothers.

He staggered into the room and collapsed in one of Luke's armchairs. "Help, I've been kidnapped." His head dropped onto the chair back and his eyes fell shut.

"Oh, Lukie, I love what you've done with the place." A gasp slipped from the woman's painted mouth. "You kept our bed?"

Emily's patience ran out. "Luke, wh-who is she?"

The woman turned heavy-lashed, wide-set eyes on Emily. "I'm his wife."

Chapter Twenty-Two

"**E**x-wife." Luke's hands balled into tight fists at his sides.

A pout turned down the corners of the woman's mouth. "You make it sound so ugly."

"You were m-m-married?" Emily couldn't keep the waver, or the weakness, from her voice any more than she could control the blasted stutter. "Wh-why didn't y-you tell m-m-me?"

With a frustrated growl, Luke shoved a hand through his hair. "There was nothing to tell."

A chill passed through Emily and she turned her head to find Luke's brother watching her with changeable green-gold eyes. Like Jack's eyes, except cold.

"Well, isn't that interesting," he murmured.

She clutched the sheet tight to her chest and scooted toward the edge of the mattress.

Vicious lines formed on either side of Luke's mouth. "You brought her here?"

The man showed Luke his palms. "Other way around. Last thing I remember I was boarding a flight to this godforsaken state, and the next thing I know, I wake up in the backseat of her car. She brought me here against my will."

"You must've blacked out." A dry smile twisted the woman's mouth. "I can't believe they let you board the plane when you were that drunk. You sure made the flight interesting, I'll say that much."

Luke swore. "Jesus, Leo, I thought you were smarter than this."

"And I thought you were a cop. What the hell are you doing leaving the damn door unlocked?"

"Oh, he locked it." The woman held up a gold metal object. "I know where he hides the spare key."

Emily's heart ached and her head followed suit. She pushed up off the bed, but her feet tangled in the sheets and she stumbled.

Luke caught her elbow. "Where are you going?"

His touch burned her skin and she jerked her arm free. "To get dressed."

The woman clicked her tongue. "Oh, dear, I haven't upset you, have I? Believe me, you have no reason to be jealous. Luke didn't love me." Her cold blue eyes speared Luke. "He isn't capable of love. It was only great sex between us."

The wrench of nausea stole Emily's breath.

Luke's grip tightened on Emily's arm and his jaw clenched. "Get her out of here. Now."

Leo hoisted himself to his feet. "All right, let's go. You've had your fun."

"Leave the key," Luke said.

The woman quickly concealed the flash of disappointment on her face with a devious smile. "Call me later. We can hook up, like the old days."

Leo hustled her through the door and yanked it shut behind them.

Silence dropped like an anvil between Luke and Emily.

He'd been married.

Had he lived here, with his wife? Had he really slept here, with her, in the same bed where Emily had been sleeping with him? Emily rubbed her forehead.

He'd been married, and he didn't tell her.

She'd told him about the guy she slept with three times in college, more than ten years ago, and he didn't bother to mention he'd had a wife? A wedding, a marriage, presumably a divorce. Any one of those things might've warranted a mention.

Whatever happened to no lying?

Guess that only applied to her.

Sick with humiliation, she fumbled through the bedsheets with shaking hands, searching for her discarded clothing.

"Let me explain," he said, an unsettling soberness in his voice.

Words piled in the back of her throat. Angry, ugly words she stood no chance of getting out. She yanked on her T-shirt and jeggings and careened toward the front door.

He hounded her steps. "Please, don't go."

She stepped into her winter boots, but didn't bother lacing them, and threw open the door.

He caught her arm. "Emily, please." He peered into her face a moment, and then brushed a strand of hair off her cheek. "Stay. Talk to me."

A lifetime of frustration and impotence welled up, closing the back of her throat. With the torment, a choked sob broke from her and she plunged out into the frigid morning.

She drove home in a haze while cruel memories snuck

up on her. She recalled the time her mom bought her a play-pretend princess gown. Her heart filled with joy, Emily had twirled so that the gown's skirts billowed out around her. She rushed to show her dad, pointing out to him all the things she loved about the dress and sharing her secret plan to one day marry a prince.

Harrison had frowned down at her. "No man's going to want you as long as you chatter like a dimwit."

His words had etched on her heart, never to be forgotten, and echoed around inside her head as she struggled to make sense of Luke's treachery.

When she tripped through the back door, Noah looked up from the kitchen table.

"What are you doing up?" he asked. "We can fend for ourselves for a day."

All she wanted to do was hide away in her bedroom and cry and scream and throw things. "I, uh, couldn't sleep."

"Mina was the same way on our wedding day."

Emily snatched up the box of muffins and tossed them on the dining table with a heavy thud. She returned to the kitchen just as the back door banged open, shattering the quiet.

Luke loomed in the doorway. He wore ancient blue jeans and a black fleece and his chest rose and fell with his labored breathing, as though he'd run to get to her.

Max appeared through the kitchen door, a crumbling doughnut in his hand. "Where are the pancakes?"

Noah plucked a plate off the stack at his elbow and passed it to him. "No pancakes today."

"It's Saturday," Max argued. "Luke makes banana pancakes on Saturdays."

Luke's eyes burned like live coals.

She scrambled around to the far side of the island. "I don't w-want to talk." Her gaze darted to the table. "Not right n-now."

"Too damn bad." He stalked toward her.

Noah's eyebrows inched upward. "Everything all right, you two?"

Drew slipped through the kitchen door carrying the box of doughnuts and settled at the table beside Max. "These were in the dining room for some reason."

Emily snapped. "Because that's wh-where you're all supposed to be eating. In the dining room. Not the kitchen. M-my kitchen."

Three pairs of eyes blinked at her.

"Everything beyond that door is my house. M-my p-p-private house." She whirled on Luke. "Y-you should have told me y-you were m-m-married."

A utensil clattered against a plate.

"You're married?" Noah said. "Jesus, a guy leaves town for a decade and a half and he misses everything."

"Divorced." Luke pressed his palms to the countertop and peered into her face. That ripple of vulnerability disturbed the emerald pools of his eyes. "And you're right, I should've told you. But it was a long time ago and I don't think about her. Ever. I'm an awful person, but there you have it. I didn't tell you because she isn't worth mentioning. She was just a mistake."

Emily flinched, his words stinging like a slap to the face. "And here I thought I was your only mistake."

"Dammit, Emily—wait—"

She slammed the door to the half-bath behind her. The intensity of the emotions whipping through her choked her, and when he looked at her with those wounded eyes, she couldn't think. So she fled.

She withdrew her cell phone from the butt pocket of her jeggings and opened a new text.

His fists pounded on the door at her back. "Emily, let me in."

Her fingers hammered out a message. *Did you love her?*

The pounding stopped and Luke's voice carried through the door. "We have a problem. Leo's home."

She hit Send.

"He's here now?" The alarm in Noah's tone carried even through the door. "Where is he?"

"I don't know. He left–" Luke's cell phone buzzed.

A short pause followed, and then he erupted. "Oh, hell no." His pounding fist thundered. "Emily, open the goddamn door, or so help me, I'm going to break it down."

Her terror pushed sudden tears to the surface. She flung open the door and bolted past him, scurrying well out of arms' reach. "How long w-w-were y-you married?"

Tension radiated off him as he circled toward her. "One month."

"H-how long ago?" She put the kitchen island between them.

"We've been divorced ten years."

"Then wh-why is she here now?" She hated the ring of anguish in her voice.

"I don't know, except there's only one thing Natalie loves more than herself, and that's drama."

Her name was Natalie. A grueling name for Emily to enunciate correctly.

"She doesn't care about me," Luke said. "Or that I'm remarrying, or even who I'm marrying. Leo's right, she's had her fun. We won't hear from her again."

He slipped around the side of the counter.

She backed away. "Wh-what happened?"

A weary sigh eased from him. "It just… it was never right for us. She grew up on the island, but she hated living here, and she hated being married to a cop."

"T-too dangerous?"

"Too boring and too poor. She didn't mind the seventy-hour workweeks or the risks, but she couldn't stand the working-class lifestyle."

He pushed into her space.

She bumped up against the refrigerator.

"Does she live here now?"

"No. She's a flight attendant and lives in Traverse City, near the airport." He leaned close. His head bent low and he inhaled deeply. "She makes an appearance once a year or so around the holidays to visit her parents. We just got lucky that she was heading home when Leo showed up on her flight and was too drunk to keep his damned mouth shut about our wedding."

Her throat worked and it took her many moments to push out the words. "Did y-you love her?"

He pulled back and a muscle twitched where his jaw met his cheekbone. "No."

"He hesitated," Drew observed casually from the table.

Luke's head whipped around. "What the fuck did I know about love?" He turned back. "I was a twenty-three-year-old with a permanent hard-on."

"God, I hate that," Max muttered.

"So I married her," Luke said. "And in less than two days, I realized I couldn't stand her. And she couldn't stand me. And the sex wasn't even all that good." He cast another glance over his shoulder. "I mean, it wasn't bad, it was sex after all, but–"

With a disgusted gasp, Emily twisted away from him.

A curse hissed through his clenched teeth and he drove a hand through his hair.

She retreated to the other side of the room. The leg of a chair scraped against the hardwood floors and set off a domino effect of chair scraping. Noah approached them while Max and Drew slipped through the kitchen door.

Noah's serious dark eyes shifted between them. "You two okay? You're supposed to be getting married in approximately six hours."

An uneasy knot twisted Emily's stomach. She always thought she'd marry and have a family one day, but only in a vague sort of way. Never in her wildest dreams could she have imagined marrying a man like Luke, or the unusual series of steps—make that missteps—that'd bring about her wedding.

"We're okay." Luke's intense green gaze remained clamped on her face. "Or, we will be."

"Do we need to deal with Leo before then?" Noah asked.

Luke dropped his head heavily. "Yeah, we better. Give me just a minute here?"

Noah backed away. "Stop by the carriage house and pick me up on your way out." He disappeared into the mudroom and the sound of the back door closing soon followed.

From across the room, Luke tracked her movements. "What are you thinking?"

Her hand flitted through the air, as if she might pluck an intelligent thought from the sky. "Haven't you dated, or married, any average-looking women?"

One corner of his mouth twitched, but no smile formed. "Not a single one."

Warmth rushed to her cheeks. "Don't you dare try to charm me. This is serious."

"I know it is." His gaze remained straight. Direct. "You wouldn't consider Natalie attractive if you knew her. She's quite possibly the ugliest woman I've ever known. She lied about everything, all the time." The hitch of vulnerability in his voice was subtle, but unmistakable. "She cheated on me."

A burst of anger expanded in her chest.

His weary sigh held a ring of defeat. "I couldn't forgive her for it, and I sure as shit wasn't going to run all over town beating up they guys she slept with, which only pissed her off more. She wanted drama, and all I wanted was her gone from my life."

The confession notched a wound on her heart. At

least now she understood his hang-up about lying.

"I wish you had told me."

"Honestly, I never once thought to do so. Our marriage was so short-lived, it's like it never happened." He held up his hands to ward off her protest. "But I should've told you. Things moved kind of fast between us and I... fucked up."

She fiddled with a dishtowel, folding and refolding it. "I'm sorry she treated you like that."

"I'm sorry I was too stupid to see it coming." He shook his head. "Man, it was like having another full-time job, dealing with all her crazy." An injured expression touched his features. "Don't you dare laugh at me. It's not funny. I was in hell."

"It's a little funny."

A smile teased his lips and he eased closer to her. "I can't believe they walked in on us."

Heat burned her face. "*That's* not funny." She smacked his arm. "Why are you smiling?"

"I'm ashamed to say it."

"You don't look ashamed. Go on and say it."

"She wanted to stir up trouble. It serves her right she got an eyeful." A wicked light came into his eyes. "What we were doing, that's something I never did with her, and I know that's going to drive her mad."

His eyelids fell just the slightest bit, and his gaze wandered to her mouth. He wet his bottom lip with his tongue.

Her stomach jumped.

"I'm sorry she ruined your wedding day, though."

"I don't care about that."

His hand slipped to her waist and he pulled her close. "Are we okay?"

She didn't know how it'd turn out for them, but she couldn't shake the sense she'd stepped into a dream. Not just since her arrival on the island, but all the years leading up to it. Her mom's illness. The loss of control. The spiral into helplessness and the dark, empty hole of hopelessness that'd ripped open inside her.

And then there he was, and the craziness didn't stop, but took on a new texture, irresistible and true, and she couldn't help but believe it'd all brought her to this moment, as if by a certain thinning of the fabric between choice and fate.

Now, in this moment, they were definitely okay. Or they would be, once they were married and he trusted her enough to open up to her.

"Promise me, no more lies," she said. Then added, "Or omissions of crucial facts."

He pressed his forehead to hers. "You have my word."

She breathed in his soothing scent.

"I have to go." He took a step back, toward the door. "I'll see you later, at the church?"

He was her prince and Harrison was wrong. She would marry him. She couldn't not marry him.

A slow sigh slipped from her. "I'll be there."

⚃

Luke collected Noah and they made their way through the frigid morning air to their vehicles parked in the driveway. Snow crunched under their feet as they trampled across the side lawn.

"Where do we start?" Noah asked.

"The bars," Luke said. "Let's split up. You start on Main Street and I'll check in at the station to make sure he hasn't already made his presence known."

"What the hell happened to him?"

The question set Luke's heart racing. "What makes you think something happened?"

"From what you guys have been saying, it sounds like Leo's gone off the deep end. I'm wondering why."

245

"He *has* gone off the deep end." Luke pulled his keys from the pocket of his fleece. "But why is that a surprise to you? It's in our DNA."

Noah's steps slowed.

Luke stopped and turned back.

Noah's dark eyes latched onto Luke's face. "That's not how it works."

"Okay." Luke twisted away.

Noah fell in step beside him. Their long strides ate the ground beneath them.

"Do you have any idea what war was like for him?"

"He won't talk about it," Luke said.

"Probably nothing good then."

A dry snort escaped Luke. "I'd say that's a safe bet."

In the driveway, Luke headed to his SUV while Noah went around to the driver side of a black crew cab truck.

In the pocket of his blue jeans, Luke's cell phone vibrated. He slid the device from his pants and opened the message from the alert system used by the county police to send out warnings and widespread calls for backup.

He cursed.

Over the hood of the truck, he met Noah's gaze. "I think I found him."

Chapter Twenty-Three

Ten minutes past the time their ceremony was to begin, the groom was missing.

At the front of the church, Maisie flung her little body across the steps to the altar and her skirt kicked up to cover her face. Isobel gently reminded her to sit like a lady while Shea tried to distract their toddler, Connor, from an impromptu striptease.

Mina finished talking with the church receptionist and when she turned toward Emily, a too-bright smile appeared frozen on her face.

"What did she say?"

"There's a church function tonight. The sooner we start the ceremony the better."

Ten minutes later, Jack and Shea roamed the church vestibule, each of them with a cell phone pressed to their ear.

The color heightened on Mina's cheeks. "He was probably held up at work."

Emily shook her head. "He didn't w-work today." She headed up the aisle.

Jack turned to her with an easy smile. "Seriously, what is Luke trying to do to me? He knows I have a thing for redheads."

Emily forced a weak smile. "Have you talked to him?"

A beat of silence greeted her question.

"We're trying to get ahold of him." Shea's brilliant blue eyes fixed on Mina. "Have you talked to Noah?"

"I'll try him again." Peering down at her cell phone, she turned away.

Jack shoved his hands into the pockets of his suit pants. "The cellular service has always been bad on the island, even before the storm knocked out a tower."

Haven had commented on the poor cellular service that morning when she'd called Emily to report her flight had landed in Traverse City and she was working on making her way to the island amidst a few more weather-related travel complications.

Nonetheless, Emily's heart started to pound. Were they hurt? Had something happened with Leo?

She went to the front doors of the church and peered out. Behind her, the brothers carried on a hushed conversation.

Understanding reached her in stages. They were worried. Worried about Luke. Not that he was unwell or in danger, but that he wasn't coming.

Fierce heat rushed into her face with her mortification.

Mina held up her cell phone. "Still no answer."

Twin scowls appeared on the brothers' faces.

"But don't worry. Noah's with him." Mina's voice clouded with uncertainty. "He'll make sure Luke–gets here soon. Safely."

Her words twisted inside Emily like a betrayal. Even Mina thought Luke might jilt her? Wishing to block out their troubled expressions, Emily wandered back to the church and lowered herself into a pew.

Luke wouldn't do that to her, he wouldn't jilt her at the altar. Just that morning, he'd had the perfect opportunity to stop the wedding and he didn't take it. She'd recalled the thread of vulnerability in his green eyes when he'd asked if she'd be there today.

She'd said yes, and he'd been relieved by it.

She stared straight ahead. That way she wouldn't see the nervous exchange between Jack and Father John when Jack informed his uncle of their suspicions.

Mina settled next to her in the pew. "I'm sure he's fine."

Emily pasted a smile on her face, but it felt strained and brittle.

"I still can't believe how fabulous you look in that dress. When Luke sees you—"

The church door banged open with enough force it bounced off the stone wall.

And then he was there, filling the doorway.

On shaky legs, Emily stood.

He strode through the vestibule, but his hurried steps slowed. He peered into each one of their faces. "What's going on?"

"You're late." Shea's tone held a sharp edge. "Where have you been?"

A commotion erupted and two more bodies stumbled into the church. The doors slammed shut behind them.

Noah, holding on to Leo, who seemed barely able to stand, cursed. "You gotta help me out here, Leo."

Leo's hand came out to grip the wall. "Got it." He swayed when Noah let go.

Shea cursed.

Noah held up a hand. "It's okay. We're okay. Well, Leo's

car is totaled and the tree he ran into had a nice gash taken out of it, but thank God he didn't kill anyone." His face twisted into a frown. "Why do you all have that weird look on your faces? What's going on?"

Leo hiccupped.

A muscle ticked along Luke's jaw. "They thought I wasn't coming."

Emily's heart lurched. "Don't b-b-be silly."

Cold fury leapt to life in his eyes. "Yes, let's don't."

"Why didn't you call someone?" A shadow of annoyance tinted Jack's voice. "We've been sitting here waiting, not knowing what was going on."

"I did call," Noah said. "There's no cell service, so I called and talked to the church receptionist."

A ripple of awkwardness passed through the group, and they watched as the receptionist approached Father John at the altar. He nodded and motioned to them, then headed down the aisle.

"I just heard," he said. "Is he all right?"

"He's drunk." Shea spat the words with disgust.

John muttered something in another language.

Leo's eyes glittered. "You have no idea."

Father John turned to Luke. "We should get started. The next group will be here any moment."

Leo staggered toward the last row church pew and collapsed onto his back with feet sticking out into the aisle. The four other brothers moved toward the altar, and Mina hurried in the direction of the vestibule.

Emily set her heels. "Can't we just... start?"

"Are you sure?"

Emily nodded.

Talons of dismay reached out to claw at her when she moved to stand beside Luke at the altar.

His anger whipped into a furious storm and radiated off him. It was the first time she'd ever looked at him and seen something ugly.

Father John came to stand before them with a warm smile. When he spoke, he sounded faraway, and her mind struggled to grasp the meaning of his words.

The ceremony passed in a haze for Emily.

When Luke placed his hand on the Bible, so did she. He felt cool and stiff to the touch. When he turned to face her, she turned also, though her gaze fixed on the column of his throat.

"I, Luke, take you, Emily, to be my wife." She detected no softness in his voice.

Her hands started to shake.

"I promise to be true to you in good times and in bad, in sickness and in health. I will love you and honor you all the days of my life."

A crude belch resounded from the back row of the church.

Father John's face flushed with anger. "Emily, do you take Luke, to have and to hold, from this day forth, until death parts you?"

"I d-do." Her voice barely rose above a whisper.

"Repeat after me. I, Emily, take you, Luke, to be my husband."

Many long seconds ticked by before she was able to utter a word. "I, Em-Emily, take y-you, Luke, to b-b-be m-my husband."

A sob built in her throat. "I promise to b-be true to you in good times and in b-b-bad, in sickness and in health."

Luke's hand closed over hers and she drew a deep, steadying breath. "I will love you and honor you all the days of my life."

Father John's strong voice carried through the church. "I now pronounce you husband and wife."

The pianist struck the piano and a joyous melody trumpeted.

Luke held out his arm and Emily slipped her hand

under the crook of his elbow. He fired a look at Shea and Jack, as if to say, *Are you happy now?*

There was little happiness in her heart when they walked back down the aisle, arm in arm, as husband and wife.

CꙄ

As Luke and Emily emerged into the chilly December air, large snowflakes wept from the sky. Church bells rang out, the peal of their chimes spilling across the hillside cemetery to drop off the cliff side and fade away over the waters of Lake Michigan.

Gray clouds loomed off shore, while waves crashed against the rock face below. Much like the anger churning inside him.

They'd thought he wasn't going to show up to his own wedding.

Worse, Emily had thought it, too. He'd seen the truth on her pale, stricken face.

He'd dedicated his entire life to being a good guy, and that was what he had to show for it? His own brothers, his wife, didn't trust he'd do the right thing?

He might've defended himself, except he didn't want to talk about what he'd been doing. He didn't want to recall the sickness that slithered through him when he first saw Leo's mangled truck. The weight of the shackles that'd clamped around his ankles, or the burden choking the breath from his body. The flashback had been one of his worst yet.

They were coming more often, more intensely, and it was taking him longer to recover from the attacks.

His jaw clenched so tightly, he couldn't speak when he opened the passenger-side door of his car for Emily.

She drew back. "Do you m-mind w-waiting a m-m-minute?"

With a shove that felt good, he slammed the car door shut and leaned against the vehicle. He rammed his hands into the pockets of his black wool coat for shelter against the cold air.

Rather than reenter the church as he expected her to do, Emily set off down the hillside. She hiked up her puffy skirts and trampled through the snow in her delicate heels. At her mother's grave, she laid her bridal bouquet of deep red roses across the tombstone and scampered back through the wet snow.

The fiery lash of his anger cooled. He needed to let it go. No matter how they'd come to it, they were married now.

The thought calmed him as she hurried up the drive.

When she approached the car, he blocked the passenger-side door, and for the first time since he'd arrived at the church, he noticed the dark shadows under her eyes and the pallor of her complexion. A deep disquiet disturbed the smooth whiskey in her eyes.

"You're beautiful." The words traveled directly from his brain to his tongue.

He wasn't referring to the way she wore her hair, down and pinned back at the sides, or the fancy dress, but the rest of her. All the parts people didn't see.

His gaze slipped down the thin column of her throat.

Her pulse scrambled. "Luke, I'm sorry–"

He stopped her with a gesture. "It's okay. Let's just get through this dinner so we can go home."

Shea had closed the pub for the night and planned a quiet dinner for the family. Luke contemplated skipping out on it altogether, but he hadn't eaten since grabbing some shitty fast food earlier in the day and she deserved some merriment on her disastrous wedding day.

They drove the short distance to the pub in silence. He parked in the back lot and helped her out of the car. His hand at the small of her back, he pulled open the pub door.

A cheer went up.

A nasty curse shot from him and he bared his teeth at the horde of bodies packed into the dimly lit room.

Shea's face appeared before him. "Sorry, man. Word got out and I couldn't stop them."

Luke looked down at Emily.

Her smile wavered. "All your friends are here. How nice."

Then the crowd rushed forward to engulf them and separated her from him.

Chapter Twenty-Four

Loud, laughing faces swam before Emily. Someone stepped down hard on her foot and she tripped. An elbow poked her in the ribs and she shrank back to the edge of the crowd.

Bodies rushed in to fill the hole left in her wake.

She retreated to a booth tucked into an alcove at the edge of the celebration and collapsed onto the hard bench.

She watched him and the way his friends interacted with him. Always flirting. Always offering him more than he asked for, but he smiled and joked with them all.

The pinch in her chest twisted with misery.

Emily shook herself. She was his wife, and she wanted him to be happy. She wanted his friends to like her. She needed to make an effort.

Someone slid into the booth across from her. She had

a familiar face, and Emily soon recalled meeting her at the pub the night she and Luke had dropped by for dinner. Jenna, the flirty one.

Emily smiled.

Jenna scowled. "You bitch."

Emily gasped.

"I'm kidding, I'm kidding." Jenna laughed. "Actually, I'm not kidding, but it isn't you personally that I hate. Any woman that married Luke was going to be despised in this town."

Jenna teetered away, and thus ended Emily's attempt to woo Luke's crowd.

Self-consciousness rushed forward to swamp her. She sensed their eyes on her. Assessing, judging. What she at first assumed were curious glances, she now suspected were something else.

They thought she wasn't good enough for him.

When another figure appeared at the table, Emily filled with apprehension. So when she looked up into a Haven's friendly face, she nearly wept with relief.

She threw her arms around her old friend. "It's so good to see y-you."

"I almost gave up." Haven's long brown hair hung in soft waves down her back and her raspy voice matched her sassy personality. "This place is nearly impossible to get to."

They sat on opposite sides of the table. "I know. I'm sorry it's been so awful for you."

Haven raised the wineglass in her hand. "I'm almost over the trauma."

Haven was much the way Emily remembered her from college, except with a solemn light behind her eyes that Emily didn't recall ever seeing before. Emily supposed she must appear similarly changed.

Haven leaned forward in the booth. "So tell me, which one is he?"

A blush touched Emily's cheeks as she scanned the crowd and pointed Luke out to her friend.

Haven's big brown eyes widened. "Holy shit, I'm just gonna say it—your husband is freaking hot."

Someone bumped Haven's arm and her wine sloshed.

Jenna fell into the booth beside Emily. "So, Emma, have you met my friend Kate?"

Emily looked up to see Kate hovering at the head of the table.

"Congratulations." Kate sank into the booth next to Haven. A shadow of pain touched her blue eyes. "I didn't know you two were even dating."

Shock rendered her mute. "Oh, well, uh..."

"It was a bit of a whirlwind romance. Love at first sight." Haven jumped in. "I mean, what's not to love, am I right, Emily?"

Haven hung a heavy emphasis on her name and Emily buried her face behind her water glass.

Luke had told her he and Kate were not a couple. Had he lied? Or had Kate harbored secret feelings for him? Guilt and unease rushed to the surface of her skin as a heated blush.

A Cheshire cat smile curled Jenna's lips and she raised her beer. "How about a toast? To love at first sight?"

A wave of nausea hit Emily and she lifted her glass.

"Wait, is that water?" Jenna peered into Emily's glass. "Why are you drinking water at your wedding reception?"

Riotous warmth flushed Emily's face. Her brain rushed ahead of her tongue and everything got jumbled up in her throat.

"Omigod," Jenna gasped. "Are you pregnant?"

Emily wanted to deny it, but then she caught the slash of pain on Kate's face and she just stared, mute.

"So that's why he married you." Jenna's softly spoken words seemed to scream at Emily.

The blood left Emily's head in a sickening rush. "N-no."

Jenna stared at her with round eyes. "How very clever of you."

A splash of liquid slapped Jenna in the face.

"Oops, I'm sorry," Haven purred. "It just slipped out of my hand."

Fury flickered to life in Jenna's eyes, and then in a flash of movement, she lunged across the table.

Chaos erupted. Haven yanked Jenna down by the hair and Jenna screamed. She kicked and flailed her arms. Kate darted from the booth.

A large body plunged into the fray. Jack clamped an arm around Haven's waist and pulled her off Jenna.

Jenna pressed a palm to her cheek and backed away.

"Holy shit." Jack gasped for air. "I think that's the hottest thing I've ever seen."

Haven twisted in his arms, craning her neck to look up at him. Her chest rose and fell with her heavy breathing. "I might say the same thing."

His hold on her firm, a seductive smile pulled up one corner of his mouth. "I don't believe we've met. Hi, I'm Jack."

"I'm Haven." She tipped her chin in the direction Jenna had fled. "She was mean to my friend."

Jack's green-gold eyes swept over Emily. "Your friend is my new sister-in-law, so I thank you."

Haven's laugh came out on a huff of air. "Are you single, Jack?"

"As a matter of fact I am, Haven." He reached up and brushed a strand of dark hair off her forehead.

"Are you going to let me go, Jack?"

His gaze fastened on her mouth. "No, I don't think I will."

Emily gaped at them. Her heart pounded in her ears, so she didn't at first register the sound of her name being said over the restaurant's loud speakers.

"Emily, where are you?"

Confused, she looked around even as people were turning to look at her. Over the wall of the crowd, she spotted Luke standing on the small stage near the front of the pub, a guitar strapped to his body.

"Come on up here, sweetheart." He teased a few bars of a song on his guitar. "Let's show these jackasses how it's done."

The blood left her head with a dizzying swoop.

╏

Luke's heart pounded its panic. He watched the color drain from her face, and with the force of a sledgehammer, realized his mistake.

He'd let his anger cloud his judgment.

Anger that his brothers thought him the kind of lowlife that'd skip out on his own wedding.

Anger that his supposed friends greeted the news of his wedding with shock and thinly veiled disbelief. Not that he'd married, but that he'd married *her*.

Then, when he watched the way they talked over her, ignored her, and finally, pushed her completely out of the way, anger had turned to cold fury.

She was miserable. He was miserable. There was only one thing to do.

Show them what he saw. What they were too blind to see. That the woman he'd married was more than all the women he'd been with before. Not only was she softhearted and smoking hot, but she was crazy talented, too.

Except she didn't join him on stage, but stood frozen at the back of the pub, her brown eyes huge in her pale face. Jack appeared at her side.

"My beautiful wife is a little shy." Luke's voice carried over the sound system. "She could use a little encouragement."

A smattering of applause rippled through the crowd. Then grew steadily louder when Emily crept forward a tiny fraction of an inch. His heart soared. He leapt down off the stage and plunged into the crowd, reaching her side in several long strides.

Her pupils had dilated to swallow all the light. He clasped his hand around hers and guided her to the stage.

He positioned her behind one of two microphones, and bringing his guitar back around, strummed the chords of a song he'd heard her singing the other day.

"You know this one, don't you, sweetheart?"

Glassy-eyed with shock, she nodded.

He leaned away from his microphone. "Emily, look at me."

Her brown eyes latched on to his face.

"Look only at me," he said. "That's my girl."

His fingers plucked the chords of the opening notes, but her cue came and went without her singing.

He repeated the short refrain. "How about we sing this first part together?"

With a deep breath, he began to sing. Soon, she joined in. Her voice at first wobbly, it grew stronger by the end of the first verse. Together, they dropped into the chorus, and their voices mingled in harmony. The quality of the sound transcended that of either of their voices unaccompanied.

At the start of the second verse, he let his vocals drop away, and her sultry voice poured over a rapt crowd. Her heart in her voice, she sang of a love she longed for and yet feared. His heart wedged in his throat and he swallowed hard to dislodge it before rejoining her at the chorus.

They eased into the concluding refrain, his vocals echoing hers in a pattern, like lovers exchanging endearments.

As Luke strummed the last chord, she came back to herself. Applause erupted and she startled. With a soft apology, she dove off the stage and charged though the cheering crowd. He bounded into the fray after her, dodging smiling faces and oblivious congratulatory pats on the back.

The cool air smacked him in the face when he shot through the back door into the dark night.

She whirled on him. The tracks of her tears on her cheeks gutted him. "Don't y-you ever do that to m-m-me again!"

"I won't. I'm sorry."

She gulped large lungfuls of air.

"Listen to them," he said softly. "They love you."

I *love you.*

The words almost slipped out. Effortlessly. Naturally.

Well, shit.

"I've never done anything like that before in m-my life. I think I might throw up."

He loved her? That wasn't part of the plan. Never, anywhere in all of this, was falling in love an acceptable part of the plan.

Her dark eyes shimmered with tears. "Are you going to make me go back in there?"

He snatched up her hand and hauled her to him. "No." He dropped kisses on her face. "I'm so proud of you."

She sagged against him and his hand slipped beneath the curtain of her hair. He tipped her head back and his mouth found hers for a long, slow taste. She tasted better than whiskey.

So he loved her. So what? He loved his brothers, his niece, and nephews.

He wasn't *in* love with her. If he were *in* love, well, that'd be a disaster. Though he'd better get some barriers erected between them before the disaster became the reality.

"I can't believe I did that." A tiny hint of wonder crept into her tone.

"You were amazing." Without letting her go, he started toward the parking lot.

She tugged on his arm. "Should we say good-bye?"

"Fuck 'em."

Her watery laugh soothed his battered heart.

Tomorrow, he'd start to work on those barriers.

"C'mon, Mrs. Nolan. Time to get you home so you can fulfill your wifely duties."

Chapter Twenty-Five

Two days after their wedding, she discovered Luke sitting on the back porch stoop, staring into the setting sun, and, despite the thirty-degree temperature, wearing no coat. She said his name, and he turned his head to look at her, but his blank stare lifted the hairs on her arms.

He'd smiled and followed her inside, but she soon spotted him stealing away to the library, a bottle of whiskey tucked under his arm.

That night, he didn't come to bed, and when she searched the house for him in the morning, she found the note he'd left her explaining he'd gone to work and would be tied up there all day.

The cycle repeated itself the next day.

The next morning, she staggered out of bed at first light and headed him off at the back door.

She caught the shadow of unease that clouded his expression before he tossed up an easy smile. "Sorry. Did I wake you?"

She shook her head. "Are y-you going to work?"

"Yeah, I'm trying to wrap a few things up before the long weekend. What about you? What are you up to today?"

"I have a doctor's appointment."

He winced. "That's today? What time?"

"Eleven."

The kitchen door swung open and Jared shuffled into the room in an undershirt and a pair of boxer briefs. "Oh, hey guys."

He trudged to the counter and plucked the carafe from the coffeemaker. While the coffee flowed, he reached around to scratch one butt cheek.

A scowl deepened the lines of fatigue around Luke's eyes.

When Jared disappeared through the kitchen door, Luke rounded on her. "Why are they still here? Shouldn't they be gone by now?"

The two weeks Max asked for had now stretched into the third week.

"They needed a few m-more days. They're supposed to be done by the end of the week."

"How long does it take to get murdered by zombies?" he muttered.

"Well, once they changed the direction of the film—"

The full force of his singular attention knocked her back a step. "When did they do that?"

"Um... a couple of weeks ago, I think."

"So they're not making a zombie horror flick?

At the snap in his tone, a shiver of alarm ran through her. "I guess not."

"What kind of movie are they making?"

She fumbled for words. "Some kind of dramatic

romantic…"

At that, a spark lit in his eyes, but he waited for her to finish.

She gulped down the fear rising in her throat. The other day, she'd witnessed a tiny glimpse of exactly one scene. There'd been some heavy breathing, and a fair bit of talk about the brightness of Honey's headlights before the stench of Will's cologne sent Emily darting for the bathroom.

"This is a small town, Emily. If they're making pornography, it will get out, and it won't go well for you, or them."

Shifting sea-green eyes speared her, as if he knew she lied and would will her confession with the brutal force of his gaze.

But she had nothing to confess. Yet. Max promised her he wasn't doing anything illegal, and she'd chosen to trust him.

She just hoped he didn't prove her wrong for doing so.

"They're not… doing that. Max promised m-me." Her palms grew clammy and she ran a hand down the thigh of her leggings.

She considered telling him about the scene she'd witnessed, but the lines of exhaustion bracketing his eyes and mouth convinced her to remain silent. Besides, in a couple of days, Max and the crew would be gone and none of it would matter.

Luke went on to work, but when Emily arrived at her doctor's office a few minutes before her appointment time, she found him reclined in a chair in the waiting room. He smiled at her and her heart gave a desperate, ravenous wrench. She'd gone too long without seeing that smile.

The doctor was an affable man who quickly put Emily at ease with his upbeat manner and relaxed way of relaying facts. According to her last period, Emily was around her ninth week with an expected due date of mid to late July.

He handed over tomes of literature for her and Luke to read and then approached her with a small, handheld device. He smoothed one end of the instrument over Emily's stomach, and a moment later, the furious echo of a heartbeat filled the room.

Listening to the light, frantic beating, laughter bubbled up, even as equal parts wonder and terror filled her. Seeking a stable point amidst her rioting emotions, she looked to Luke.

His complexion pale, his eyes appeared glazed, like glassy jewels. The mix of emotions she expected to see on his face was absent, and instead he appeared expressionless. Blank.

Their appointment ended and at her car, he dropped a kiss on her forehead. "I'll probably have to work late again." An emptiness rode the top of his voice. "Text me if you need me."

She didn't need him, though an aching hollowness opened up in the center of her chest and stayed with her throughout the day.

Late that night, she woke from a dreamless sleep when he moved over her. The warmth from his skin soothed her weary bones and the press of his erection between her legs aroused her longing for him.

He eased himself inside her and she bit down on her bottom lip to stifle her needy moans. Buried to the hilt, he peered into her face. His eyes blazed.

Then he started to pump his hips. Long, languid strokes turned urgent and fierce. He drove into her, again and again, while his green gaze bored into her.

She swallowed back a sob as sensation tore through her. He gripped her hips and plunged deeper, wresting all the fear and sorrow from her. A tear leaked out and she squeezed her eyes shut. She whispered his name and when she found the courage to look at him, she watched as something in his eyes shifted, from desperate to pleading.

Her orgasm shattered over her, but no joy came with her release.

He dropped his head to her shoulder. With one last series of pounding thrusts and a guttural growl, he emptied himself inside her.

She toyed with the hair at his nape while their breathing slowed. He lifted his head, but her weak smile fell on his back as he rolled off her and stood.

"Wh-where are you going?"

"I've got some paperwork to catch up on." He pulled a pair of running pants over his lean hips.

"Right now? But you just got home."

He was already at the bedroom door. "Don't worry about me. Get some sleep."

The door eased shut behind him.

⚃

On Friday, two days before Christmas, Max finally wrapped filming and the crew began to leave the inn.

Will was the first to go, and Emily inhaled a deep breath of cologne-free air once he'd gone. Jared and Ian left shortly thereafter, confiscating the box of doughnuts on their way out. Around lunchtime, Drew picked up Honey, and Max, having decided to stay at the inn another week, was closeted away in his room upstairs working on film edits.

The estate didn't remain quiet for long.

Luke and Emily celebrated Christmas with Noah and Mina, and Shea and Isobel. While Shea and Isobel's teenage son, Finn, hid behind a hoodie and an electronic device, the uncontainable excitement of Maisie and Connor delivered a smile to Emily's lips. Though it was quickly squashed by the obvious frustration and exhaustion of their parents.

Throughout the day, Luke was kind and charming, and that night, he seemed determined to give her as many orgasms as a girl could possibly withstand. Emily opened for him eagerly, hoping that he might taste her love for him and it would turn his heart toward her.

Afterwards, he slipped from her bed, mumbling something about work and the library.

The weight of her loneliness pressed down on her. When she'd agreed to marry him, she'd expected the loneliness would end. Instead, she wasn't sure if she'd ever felt more alone in all her life.

A week later, on New Year's Eve, Noah and Mina had gone out, and Luke was on duty. So two weeks after her wedding day and two months pregnant, Emily sat home alone.

The Christmas tree she'd dragged home remained propped up before the front window in her living room. She wandered over to it and fingered a few of the ornaments she'd brought with her from the house in Tucson.

Her favorite, a red bulb with a small photograph of her and her mom, hung on a branch at the front of the tree. She peered at the photo. She'd probably been in first or second grade when the picture was taken, and her mom, newly divorced.

She recalled feeling such joy. Harrison had left and Christmas grew near. The anticipation and presents were great, but for Emily, the elation of staying home from school for two weeks was intoxicating. No speech therapy, no teasing schoolmates, no terrorizing dread.

Her thumb brushed over a small button on the ornament and the long-ago recording of Emily and Audrey singing a Christmas carol filled the quiet room.

The singing stopped and Emily's second- or third-grade voice carried through the crappy speaker.

"I love you, Mama."

"I love you, baby girl."

It was the only recording she had of her mom's voice.

Tears falling, Emily pushed the button again.

ᥴ୫

Turned out, there was a reason Luke only drank whiskey at home. Alone.

He was a mean drunk.

The knot between his shoulder blades ached and he rolled his head, trying to chase it away. He should be happy. After all the delays and rounds of second and third interviews, he was perfectly positioned for the job he'd spent the last ten years working toward.

Not only that, but in the two weeks since he and Emily married, he'd managed to put a little distance between them. A fact that should calm him. But the more space he wedged between them, the more lost and empty he became.

An uneasy churning in his gut lingered, and he attempted to drown it, once and for all, with alcohol. More alcohol. As much as it took.

A group of men Luke knew to be fishermen from the wharf played pool at one of the tables in the back. Justin Sloane was among them.

"You like that, Jimmy?" Sloane's voice rose above the pub noise to reach Luke. "Wish you had my skills, don't ya? Watch this—hey, hey, Tommy, watch this one."

Luke sipped his whiskey and tried to ignore the little prick.

God, he missed Anthony. Big-hearted and teller of outrageous stories Anthony.

Sloane kept it up, and soon guys started slinking away from the pool table to avoid the blowhard. Good,

269

hardworking guys didn't deserve Justin ruining one of their rare nights out to relax.

Drink in hand, Luke slid off his barstool and approached the pool table. He chatted with Tommy and JJ until Sloane barked at them.

"Hey, JJ, you done stroking your stick over there? It's your shot, man."

With a grimace, JJ stepped up to the table. He sunk two balls before missing.

A sleazy grin split Sloane's face. "Another one bites the dust. Who's next? How about you, Gary? You ready for your ass whooping?"

Gary held up his hand. "I'm going to sit this one out."

Sloane nagged Gary for a bit, coming around the pool table to stand in the man's personal space.

"Hey, Sloane," Luke jumped in. "I overheard Big Mike taking bets on the game this weekend."

"And?" Sloane rubbed chalk on the tip of his pool stick.

"And I thought you might want to get in on it, that's all." Even though Sloane stood a short distance from him, Luke had trouble focusing on his bullish features.

"First, I'm gonna finish taking JJ's fifty bucks," Sloane said. "Then I'm gonna take Gary's fifty bucks, and then Tommy's fifty bucks."

Luke's hand balled into a fist. "I think they'll probably hand over the money just to get rid of you."

The men howled with laughter.

Color rose on Sloane's cheeks. "You think so?"

"I do." Luke sipped his whiskey.

"What the hell are you doing here anyway, Nolan? Lost interest in your little wife already?"

Luke set his tumbler on the ledge. "Don't talk about my wife."

One of Sloane's eyebrows shot up. "Don't get mad at me. You're the one that knocked her up and had to marry her."

Luke's fist crashed into his weak jaw. The men scattered when Sloane stumbled back.

He maintained his feet and lunged, his fist connecting with Luke's lip.

Luke laughed, the stinging pain a welcome relief to the blinding panic and excruciating numbness. He planted his shoulder in Justin's chest and swept his legs out from under him. The prick hit the floor and Luke went for his throat.

But hands grasped him from behind and pulled him away.

"What do you think you're doing?" Shea bellowed in his ear.

Disappointment slashed through Luke. "Just having some fun."

Sloane staggered to his feet. "What the fuck is wrong with you?"

Luke shook the ache from his hand. "C'mon, admit it, that felt good, didn't it?"

"Fuck you." Sloane touched the red welt on his cheek.

"You've been wanting to do that as long as I have."

Sloane's dark eyes burned bright. "You're gonna regret this, Nolan."

"Not half as much as I enjoyed it."

Firm hands clamped down on his shoulders. The room tipped on its axis and Luke twisted his body, trying to gain steady ground.

Cool night air smacked into him when Shea shoved him through the pub door and sent him hurtling into the parking lot. He slid on the loose gravel and his stomach pitched.

"He doesn't look too good," Noah said.

Luke tried to stand but rocked back. He fell against the brick wall.

Shea planted his hands on his hips. "What the hell has gotten into you?"

"I'm in love." Luke spit a splotch of blood onto the ground. "With my wife."

Chapter Twenty-Six

"**H**ow unfortunate for you."

While Shea chuckled, Luke glared at Noah's smug face. "It's not funny."

Noah's expression turned serious. "No, you're right, it's not funny. I share the same misfortune, and I'm not gonna lie to you, it's a terrible fate."

Behind him, Shea stared at the pavement, shaking his head. "Nothing can prepare a man for that kind of misery."

Luke's head dropped back against the hard brick of the building. "You guys are a big help."

"Can I make a suggestion?"

Luke waved Noah on.

"Give up."

Luke groaned.

"No, I mean it. It's a losing battle that you stand no

chance of winning. Why fight it?"

Shea's boots shuffled over the asphalt as he shifted his weight. "Well, there's always the possibility for makeup sex."

"Fair point," Noah conceded.

A rush of anger and terror flooded Luke.

Just then, the pub door opened and noise from inside spilled out with the bartender, Tony. "Hey, Shea, that new tap's jammed again. Can you come take a look?"

"You got this?" Shea said.

Noah inclined his head and Shea disappeared behind the pub door.

Darkness churned inside Luke, causing the world to tilt to one side. His back against the wall, he sank to the ground. He slung an arm across his knees and dropped his head.

Into the silence, Noah asked, "Would it be so bad if you just love her?"

"Yes." He couldn't think of a worse fate.

"Why?"

Luke lifted his heavy head. "You wouldn't understand."

"Try me anyway."

The words rushed to the surface and propelled into the night air. "Because I'll ruin her. Or she'll ruin me. Shit, she already has."

The bastard laughed, and Luke considered planting a fist into his jaw as well.

"Yeah, you two are a couple of real toxic personalities," Noah said. "You know, now that you mention it, I can already see your corrupting influence on her. She's becoming a tyrant. The other day, she even made us eat off plates."

"Very funny."

"I'm sorry, I'm done." Noah eased himself to the ground to sit beside Luke. "What's got you so convinced you'll ruin her?"

"Darth Vader." Luke laid his head against the wall. "I understood him. He was the only one that made sense to me."

"That's hardly–"

"More serial killers are born in November than any other month."

"I was born in November," Noah said dryly.

"I know that. We both were. Convinced yet?"

"Nearly. What else you got?"

Luke stared into his brother's face for a long moment while the words rolled around in his mouth like sour balls. "I'm the most like him."

Noah's gaze glittered. "Like who?" he asked carefully.

"Dad."

The air changed, as if a live wire suddenly ran between them.

"He was weak," Luke said.

"You think you're weak?"

"I–" Luke swallowed back bile. "I killed a kid."

Noah's beat of silence blared like a foghorn. "What happened?"

"School shooting. He trapped them in the lunchroom. Started picking them off as they ran. At the first clear shot, I took him out."

"That's nothing like Dad." Noah was shaking his head. "Not the same thing at all."

"I'd do it again." The blood in Luke's veins turned to ice. "In a heartbeat. For her. If someone hurt her, or tried to, I'd kill them. I'd do it gladly, and then I'd dance on their fucking grave."

Rather than recoil, Noah's expression turned thoughtful. "I don't think that makes you like him."

Probably not. It made him a thousand times worse.

"You're a protector. A shield. Dad wasn't a shield." Noah's tone hardened. "You're right, he was weak. Too weak to be a shield. All he knew was how to lash out and strike. He was a sword. The difference between you two is night and day, right and wrong."

"The end result is the same."

"What's the end result?"

"I've tried to politely self-destruct, but it's not working." Luke shoved a hand through his hair. "Either I'm going to take her down with me or–" He bit back the words.

"Or what?"

Bile rose in his throat. "She'll leave me."

"I don't think you have to worry about that. Not yet. Look, the way I see it, you have a choice–"

"What choice?" His voice pitched high with his anger. "Leave her?"

"No, of course not. There are people who can help–"

A growl of frustration tore from Luke. "I've tried it. It didn't work. The weakness... it's a part of me."

"Luke, listen to me. You are not Daniel. In fact, I don't think you could be more unlike him. You're the peacemaker. Like Mom."

"You didn't live with him."

"I did." Steel wrapped around Noah's statement. "I was his favorite punching bag, remember?"

"But then you left, and Shea moved out to get his own place. Jack went to live with the Thompsons. It was just Leo and me, and we're both exactly like him."

Noah's silence was damning.

"You saw it, too." Luke's voice shook. "With Leo. You know I'm right."

"Let's take care of you before we move on to deal with Leo."

"Don't you get it, there's nothing to deal with. We can't be fixed."

"That's not how it works. You're soldiers, fighters, and with fighters, there's always a chance."

Luke tried to focus on one of the Noah's sitting beside

him. "How do you know so much about it? You work with soldiers overseas or something?"

A pensive quiet overcame his brother, until finally, he said, "I married one."

From there, Luke's world faded to black. He recalled glimpses of the ride home, snippets of conversation with Noah.

Then he was at the inn, pinned beneath huge brown eyes.

"Wh-what happened?"

He fell into a chair at the table. "Nothing."

"You're bleeding." Her fingers brushed the corner of his mouth. "Someone hit you?"

He jerked his head back. "Stop it. I'm fine."

She recoiled at the sharp bite in his tone. He wanted to pursue her, soothe her, but he didn't.

"You should just tell her." Noah settled in a chair with a bag of chips. "Save yourself the grief."

Luke groaned. "Get out."

"He got into a fight at the pub." Noah crunched happily.

"The pub? I thought you w-were working tonight."

"It was quiet. I got out a little early." He glared at his brother. "You told on me?"

"What, are we seven?" Noah turned to Emily. "He got in a fight with another cop. Weird fraternity of brothers thing."

Her soft gasp landed as a brutal gash on Luke's heart. "Which cop? Wh-why?"

Noah frowned. "Didn't catch his name. Unless it was pissant or cocksucker."

"Noah, go home."

"All right, I'm going." Noah scooped up his chips and pushed to his feet. "Talk to your wife, man."

Then Noah was gone and Emily stood before him. She pressed a warm washcloth to his lip.

"Are you sure y-you're okay?"

"I'm fine. I drank too much and let Sloane get to me. The guy's been a thorn in my side for months now and it just sort of built up."

"It's not like you to get into a fight."

"Yeah, well, I'm a complicated man." He was a broken man, and he didn't know how to fit the pieces of himself back together again.

He lurched to his feet. "I'm going to grab a shower and crash."

On unsteady legs, he staggered toward the suite and twisted the doorknob. The dread clamped like a vise around his chest cavity when he closed the door behind him, shutting her out.

ᠪ

Luke woke with a fierce headache and a raging attack of conscience.

Beside him, the bed was empty. With a groan, he left the sanctuary of slumber. In need of a jolt, he pulled his blue jeans on over his boxers and trudged to the kitchen. The carafe was missing from its perch in the coffeemaker, so he shuffled into the dining room, and at the buffet, filled a mug with steaming coffee.

Voices carried to him from the foyer.

"It's so peaceful here." He didn't recognize the woman's voice.

"It is." Mina said. "I'm so excited about this idea."

He scratched the scruff on his cheek and wandered closer.

A waiflike woman with brown hair stood beside Mina beneath the crystal chandelier. "I'm not sure which is more beautiful, the property, or the house itself. It's the perfect place to heal after a trauma."

Luke froze. His sluggish brain grappled with the

meaning of their words.

"I can't believe you renovated this place all by yourself," the waif said.

Mina smiled. "I had help. My cousin helped with the decorating. She owns the house now and runs the inn."

Max bounded down the stairs and swept past them on his way into the dining room. He grunted at Luke when he passed by.

Mina noticed him then. "I didn't hear you come in. Luke, this is Chloe Smallwood. She's a counselor. Her office is downtown, not far from the station. Chloe, this is Luke."

That was all she said by way of his introduction, as if the counselor already knew exactly who he was.

His mind raced with panicked thoughts. This had Noah written all over it. He'd told his brother too much and the bastard had manufactured an opportunity to get a head shrink in front of Luke as quickly as possible.

"It's nice to meet you." Chloe held out her tiny hand to him.

He folded his arms over his chest. "What are you doing here?"

"Uh, I was just showing her the house," Mina said.

"She's seen it."

Both women stilled.

An apple in hand, Max appeared at Luke's side. "Everything all right?"

"Everything's fucking fine." Luke's muscles bunched.

"Chloe's interested in reserving the house for an event." A slight tremble tinged Mina's voice.

"What kind of an event?"

Max crunched into the apple, the noise like the crack of a firework exploding.

The counselor's mouth was moving. "I want to establish a retreat program for persons suffering post-traumatic stress disorder and other trauma-related disruptions."

Her words embedded like a sliver under his skin. "Is that right?"

Mina's nervous gaze darted between him and Chloe. "She's created a program based on texts written thousands of years ago describing treatments for ancient warriors returning from battle. Cool, huh?"

"We're not interested."

He didn't understand what was happening to him, or why panic roared through him. All he knew was that he wanted the counselor and her damn knowing eyes gone.

"Since when did you take over event booking, too?" Max wanted to know.

Hectic color stained Mina's cheeks. "When I mentioned it to Emily, she was excited about the idea."

Luke pushed into Chloe's space. "It's time for you to leave. Now."

The color drained from her tiny face.

Max slid between them. "Why don't I show her the way out?" His features carefully blanked, he held Luke's gaze. "Would that be all right?"

Luke gave him a curt nod.

Max placed a protective hand on the small of Chloe's back and they disappeared through the front door.

Luke sensed Mina's huge, shock-filled eyes on him. A wave of shame and regret stole his breath and nearly dropped him to his knees.

Without another word, he strode from the room.

Chapter Twenty-Seven

Winter hit the island hard. Snow fell from the sky in a relentless onslaught and the churning waters of the lake calmed, crept, and finally froze. By mid-February, ice shrouded the harbor and coastline, and a bone-deep chill had settled in Emily's body.

Wrapped in the quilt from her bed, she sat at the kitchen table and stared unseeing into her coffee. At her elbow sat an invitation from Max to the premiere of his movie. It'd debuted at a film festival in Traverse City the day before, but she hadn't attended.

At four months pregnant, her belly had begun to show and she couldn't imagine a dress that wouldn't make her look like a bright-haired whale. Not to mention, as the lake iced over, the ferry had begun to run infrequently and she wasn't sure she'd have been able to get off the island.

Mainly, she didn't have the heart for going.

Loneliness gnawed at her as Luke continued to withdraw, and a tender wound had formed on her heart. Her only solace, and it wasn't much of one, was the fact that by now she'd been married to Luke twice as long as Natalie had.

A noise sounded at the back door and a moment later Mina floated into the room.

"Hey, Em, what's up?" At the table, she flipped open the box from the bakery. "Are there any glazed ones in here?"

The tears that came too often with too little to provoke them threatened.

Mina abandoned the box and sank into a chair. "What is it? Did I say something?"

Emily shook her head. "It's Luke, he's... he's m-m-miserable."

Mina didn't disagree. "Maybe it's stress at work. His job must be hard."

Emily nodded. "I've tried talking to him about that, but he shuts m-me out. Even before the wedding..." Her fears rose up to consume her. "Wh-what if it isn't work? Wh-what if he didn't want to m-marry me?"

Mina shook her head. "No way. Luke isn't about to do something he doesn't want to do. Not without a gun pointed to his head."

Emily blanched.

Mina's eyes grew wide with panic. "I'm sorry. I didn't mean the baby..."

When Emily spoke, her voice barely rose above a whisper. "You know?"

"I know. Small town and all that." Mina's eyes shimmered. "Why didn't you tell me?" A twinge of hurt threaded her tone.

"I wanted to, but... I didn't want to hurt you... after..."

Mina's throat worked. "After I miscarried. I

understand. I do."

"I'm s-sorry, Mina. For everything."

"Me, too." Mina squeezed her arm.

Their misery hung heavy in the room. Emily's heart ached to see the anguish on her cousin's face. She didn't know any words to take away Mina's pain, but she wished to make her understand, at least, that she hadn't shut her out to be cruel.

"I was afraid if I told y-y-you the truth, then I'd be forced to think about why I was marrying Luke." Emily's voice wavered and she cleared her throat. "And if I thought too m-much about it, I'd have to admit the p-pregnancy was the only reason he p-proposed, and I was so desperate and scared and lonely, I let myself believe his p-proposal was real."

Mina lifted her shoulders. "He's a guy. Maybe he doesn't show it, but he cares about you, Em. I can see that he does."

Emily sniffled and nodded, wanting with all her heart to believe Mina's words.

A determined frown came over Mina's face. "We're married to brothers and that makes us sisters. We have to promise each other, no matter what, we'll be there for each other to talk, or listen, or plot revenge. Whatever is necessary."

Her words plucked Emily like a tuning fork and startled a laugh from her.

Since her mom became ill, she'd had no one with which she'd shared her inner world. Not her heart or her fears. Nothing of her true self. Even before that, her social phobias caused her to hold herself back, keeping people away so that they couldn't hurt her. If they didn't know her, the real her, they couldn't reject her.

Harrison's cruelty had changed her at the core and made her suspect she lacked some essential quality, which made her unlovable. So she made sure no one ever got close enough to confirm her fear one way or the other.

She'd moved to the island because she craved a connection with Mina. Along the way, she'd collected a husband and a baby. But how could any of them come to love her if she never let them know her?

The real her.

Though she'd thought so at one time, she now knew Luke wasn't without insecurities. Maybe he was afraid of opening up to her. Maybe, if she opened her heart to him, he'd do the same, and then he'd begin to trust her with his worries. Maybe, if he knew she loved him, he'd open his heart to her. Maybe her love would help him conquer whatever demons chased him.

Maybe it'd make him happy.

And maybe, just maybe, he'd love her back.

An urgency she couldn't explain gripped her. She pushed to her feet. "I have to go."

Mina looked up at her. "Right now?"

"I have to find Luke. There's s-something I have to tell him."

She couldn't wait a single moment more to tell him what was in her heart, not when he was hurting and it might give him some comfort.

She didn't notice the wrinkle of worry creasing Mina's brow.

Three hours later, frustration eroded her fantasy of rescuing him. He wouldn't answer her texts, or pick up her call when she did the previously unthinkable and phoned him.

She had to find him right away. But how?

Her spine snapped straight when a thought struck.

CB

Emily crawled down Main Street in the sedan, her fifth

pass through downtown in the last hour. As she approached the traffic light, it switched to yellow and she slowed the car to a stop. Craning her neck, she peered down the side streets in search of his SUV. Dejected, she slung back in her seat.

That's when she saw him, pulling up to the stoplight opposite her.

Her heart tripped into an erratic rhythm.

She used to pray for courage. When kids teased her, or her teachers grew frustrated with what they viewed as laziness or defiance, she'd imagined saying bold things. Something clever and quick to knock them back or prove their assumptions wrong.

When her mom grew sick and the doctors kept saying there was nothing they could do, Emily prayed for the courage to fight them. To demand they not give up on Audrey. On them.

She hadn't found the strength to be brave then, but this time would be different. No matter how difficult, she'd find a way. For him.

The light flicked to green, but she stayed with her foot on the brake pedal while Luke and two more cars progressed through the intersection. Behind her, a car horn blared.

Chewing her bottom lip, she eased the Jetta forward, then whipped the steering wheel hard to the left and executed a U-turn beneath the traffic light.

The sedan following her rocked to a jerky stop. More horns blared. Emily ignored the over-permed, gray-haired woman flipping her the bird as she passed by and pressed down on the gas pedal with steady pressure until she caught up with Luke's SUV.

She continued to push down on the accelerator, nudging the nose of her car as close to his rear bumper as she dared. His head bobbled back and forth between the road and the rearview mirror. He lifted a hand, as if in question.

With a hard stomp on the accelerator, she swallowed her fear and swung the car out into the passing lane. She breezed by him, topping out at forty-two miles per hour.

Seventeen miles per hour over the posted legal limit.

A stop sign came into view and she slowed, but clearly did not come to a complete stop, before turning right onto Lakeshore Drive. In her rearview, he stopped at the sign, and paused, as if contemplating whether to follow.

She couldn't give him the option not to.

She punched the accelerator. The Jetta's engine whimpered and the car lurched forward on the winding coastal drive.

He pursued.

She had him right where she wanted him. Her sole focus shifted to the upcoming turn. At the last possible moment, she cranked the steering wheel hard and–without indicating her intention with the car's turn signal–whipped into her driveway.

In front of the house, she threw the car in park and scrambled out from behind the wheel.

His SUV ambled up the long, winding drive until finally he rolled to a stop beside her. A pair of mirrored sunglasses masked his gaze and the white stick of a lollipop dangled from his lips.

With a soft electric whir, he lowered the window. "What are you doing?"

She swallowed the lump of terror that rose up to clog her throat.

You're a piranha.

The memory twisted.

He'd touched more than her body. He'd stolen so many of her fears and disappointments. Destroyed her misconceptions about herself. No matter what happened between them, she'd be eternally grateful to him for that.

With her nervous hesitation, he shot from the car. He

yanked the sunglasses off his face and green eyes knocked into her. "What is it? What's wrong?"

"I-I-I-I love y-you." The words burst from her to hang in the air between them.

He stood frozen for a long painful moment. Then he eased slightly back. Away from her.

In the heavy silence, her skin stretched tight and the air passages in her lungs constricted. "I just w-wanted you to know. Y-y-you don't have to say it back."

"That wasn't part of the deal."

She flinched as though struck, and stumbled back a step. He didn't love her. He liked her, and possibly, he even cared for her, but he didn't love her. And the feelings she thought she'd seen weren't his feelings, but her own feelings reflecting back at her.

He. Didn't. Love. Her.

Harrison was right.

"I didn't deceive you, Emily."

"I know."

She wanted to be mad at him for making her believe, but she couldn't. He hadn't done this, she had. He'd proposed because he was an honorable man, and she'd let herself believe his proposal was real because she couldn't bear to think otherwise.

He'd proposed, but it was a lie, and she'd let herself believe the lie because she wanted so badly to belong to someone. Anyone. Even if they didn't belong to her.

With his silence, a chill seeped under her skin.

Backing away, she started to shake. "I'm sorry. I m-misunderstood. It's m-my fault. I thought I could do this, but I was wrong."

"What do you mean?"

She raced up the porch steps, fumbling for her keys.

His hand came down over the lock to stop her from unbolting the door. "What does that mean, you thought you could do this?"

She didn't want to be near him while the truth twisted and tormented her. "I'm going away."

A long moment passed in which he didn't speak or move. His face changed and a Luke she didn't recognize emerged. Not the smooth charmer or the cool cop. This Luke was wild. Frantic.

And angry.

So very, very angry.

Rage rolled off him in waves and threatened to pull her down with the undertow. "You're leaving me?"

"I don't w-want to be the only o-o-one in love."

Hot fury blazed in his eyes. "Have I not given you enough? Have I mistreated you in some way?"

"No, of course not."

"Then stop this." He turned toward his car. "I'll see you for dinner."

She watched his back as he retreated down the porch steps. Natalie's words ricocheted around in her mind.

He isn't capable of love.

Maybe it was true and he'd never love her. He'd never loved any of them. Not Kate. Or Natalie. Certainly not Emily.

"No." With vicious swipes, she wiped the wetness from her cheeks. "I want more."

"More what?" His voice broke with his frustration.

"More of y-you."

His eyes glittered. "You want me to cut out my heart and give it to you?"

"Yes." The word flew from her. "I want your heart."

All the hot fury in him cooled in an instant. "That isn't going to happen."

Her heart cracked open and she gasped with the pain.

His head bent, and it took her a moment to realize he'd become riveted by something at her feet. She looked down to see that morning's newspaper. On the front page was a picture of her house beneath large black typeface.

He crouched down and rescued the paper from the snow. Reading, he unfolded it.

His face darkened.

When his gaze snapped to her face, she shrunk back. A muscle ticked along his jaw. He turned the paper, holding it over his chest.

The headline screamed at her.

House of Porn?
Allegations surround controversial new movie filmed on Thief Island

Words jammed in her throat.

He spoke in a low, dangerous tone. "You lied to me."

"No. I didn't m-m-mean to. M-Max, after he changed the script I was w-w-worried, but—"

Betrayal slashed across his features.

She wanted to scream, to beg him to understand, to say all the words, any words, that would make things right between them again.

As always, no words were available to her.

He whipped the paper to the ground with a violent snap.

Cold green eyes lashed her. "You're right, it's best if you go."

Chapter Twenty-Eight

The days passed in a haze of despair and whiskey, with sprinklings of work and sleep.

He stared into the bottle of amber liquid, seeing only tormented whiskey-colored eyes. His grip tightened on the bottle's neck.

Whiskey mixed with agony. The memory of her soft moans invaded his mind and tunneled through his veins.

She'd lied to him. It was the one thing he couldn't tolerate.

Through the murky alleys of his alcohol-addled mind, he fought to recall what she had admitted to, exactly.

Suspicions. She'd had them. Maybe.

He'd glimpsed the guilt in her eyes and, drowning under the weight of her abandonment, he'd lashed out. As long as she was there, he had a chance of finding his way out of the dark tunnel. Eventually.

But if she were gone, there was no hope.

So like a snarling dog with a bone, he'd latched on to the idea that she'd lied to him because it was far easier to send her away than it was to watch her leave him.

No matter how they'd come to it, the fact was, she was gone, and with the loss, something inside him had snapped.

Was it the same something that'd twisted his dad's mind after Luke's mom died? It seemed likely, for the weakness was in the DNA, whether or not Noah believed it.

The fear had formed early and resided deep in Luke's heart, that no matter how far he ran, or how sophisticated the mask of charm, he might never be able to escape his fate. He was not one of the good guys, and one day that truth would be revealed.

This was that day.

Because she wasn't there.

Because he'd told her to get out and confirmed his fear.

He was weak, too weak to overcome the coding of his DNA.

He lifted the bottle to his lips. The liquor's stench assaulted his nostrils. He didn't want whiskey.

He wanted his wife.

When the sun peeked above the horizon, he stared into its fiery flame.

The bottle sat untouched at his feet.

ڃ

Get up.

I can't.

You must. The baby needs you to be strong and well.

So Emily got up. She moved through the empty house with heavy legs and a shattered heart, like one of the soulless zombies in Max's movie.

A groan of disgust ripped through her as she recalled the article in the newspaper.

Written by a local journalist who'd attended Max's movie premiere, the column had raised an array of disturbing questions. Was the sexually charged erotic drama a form of artistic expression, or did it cross the line into pornography? Was the filmmaker, a shadowy figure whose mysterious past was locked away behind a closed juvenile record, a budding porn king?

Viewers would have to decide for themselves, the article concluded, noting the controversial film, having gone straight to DVD, was available for purchase at most retail outlets.

She closed her eyes and rubbed her temples.

Regrets. That was all she had now. She should not have trusted Max and she should have told Luke about her suspicions when he'd asked.

Instead, she'd acted like a coward and it'd cost her the only man she'd ever loved. Though in truth, she'd likely lost Luke long before Max and his movie came into play. Or maybe he was never really hers to lose.

All the heartaches she'd endured in her life hadn't prepared her for the devastation of his rejection. Better that it happened now, she told herself, before the baby came and it was too late. Or too hard. Or too... sad.

A soft knock sounded on the door to her suite. Emily climbed off the sofa and shuffled to the door.

Mina's big blue eyes swept her from head to toe. "How are you doing? Did you talk to Luke?"

In answer, silent tears streamed down Emily's cheeks.

Mina wrapped Emily in her arms and hugged her, a deep-tissue squeeze that set loose the flood of Emily's tears.

೫

The jingle of his cell phone stirred him from a restless sleep.

"Yeah." His throat croaked with dryness.

"You're late, Detective Nolan." Chief's voice crackled over the connection. "Get your ass out of bed and to my office. Now."

Given Cynthia's tone and his general apathy, Luke skipped the shower and drove to the station. Once there, he ignored Newberry at the front desk and took a straight path to the Chief's office.

As he approached, Sloane slipped through the door.

A sneer curled the bastard's lip. "Let's see you sweet talk your way out of this one."

Luke's hands began to shake and he knotted his fists into tight balls. Cynthia looked up from her desk when Luke knocked. Her expression turned sour.

She lifted a copy of the Thief Island Gazette. "Did you know about this?"

"Did I know what exactly?"

"That this movie was being made?"

"I knew *a* movie was being made."

"The production of pornography is against city ordinance."

"I know that, too."

She eased back and folded her hands over her abdomen. "Were you or were you not aware that a pornographic film—?"

He interjected. "Alleged pornographic film."

Cynthia heaved a sigh. "An alleged pornographic film was being made at a house owned by your wife?"

He scratched his head. "There are a lot of questions packed into that one sentence."

Cynthia leveled him with a look. "A warrant has been issued for your wife's arrest."

Her statement hit him straight in the chest. A kill shot.

"How? The film isn't even porn. Who–?" Luke stopped talking when realization struck.

Sloane.

Luke cursed. All this for a bar fight? What a fucking pussy.

"The charges are serious, Detective."

He held her gaze while panic rioted through his veins. "The charges are bullshit."

"Still, as Lieutenant, this could be problematic for you."

He blinked several times. "That'd be true, if I were Lieutenant."

She leaned back in her chair and folded her hands over her abdomen. "I thought I'd introduce you as such when you're honored at the ball next month."

He bit back a curse. He'd forgotten about that stupid ball with its stupid award. Of course, he'd forgotten.

Well, shit.

"Let's try to resolve this matter with your wife by then, shall we, Lieutenant?"

℅

His knuckles white on the steering wheel, Luke raced to the inn.

Truth be told, the thought of arresting Emily held some appeal. At least he'd get to be near her, and touch her again.

But that was a little like finding the silver lining in a tornado cloud.

With a severe crank of the wheel, he barreled up her driveway and skid to a stop on the gravel. He stomped up the porch stairs and pounded on the front door with his fist. When she didn't open, he pounded again and bellowed her name.

Nothing.

Frustrated impotence roared through him and he leaned over the porch balustrade to peer through the pristine glass of the bay window. The one replaced only a few months ago after the rock crashed through it.

As he stared into the empty house, the possibility of life without her opened before him like an abyss. The truth slammed into with the force of a cannon blast.

Loving her didn't' make him weak. Losing her did.

When he met her, he was only half a man, but she'd looked beyond his face, into his heart, and found the other pieces of him. The parts he'd thought lost, or missing. The parts that, when reclaimed, made him whole. Made him the man he wanted to be, but wasn't.

Not without her.

Turning away from the house, his gaze searched the premises with frantic desperation. Through the haze of his panic, he realized her sedan was nowhere in sight.

He plunged through the snow to the carriage house and banged on the door.

When his fists summoned a response, he growled at his sister-in-law. "Where is she?"

Mina's blue eyes grew huge in her small face as her gaze swept over him. He hadn't slept and he couldn't recall the last time he'd eaten. Or showered.

"Who?"

His fists clenched at his sides. "Do not fuck with me. I need to find my wife."

She turned her back to him. At the dining table, she dropped into a chair and took a tiny bite of a bagel.

"There's a warrant out for her arrest."

The bagel rattled onto the plate. "What for?"

"I need you to tell me where she is."

"So you can arrest her?"

His gaze slid away.

Her expression pinched with annoyance. "Sorry, I can't help you."

He bit down on the volcanic anger seething inside him. "You wouldn't aid and abet an alleged criminal, would you?"

"Damn straight I would."

"I want to help her. Please, tell me where she is."

Her features softened. "Even if I wanted to, I can't. I have no idea where she went."

A frustrated groan tore from him and he slumped into a chair at the table. "It's like she's vanished. I've searched this entire island and she's nowhere to be found."

"Oh, she's not on the island. She left."

His hand arrested in his hair midsweep, elbow pointed to the ceiling. "She what?"

"She left the island. She said she might go to Boston or New Orleans. Maybe Seattle. I don't think she'd go back to Tucson," she mused. "Maybe check with Haven."

He stared, mute, while his world crashed down around him.

She couldn't leave. He wasn't ready to let her go. They might be estranged, but he expected to be able to see her around town. To be tormented by her nearness.

Mina misunderstood his silence.

"Haven Callahan. Her friend. She was at your wedding."

"I know who Haven is," he snapped. "When did she leave?"

Mina shrugged. "After she talked to you–"

"That was three days ago! She could be anywhere in the fucking world by now."

He'd lost her. Panic rose up to choke him and he gripped the edge of the table to keep the world from dumping him over.

"Don't worry. She said she'll be back."

"When? When will she be back?"

"She didn't say, but she was adamant." Her voice gentled. "She won't keep the baby from you."

The words twisted like a knife. He cursed and dropped his head into his hands.

"You know, you can be a good dad without being married to her."

He reared back. "Why does everyone think that's the only reason I married her?"

Her cheeks flushed a deep shade of pink but she held his gaze directly. "Isn't it?"

With the upwelling of molten fury, he surged to his feet.

The muted buzz of a vibrating cell phone cut short his explosion of anger.

Mina snatched the phone off the table and read the display. He watched her face change.

"Who is it?" He lunged forward. "Is it Emily?"

Mina twisted to keep the phone from his grasp. She pressed the button to accept the call and raised the phone to her ear. "Hey, Em, what's up? Where are you?"

Mina swatted at his hand. Her brow crinkled. "Slow down. What's wrong? Are you okay?"

The blood curdled in his veins.

"Yes, I'm alone." She bit her lip on the lie.

As she listened, her face drained of color. She lifted a hand to cover her lips. "No, I know. I know you didn't do it. What can I do?" She listened. "Okay. Okay, I'm on my way."

She didn't hang up and after a beat of silence, her eyes locked with his. "I promise, I won't tell Luke."

With a shaking hand, she disconnected the call, and he braced himself before she uttered the awful, ugly words.

She gulped. "Emily's been arrested."

Chapter Twenty-Nine

Thank God.

It was his first thought. Though blasphemous, at least now he could get to her.

Mina crammed her feet into her snow boots. "She sounds really freaked out."

"How long has she been there?" he asked, his feet already moving.

He had to get to her.

"I don't know. Not long I don't think." Mina snatched her coat off a hook by the door and pulled the door shut behind them.

A snarl of emotions, intense and chaotic, roared through him. He had no control over them. "Why the hell didn't she call me?"

"I don't know." She chased him down the porch stairs and caught up to him in the side yard. "Remember she asked me not to tell you about this? Why don't I go alone and—"

He slammed the car door on her words and jammed the key into the ignition. She fell into the passenger seat a split second before he punched the accelerator.

His pregnant wife sat locked in a jail cell. Was she scared? Hurt or hungry? Had she slept at all or had worry stolen her peace?

So consumed by his racing thoughts, he was vaguely aware of Mina talking into her cell phone while he drove.

He whipped into the station parking lot and stalked up the front walk, his sister-in-law dogging his heels. Noah waited for them at the front entrance, a cell phone pressed to his ear.

"What do we know?" He angled the phone away from his mouth. "Anything?"

Luke gave a shake of his head and swept inside the police station.

At the front desk, Newberry's head came up. When he saw Luke's face, he paled.

"Where is she?" Luke barked.

Newberry didn't get a chance to answer. The door to the jail cell opened and Sloane emerged."Ah, good, I'm glad you're here. Maybe you can get our little jailbird to sing." A pained grimace contorted Sloane's bullish features. "Not much of a talker, is she?"

Luke's hand shot out and clamped around the bastard's neck. "You son of a bitch. You did this to her?"

Sloane's eyes grew wide with shock and a bemused smile curled his lips. "Just doing my job." The words rasped from him.

Luke wanted to kill. He could do it, too. All he had to do was squeeze until Justin's airway passages became blocked, or his larynx was crushed. It wouldn't be hard and Luke wouldn't regret it, even if it made him a murderer, like his father.

"What'd you do?" Luke asked. "Call your daddy? Get him to issue a warrant even though you have shit for evidence?"

From Sloane's expression, Luke knew he hit upon the truth. "I have evidence. I have the movie."

"That doesn't prove shit." Luke's grip tightened. "She had nothing to do with that movie."

"It's her house," Justin wheezed. "She's an accomplice, at least."

Justin's eyes bulged and Luke watched the fear stir in them.

"Luke." Noah's voice pierced the haze of his fury. "Emily needs you."

With a hard shove, Luke knocked Sloane against the cement wall.

"Buzz me in." He barked the order to Newberry over the sound of Sloane's coughing.

The latch remained locked. Luke glowered at the rookie over his shoulder. "Buzz. Me. In. Now."

The door to the station entrance swung open and Cynthia shuffled through with a chilly breeze.

Her serious dark eyes quickly assessed the gathered crowd before clamping on Luke. "Is there a problem here, Officer Newberry?"

"No, ma'am."

With a harsh buzz, the latch gave way. Luke plunged into the jail.

"You can't go back there—"

He ignored Cynthia and stalked down the row of empty cells until he found her.

She sat on the gray-covered cot, her legs folded in front of her. Her head came up when he said her name. Her eyes looked huge in her pale face.

He drowned in whiskey.

Her feet eased to the floor and she tipped forward, but didn't stand.

He gripped the iron bars. "Are you all right?"

The cot creaked when she pushed to her feet.

"Are you hurt?" he asked.

With small, hesitant steps, she crossed to him. Her hands came up and she wrapped her fingers around the bars, a fraction below his white-knuckled fists.

The sleeves of her sweatshirt drooped and exposed her wrists. No marks or bruises marred her skin. A slow hiss of relief slipped from him. "You're not hurt?"

She shook her head.

He covered her hands, which felt cold and small beneath his. "You're okay?"

She nodded.

"Then why are you crying, sweetheart?"

Her mouth moved as she struggled for words. "Y-you came. For m-me?"

The pain wrenching his heart pulled a groan from him. She'd thought he wouldn't come for her.

He shoved both hands between the bars and gripped her head in his hands. "You are my wife." His voice croaked. "You are my life."

A broken sob tore from her.

"I will always come for you." He wiped away her tears with the palms of his hands.

"B-but y-you said—"

"I know. I know what I said. I was lying." He swallowed his heart with a painful gulp. "I can't lose you, Em. I'm not strong enough. I thought if I could stop myself from falling in love with you, it wouldn't hurt so much. But I couldn't stop myself..."

He swallowed her sobs when he kissed her, a wholly unsatisfying kiss with the cell bars pressing into the sides of his face. Her tears tasted salty on his tongue.

"Detective Nolan," Cynthia's big voice boomed. "What do you think you're doing?"

"That's his wife." Sloane nipped at her heels.

Cynthia's steps slowed, and she glared down at Sloane. He squirmed.

Her gaze shifted to Luke, and then to Emily.

Luke straightened away from the jail. "She was not directly involved in the film's production. I verified the film permits myself—"

"You knew your wife was making a porno?" Sloane crowed. "That makes you an accessory. I suspected you of a lot of things, Nolan, but not a pornographer. Never that."

Cynthia rolled her eyes. "Stand down, Justin." She fixed Luke with a pointed look. "I trust Mrs. Nolan's lawyer will want to help sort all this out when he or she arrives."

"He should be here any minute." At least, Luke hoped Noah had called Shea. "But for the record, this whole thing is a mistake. Officer Sloane has a vendetta and he's using my wife to try to get to me."

"That's a lie," Sloane spat.

"Why don't you go check to see if Mrs. Nolan's lawyer has arrived?"

"But—"

"Do it now, Justin."

With a scowl, Sloane slithered away, but when he pulled back the steel cellblock door, a surge of noise filled the jail.

"Oh, for the love," Cynthia muttered.

Luke was aware of Sloane's protests before the Mayor of Thief Island burst into the jail. A crush of bodies followed Drew Alexander down the hall toward them. Shea nipped at his heels while Honey and Mina hurried along behind them. Noah, his arm flung across Newberry's shoulders, trailed at the rear.

Drew held his arms wide as he approached. "Chief Brown, I apologize for my obstinacy, but I wanted to make you aware of the discussions which took place at our last city council meeting."

"With all due respect, Mr. Mayor, this is not a good time," Cynthia said. "If you'll wait in my office, I'll be right with you."

Emily squeezed his hand and Luke looked down into her face. His heart lifted, and unbelievably, a smile found its way to his lips.

"I won't take more than a few minutes of your time," Drew was saying. "It involves a change to city ordinance banning the production of certain salacious material."

Cynthia's expression turned wry. "Is that right?"

"Did you know this island had an ordinance on the books which was so narrowly written that several films honored over the years by the Academy Awards likely could not have legally been made here?"

"I can honestly say I did not know that," Cynthia deadpanned.

"It's shocking, isn't it? To think, such censorship was allowed to crush artistic expression. Not to mention the missed opportunities for economic growth. With all our diverse little island has to offer, from beaches and sand dunes to forests and an idyllic downtown, we're a desirable locale for many a filmmaker." Drew slipped his hands into the front pockets of his slacks. "Anyway, I put forth a measure to immediately rectify this gross oversight, and after a spirited debate, the council voted to temporarily lift the ban. We're gonna see how it goes. Even ol' Thackery approved the measure."

"What a wise action," Cynthia said dryly.

Drew flashed a surprisingly charming smile. "You flatter. Which I'm sure has nothing to do with the fact that I appoint you to your post, Chief Brown."

"You can't do that," Sloane seethed.

Drew sliced him with a look. "Actually, I can. That's how governance works." He lifted an eyebrow at Cynthia. "Maybe it's time we reevaluate the officer continuing education program."

Cynthia executed a weak smile. "I think everything here is under control. Thank you, Mr. Mayor. Why don't we talk in my office for a moment? I can update you on a few changes in our office."

"You're still going to give him that stupid award?" Sloane gaped at her. "He doesn't deserve it. He's not a hero, he's a criminal."

"That's not t-true!" The words burst from Emily and all attention swung to her. She shrunk back. "No o-o-one wh-wh-who knows him w-w-would say something so b-blatantly untrue."

The torturous stutter left a gash on his heart.

Her eyes darted back and forth in full panic for a moment, and then latched on to his face. "He's a good m-m-man, and a good cop. He's the b-best m-m-man I've ever known. B-because he cares about p-people, and-and-and he w-w-would do anything to h-help them."

He understood how wounding the moment must be for her. "Emily, it's okay."

"He's the b-best kind of m-man." She cast a measuring look at Sloane. "A real m-m-man. He'd do anything to h-h-help o-others and I love h-him for that."

Her declaration hit him like a punch in the gut, and as she stuttered and stammered her way through more horrid platitudes, something inside him shifted. Changed.

His heart filled. There was no stopping the onslaught. It spilled over, drenching him in the knowledge of her love, and he realized if a woman as smart and sweet as Emily Cole Nolan thought him worthy of love, then he must be.

All the self-doubt and hatred that'd built up over the past year—no, over a lifetime—vanished like the stars at dawn.

"He gave a h-homeless m-man shoes."

"Aw, how sweet." Sloane's tongue dripped with

sarcasm. "He's a cop, not a charity worker."

"I know that," Emily said. "B-but cops are supposed to serve and p-protect, right? Not only arrest people. He deserves that award, and-and he deserves to be Lieutenant."

Disgust curled Sloane's lip when he looked to Cynthia. "You're giving him the job?"

"No, I'm not," Cynthia said.

Emily flinched. "Please don't punish him for my actions. We're not staying married."

Terror seized him. "The hell we aren't," he growled.

Cynthia covered her laughter with a cough. "Are you going to tell them or am I?"

Luke rolled his shoulders. "I didn't get the job."

"I offered the position to Detective Nolan," Cynthia said. "He turned me down. Not only that, but he resigned from the force."

"*What?*" Emily's voice pitched to shrill levels. "Why?"

"I believe the reason given had something to do with you, Mrs. Nolan."

Luke opened his mouth to protest.

"What was it you said, Detective?" Cynthia was enjoying herself now. "If I laid a finger on your wife you'd cut off my balls and feed them to the patrons at your brother's pub?"

Drew snickered.

"Then he tendered his resignation, effective the moment I kissed his hairy white ass. Is that about right, Detective?"

Luke scratched a phantom itch on his collarbone. "Yeah, something like that."

"I don't understand." Emily gazed up at him with huge brown eyes.

"I need to step away for a while." He reached through the cell bars and stroked her cheek. "But you're going to have to start paying me for my services."

Cynthia clapped her hands together. "If any of you are Mrs. Nolan's attorney, can you step to the front desk so we can resolve this matter? Officer Newberry, can you assist with the release?"

Newberry slipped out of the jail, and a moment later, the latch to Emily's cell gave way. Luke swung open the door and she shot into his arms.

He cradled her head in both his hands and kissed the tiny freckle on her cheekbone, under her right eye. "We're not getting a divorce. I'll never agree to it."

A watery laugh bubbled out of her as he dropped more kisses on her face, her forehead, and the tip of her nose.

She turned her face away, and to their attentive audience said, "His ass isn't hairy."

Chapter Thirty

The temperature climbed above fifty degrees and the rich, loamy scent of spring filled the air. Outside to greet their new guests, Emily shucked her sweatshirt and turned her face toward the sun. Only a few months ago, fifty degrees had hit her like an arctic blast. Now, warmth spread through her and eased the aching from her bones.

Luke bounded down the porch stairs. The shadows that'd stalked him seemed to have lifted.

One hand slipped around her waist while the other smoothed over her large belly. "How's he doing today?"

"He's active. I think he's excited, too."

An ultrasound showed the baby to be developing well and in perfect health. It also showed they were having a boy. With the news, the wonder-terror had returned with the intensity of a thousand white-hot suns. What did she know about raising a little boy?

But then she remembered she didn't have to do it alone. Luke was there, and he had enough confidence for ten people. And she had Luke's brothers, and Mina, and Isobel was becoming a dear friend very quickly.

One thing Emily knew for certain, her baby would be loved.

Luke took a long taste of her mouth. "And how are you today, Mrs. Nolan?"

She laid her head on his shoulder. "I'm perfect."

A car turned and ambled up the drive. When it rolled to a stop in front of the house, Luke went around to the driver-side door.

Leo unfolded from the car.

At his appearance, Emily's heart squeezed. He was thin, gaunt even, and his eyes appeared sunken in his too-thin face.

He was the first of their weekend guests, though Leo would be staying with them after the others left next week.

It'd be their third time hosting the retreat. Luke had worked with Chloe Smallwood to plan the program and bring it to fruition. This weekend's group was their most diverse yet and included military and law enforcement personnel, as well as rape survivors.

Warriors from every battlefield, Luke had said when he first told her about the idea.

The brothers stood at the car for a time, talking, until finally, they moved to join her on the front porch.

A light twinkled in Luke's emerald eyes when he smiled at her. "You'll never guess what happened."

"What happened?" she repeated.

"They lost Leo's luggage."

Leo glowered at him, though his scowl held no bite. "He told me I'm lucky."

Luke lifted one shoulder. "You could've found your things thrown all over the airport terminal."

Heat rushed into Emily's cheeks. "Speaking of, y-you still haven't returned BOB to m-me."

Luke slung his arm over her shoulders and pulled her close into his side. "You and BOB are through. I'm entirely too insecure to share you with another man."

"Who's Bob?" Leo asked.

Emily laughed and slipped her arms around Luke's waist as they walked with Leo into the house.

It struck her then that her whole world, when snuggled tight, fit inside of her arms.

♋

Luke lay in their bed, awaiting her return.

When finally she waddled back into the bedroom, her belly heavy and round in front of her, his heart squeezed.

He stretched, filching a prepackaged cookie from the plate she carried. "Hey, guess what? There's a plot."

"Really?" The mattress dipped when she climbed onto the bed and a wisp of her scent teased his nostrils. "What's happening?"

"So Serena has made the tough choice to sell her virginity to the highest bidder."

Emily's pouty mouth twisted into a wry frown. "Tough choice, huh?"

"Her little brother has a rare form of cancer and she has to come up with the money to pay for his treatment."

"Okay, that is a good reason." She adjusted a pillow behind her back.

He bit into a cookie and hit play to resume the movie. "The highest bidder is some old dude named Roger and she's arrived at his beach house mansion to make good on the deal." He held up the cookie. "You know, these aren't that bad."

"I told you so."

He placed one hand on her bare leg. "I've learned

there's a place for cheap and easy in my life after all."

She slapped his arm. "What happened when Serena got to Roger's mansion? Did they do it?"

Luke shook his head. "Not yet. Roger's son, Chase, saw her first. Now he's pretending to be Roger."

Emily snuggled down under the quilt. "How stupid is Serena if she can't tell the difference between a sixty-year-old and a twenty-year-old?"

The scene changed to a dark night on the beach.

Luke frowned at the TV. "They weren't supposed to film on the beach. That's a permit violation."

"Max appealed and won. I think Drew may have used his influence on that one, too."

"He's a real servant to the public, isn't he?"

On the TV screen, Honey emerged from the lake. Water sloughed off her naked body. On shore, a man waited for her.

Emily peered at the TV. "Is that a boom mike?"

"You're looking at the scenery?"

"I've already seen Honey naked. I gather from your familiarity with her resume, so have you."

"Lucky for you, I don't get tired of looking at naked women."

Honey's voice carried through the TV. "I seem to have misplaced my clothes."

"You don't need them." Will snatched Honey to him and kissed her.

"I like this guy." Luke took another bite of his cookie.

Emily frowned. "His delivery isn't the only thing that's a little stiff."

With his bark of laughter, he choked on a chocolate chip.

Soft moans and grunts offset the slippery sounds of their kissing.

"Are they actually doing it?"

"Max told me Will's wearing a skin-colored banana

hammock." Her nose crinkled adorably. "Knowing them kind of ruins it."

Luke tilted his head to the side as the couple on the screen rolled in the sand. "Yeah, you're right, it kinda does."

He hit the Fast-Forward button until the scene changed. Honey and Will had moved to the library and were doing it on the desk.

"Do you think we missed a plot point or something?" he asked.

Emily flushed pink all over. "I thought the skinny dipping was just a coincidence." She tucked a soft strand of her light hair behind her ear. "You don't think...? Max didn't... know that we... Did he?"

Luke frowned, chasing his memory. "Was he even here for your little skinny dip?"

Her shoulders relaxed. "Yeah, you're right."

"I guess we just picked all the best places to have sex."

She crunched on a cookie and a crease puckered her brow while she chewed. "I really need to clean that desk."

"You're thinking about cleaning?"

She winced. "Sorry. Fast-forward some more."

Images rushed by, until Honey and Will emerged on the screen with their clothes on, and Luke hit the Play button.

They were arguing, as somehow Serena had found out Chase wasn't Roger. Through tears, Honey told Will she didn't care he lied because she was in love with him. Then they did it again.

"Oh, good." Emily breathed a relieved sigh. "We never did it on that balcony."

"We need to correct that grievous oversight."

She titled her head to the side and watched the action on the screen for a long moment. "She looks kind of bored."

He hit Fast-Forward.

"Sex never lasts this long," he felt compelled to point out.

He stopped the video. Serena stood in the foyer, a suitcase at her feet. When Chase appeared, she wanted to know why he didn't have his suitcase. They were going to miss their flight to Vegas. Chase told Serena he couldn't marry her. He would marry Mitzi, the daughter of his father's business partner, as the families arranged years ago.

The credits rolled. He hit the Power button and the TV went dark.

"Wow, twist ending." She snuggled into his side.

He ran a hand over her ginormous belly. "I can't believe I married a woman who will watch porn with me."

"It's not porn. There's a plot."

"If you say so."

"I do say so. And if you're counting up my virtues, don't forget I bake, too," she said proudly.

"That's pushing it."

He buried his face in her hair.

For years on the force, he'd had to find little ways to lie to himself, to try to convince himself that some goodness remained in this world.

Now, he didn't have to lie.

With a deep breath, he drew her inside him.

He was no longer a cop. At one time, the mere possibility of that happening would've destroyed him, and at first, it'd been hard. He didn't know how to be anything other than a cop. He didn't know how to do anything other than fight for the good guys.

He'd had a different story planned for himself, one with a different ending.

But this one would do.

The background noise had faded somewhat. He had them, and somehow, it was enough to fill the hole. To erase the void that'd opened up inside him the day a disturbed kid lashed out.

And while he'd never regain what was lost that day, he'd made some peace with it. What if one of the children at that school, facing the other end of that gun, had belonged to him and Emily? There were no winners, no heroes, in such tragedies. Only anguish.

His arms tightened around them.

He was no longer just a cop.

Now, he had options.

He was an inn owner. A community activist.

He was a brother and an uncle.

Soon, he'd be a dad.

He was Emily's husband.

And it was enough.

It was everything.

THE END

ABOUT THE AUTHOR

Amy Olle writes sexy contemporary romances filled with hope, heart, and humor. Her debut novel, *Beautiful Ruin*, is the first book in the series about the five Irish-born Nolan brothers sent as children to live with family on a remote island in northern Michigan. She is delighted to put her Psychology degrees to good use writing romance.

Amy lives in Michigan with her longsuffering husband, brilliant son, and (female) turtle named George.

Amy loves connecting with readers! Find her on the web at www.amyolle.com.